THE JURY'S OUT

THE JURY'S OUT

A lawyer's tales from courts and jails

Anthony Harkavy

Published in 2023 by Best Books and Films
an imprint of Psychology News Press
92a Hoxton Street, London N1 6LP

dcpsychologynews@gmail.com

www.bestbooksandfilms.com

Typeset by Keyboard Services, Luton, Beds.
Printed by Balto Print in Lithuania.

This book is also available in Kindle and Ebook formats.

Contact David Cohen at dcpsychologynews@gmail.com
or 07824 314189 for more information

ISBN 978-0-907633-33-4

Contents

Author's Introductory Note

For the purposes only of providing credibility and authority to this collection of short stories, allow me to give you some of my relevant career experience. Qualifying as a solicitor in 1963, I spent the first few years as a partner in a small private practice taking whatever work I could attract. In my case it involved the representation of clients charged with criminal offences. Gradually my clientèle widened to include a more commercially based civil and matrimonial practice which, although more lucrative-and some would say more respectable – left behind the incomparable thrill of a jury trial, where, rather like the institution of freemasonry, the deliberations of the jury within the confines of its jury room, are undertaken under conditions of strict secrecy enshrined in law. I daresay many, like me, would be fascinated to be able to eavesdrop on those conversations which would explain the occasional perversity of the verdicts, and in 'What Would I Have Done?' I make an attempt to circumnavigate the restrictions.

Many of my tales describe the advocacy skills performed by Anthony Harrison, my fictional aspirational alter ego, who, as solicitor/advocate enjoys special rights of audience in a Crown Court in the same way as does a barrister, and where I recreate the drama, suspense and excitement of attempting to win the unwinnable against all the odds – the verdict frequently being on a knife-edge.

Following my retirement in 1998 I took the opportunity to try to give something back to society by volunteering to become a member of the Independent Monitoring Board – IMB – a statutory, unpaid body of persons appointed to oversee, and report on – the management of prisons with a particular focus on the welfare of prisoners and enforcement of their rights. Each UK prison is served by the presence of its own IMB consisting of ten or so dedicated members of the community who often, in the face of almost intolerable provocation, undertake their legal responsibilities towards insufferably demanding, and occasionally threatening, prisoners with a degree of heroism. Between 2003 and 2018, aided by my legal training which was by no means indispensable but nevertheless helpful, I served for a total of 13 years – three as Chairman – which gave me an insight into human behaviour which those who have never been inside a jail, will never have enjoyed the privilege of gaining. Thus I have been able to witness both the best, as well as the worst, of humanity and to recognise that compassion is not the sole preserve of the law abiding. A rich source of writer's material which is represented in several of my stories – see for instance 'CSRA'. Additionally, and while not strictly within the parameters of the theme of this collection, I could not resist straying from the path which I set myself by including '*Pro Bono*' because it so typically illustrates all which is good in the world generally, and in my profession in particular.

So this collection endeavours principally, to entertain, but also to inform as well as be thought provoking. All, bar the self evidently true 'The Statement' and 'A Matter of Disguise', which is too outrageous to pass the fiction plausibility threshold, are inspired by elements of truth and thus, I hope, bear the hallmark of reality.

I doubt that any of these stories would ever have seen the light of day in this setting without the positive reaction of all those recipients of the first productions – friends and acquaintances alike – who have been so encouraging. I mention no names in the interests of confidentiality. Except for one. Jeremy Robson. A close friend for 70 years. A distinguished poet and former publisher, who, in 2013, set me on the writing road as a result of his published lyrical poem of a remarkable event on the concourse of King's Cross station which inspired me to write my own prose version. The start of it all.   *Anthony Harkavy*

Wrong Call

Her Majesty's Prison Birkinghurst, set in one of the least populated areas of Hertfordshire, is a low security jail housing 1000 or so inmates who have been convicted of the entire panoply of crimes. Those who have not, nor are ever likely to, set foot in a prison see it as a cushy number. Free accommodation. Free meals. Free central heating. Free hot showers. Free clothing. Free bedding. Colour in cell television – albeit at a cost of one pound per week. A potential weekly income of £20 – for some with the plum jobs – and for others enough to live well above the poverty line. No expenses. And worse, in the opinion of those who don't have the least progressive instinct, let alone compassion, the prison does not offer the remotest presence of a punishment regime even for those prisoners who may have committed the most unspeakable of crimes.

The reality is somewhat different. A world alien to the relative civilization of the free. A population of gangsters – literally, with a minimum of 15 gangs at war with each other, arising from events which survive life on the outside – for a start. Violence lurks round every corner. Bullies abound. And for every one of those there appears to be a victim. Maybe unable to read or write or otherwise with learning difficulties and so vulnerable and easily intimidated. Perhaps with substance addiction and unable to resist the offer of a free spliff – or something more potent – in return for unmentionable favours. Survival of the fittest. Misery for the weakest. A jungle.

George was 40 years old. Unmarried. Unemployed as a result of chronic mental health issues. Doing four years for five Tesco burglaries

1

committed over three weeks. With a schizophrenic mother – living in council accommodation – of whom he was the sole carer, who felt compelled to steal in order to alleviate the harsh impact of recent benefit cuts. Four years in prison was not the most liberal and compassionate of sentences; the judge was miserable and dyspeptic and his barrister less than inspired to plead effectively for a measure of leniency. So, George got four years, two at Birkinghurst and the remaining two years to be served outside prison on licence – which requires good behaviour as a condition for remaining free. Any material, or sometimes less than material, infraction means recall; in other words – back inside.

George had the misfortune to be allocated a prison cell in Compton Block, whose previous occupant had vacated it on his release while remaining in debt to the tune of £100 to 'Big Ron', a prisoner whose ability to avoid detection in the supply of mobile phones and drugs was matched by his ruthlessness in enforcing satisfaction of unpaid liabilities. You didn't mess with Big Ron who had an army of enforcers. There was also a strange prevailing custom, such 'inherited' debts were assumed to attach to the debtor's cell. So, George was welcomed with a £100 demand within an hour of arrival. He protested it was unfair and that he had no money. His appeal for sympathy attracted threats of violence if he did not pay up at once.

'But' – it was suggested – 'there is another way.' That other way did not – at least initially – find favour with George.

The next day, when walking in the corridor outside his cell at a time when nobody else was present, he was aware of heavy, foul smelling breath on his neck. First stench then a sharp end of a blade placed with a degree of finesse coupled with menace, alongside his carotid artery. George froze.

'Don't dare fucking turn round. Big Ron suggests that you might like to reconsider.' And he was gone. Abject terror. Paralysed by fear George did not move for the next two minutes.

'Maybe it's just an empty threat,' he told himself. 'They're only trying to scare me.'

But any such hopes were dashed the following day on opening an envelope pushed under his cell door which contained a photograph of a prisoner's hand being mangled by a pair of pliers inscribed in capital letters: 'WHO DO YOU THINK MIGHT BE NEXT? THINK ABOUT IT'.

When prison staff raided George's cell six weeks later, they discovered a cornucopia of illicit items. Three mobile phones, a sim card and a charger, as well as six tiny, but highly potent, packets of spice – the in vogue synthetic cannabinoid drug. Some haul. Criminal offences which, on conviction, could attract a substantial prison sentence to add on to his current one. Caught red handed and in the depths of profound despair, George was near breaking point. His explanations that he was the reluctant custodian of the illicit items were initially greeted with scepticism. But when he emphasised that his loss of the items belonging to another prisoner would result in a debt of something like £2500 – a mobile phone has a ransom price alone of £500 – he was listened to. As he explained to Officer Stanwell who had led the raid, he was only holding the items to help an anonymous prisoner – who wanted to make sure that his own cell was 'clean' – in satisfaction of a contrived debt. 'Terrified' doesn't begin to describe his mental state.

'Please,' implored George, 'let me go to the segregation block for my own safety. I haven't a hope in hell of paying two and half grand and my life will be hell if I stay on the wing.'

'Tell you what George,' Officer Stanwell said in a smarmy kind of way, 'tell us who the real owner is, and we will consider it.'

'Are you mad? Asking me to grass up someone is like asking me to write my own suicide note.'

'In that case we can't help,' Stanwell answered. It was like authorized blackmail. Don't grass and suffer the consequences of oppressive debt plus a possible further prison sentence for offences for which he was not

3

responsible – morally at least – or grass, with all that that entails, and we will keep you safe. The choice was made for him. Against his better judgement he revealed it was Big Ron. He was taken to segregation safety. He gave a huge sigh of relief. But he also had equally huge misgivings.

The procedures attached to the segregation of prisoners are, in theory, designed to ensure that they remain as unaffected as is practical by any adverse impact of isolation. Solitude may be all very well – it can be life enhancing – but in many situations, and even when endured for a relatively short period, can be damaging to one's mental wellbeing involving risks of depression and self-harm. For someone with existing mental health issues those risks are exacerbated for obvious reasons. At least every 14 days each segregated prisoner must go before a review panel – presided over by a prison governor and attended by a healthcare worker and a member of the Independent Monitoring Board. The idea is to check whether continued segregation is in his best interests. George was first reviewed two days after he was segregated. The panel consisted of a newly appointed, some might say green, governor, Julie Manners, balanced by Bernice Weller, a nurse with 30 years of prison experience, as well as an IMB member in attendance to observe the propriety of the proceedings.

George was beside himself. Shaking with fear. Fear for the consequences of grassing. Fear resulting from his inability to make even modest inroads into settling his unmanageable debt. Fear for his future. Sheer desperation. Tears of misery flowed. He felt utterly helpless. Deserted. Hung out to dry. The governor sympathetically suggested that he remain in 'the block' (as the segregation unit is known) pending a transfer out to another prison where he could start with a clean slate. An eminently sensible suggestion one might well think. But the nurse was no shrinking violet. She had years of experience and claimed a profound insight into the effects of isolation having read many articles on the subject. She knew it all.

'It is plainly not in this prisoner's interests,' she proclaimed, 'to keep him down here a moment longer and I emphatically decline to sign the associated paperwork – everything in a jail is paperwork – which authorizes his continued segregation. His mental state is too fragile.' Honest and sincere? Certainly. Over-confident? Undeniably.

'Where do you suggest he is located?' asked the governor.

'That's not my responsibility,' the nurse replied.

The governor had a dilemma. Lock him up in segregation in disregard of medical advice, and expose him to risk of cutting himself or worse. Release him back to the normal wing and you expose him to the risk of attack. Who would be a prison governor? Yielding to the overpowering personality of the nurse, whose advice was dispensed with the very best of intentions, albeit tainted by arrogance, and despite George's desperate entreaties – 'Please guv, I beg you, don't send me back, please' – Julie located George to cell E-17 Edrich wing thinking he would be safe from any threats emanating from Compton.

But in a jail, bush telegraph operates. One whisper and it reverberates everywhere. Wings have no boundaries. As George well suspected.

The door of cell E-17 was unlocked by a prison officer at 6.45 the following morning. The sight of George hanging by a ligature from a bar above his bed caused pandemonium. Alarm bells ringing. Shouting. He was cut down. The administration of CPR. But in vain. George was dead. The governor's decision to protect George from himself had backfired. Neither she nor the nurse had considered the ultimate risk: George's inability to cope with his overwhelming, and, unendurable, terror at the prospect of being the victim of reprisal. All the studies, all the science, all the learned academic papers which influenced the nurse's advice, proved to be a terrible distraction from the obvious. 'Wrong call' was the coroner's verdict.

The nurse was unrepentant. 'I was doing my job.' The governor remained distraught. The Independent Monitoring Board member heartbroken.

A Matter of Self Defence

When Mildred Grayson set off to work on that auspicious Monday morning in the second week of March 2017, little could she foretell the events which would change the rest of her life. She was 46 years old, five feet one inches tall, bespectacled with a slightly donnish expression, soberly dressed, lived alone in a two bedroomed cottage in the Worcestershire village of Luscombe she had inherited from an aunt.

Mildred was unmarried and seemed likely to remain so. For 25 years she had been the Librarian to the Windsgate Civic Library – a seven-mile drive from her home.

'Librarian', as a description, does scant justice to the esteem in which she was held. She loved literature and books, from Plato's *Republic* to Enid Blyton's *Book of Naughty Children* and, via the works of Shakespeare, Dickens, J K Rowling, Sebastian Faulks, to David Attenborough. Very few publications escaped her attention.

She could place the section and shelf of almost every work, without a second's hesitation. With an encyclopaedic knowledge of the Library's contents, she had acquired the reputation as the town's soul of learning to be treasured by past, present and future generations.

She was the figurehead of the successful campaign launched against the proposed library closure in 2014 and had won the hearts and minds of the entire local population. Not that she was confrontational in her tactics. On the contrary, she had set about the task with a degree of reason and persuasion which not only led to a famous victory, but also gained both the respect and admiration of the abolitionists. The nearest that she ever came to visible irritation, were first, the occasions when

Mrs. Fortescue, an 88-year-old widow, with ever increasing frequency, would forget to return, within time, her copies of Barbara Taylor Bradford novels – 'I'll let it go this time Martha, but don't expect me to waive the fine in future' (which she always did). The second irritant was the excessive noise from the adjacent site on which a nine-storey block of flats had been being built for the previous 15 months. No one knew when the block would be completed.

Otherwise, she was the epitome of gentle, generous – of spirit – civilised, refinement.

The traffic was unusually light in the early morning of 6th March 2017, and Mildred had little difficulty in reaching 30 mph in her 1957 Morris Minor as she approached the Luscombe bridge, which is too narrow to allow vehicles approaching each other from the opposite side to pass. Cars coming from her direction when travelling to her Library had priority.

'I'm in good time,' she was telling herself. As she always was. She had missed the Library opening time of 9am only once, and that was due to a broken-down bus on the other side of the bridge. Otherwise, residents said that one's clock would be set by the exact time at which Mildred introduced her key into the Library's front door. Historians of philosophy will know the same was said of Immanuel Kant. You could also set the time by his walk.

Mildred slowed down to 20 mph on her approach to the bridge. She was horrified to see a dog running from the left-hand side of the road without any regard for Mildred's car. Feeling a sickening thud which made her to slam on her brakes. She stopped just short of the bridge and jumped out. This young German Shepherd was lying prone two yards in front of her car in the centre of the road. Never having had a pet and having not an inkling as to how to treat a dog with any serious injury, she did not, to her everlasting credit, panic.

She carefully approached the irregularly breathing animal. She cuddled it. And stroked it. And kissed it. And spoke to it in soothing tones while it whimpered. The motorist immediately behind, a thickset, six-foot one-inch, heavily tattooed brute whose acquaintance in a dark alley one might prefer to avoid, joined her.

'My name is Bill. Keep stroking and talking luv. I've just googled local vets and will do my best.' After ten minutes of trying, he finally found a vet who estimated a half an hour journey to get to the scene. 'Meanwhile she told me on no account to move the animal; it could prove fatal.'

The initial sympathy of queuing motorists began to wane. Tempers began to fray. The traffic was mounting both ways. Mutterings of 'how are we expected to get to work?', 'it's only a dog for heaven's sake', 'just move the fucking creature' were some of the more genteel comments.

The chauffeur of a Bentley five cars behind came up and explained that his boss was going frantic because he had an important takeover meeting to start at 8.45 and if he missed it the whole deal might well abort. Mildred politely rejected his offer of £1000 in cash to move the dog.

One hooter. And then another. Followed by a cacophony made no difference.

Mildred, fortified by the presence of Bill, was not for turning. After 15 minutes a police car, blue light flashing and siren screaming, raced up to the scene – much to the relief of the complaining drivers. 'What have we here?' asked the Police Officer – a man in his early fifties who had seen serious crime, serious trouble by comparison to which this incident was a stroll in the park. 'Come on miss; let's get this dog moved.'

'Sorry officer, but you can see what a bad way he is in. A vet will be here in 15 minutes or so and I have been advised not to move the dog under pain of its potential death.'

'Your name, madam?'

'Mildred Grayson.'

'The dog cannot – cannot – be moved,' explained Bill, in a marginally threatening tone.

'Your name sir? And don't come that tone with me.'

'William Manners. But you can call me Bill if you like. The dog stays where he is.'

At which point the police officer approached the dog and made as if to move him. For the rest of her life Mildred would fail to understand her reaction. As the officer bent down, she drew her hand back and slapped his face with a power and strength that she had never realised she had. The policeman froze. About to arrest her, he was confronted with Bill who firmly interposed himself.

'Don't you fucking dare mate. I've just come out after doing ten years for grievous bodily harm, and if you think I'm fucking scared of you, think again.'

Mildred, who had only previously encountered such language in the works of Chaucer, resumed tending the dog. Drops of blood were beginning to seep from his jaws and on to Mildred's coat, his whimpering rose in volume to howls of pain, cries of desperation and helplessness. The plaintive expression in his eyes, as if to suggest an absolute trust in Mildred's ability to keep him alive, was touching.

The police officer, handkerchief on cheek to mop up the blood flowing from his own injuries, thwarted from performing his duties, was fulminating for fully ten minutes before Sarah Johnston, the vet, arrived She calmly and rapidly managed to administer the necessary pain killers to stabilise and sedate the dog, and bind him to a stretcher which she carried to her animal ambulance and then drive him back to her surgery. After restoring the traffic flow and taking Mildred's and Bill's particulars, the policeman left with a 'You haven't heard the last of this – both of you. My name is Dave Richards.'

The local press had a field day. 'Librarian saves the life of a German Shepherd, helped by quick thinking recently released convict'. The dog had survived. Its owners were 'over the moon'. Mildred, delighted though she was, had no interest in any publicity. Statements and photographs were out. That day's traumatic events were enough. She was emotionally exhausted.

She had never been in court before. The charge read out to Mildred as she stood in the dock of Worcester Magistrates Court on Monday 3rd July 2017. 'Mildred Grayson. You are charged with the assault of a police officer in the execution of his duty. Namely that on Monday 6th March 2017 at approximately 8.27am you did unlawfully strike, and thereby assault, Police Constable David Richards whilst attempting to perform his duties. How do you plead?'

District Judge Lady Audrey Mattheson was presiding. A charitable description might be 'unyielding'. An uncharitable – and more realistic – one being nasty, vicious, vindictive, police worshipping and a disgrace to the Bench. She had only survived in office because her brother-in-law had been the Attorney General of Bermuda with influence in the corridors of minor legal powers.

The arrival of the summons came as no surprise to Mildred. The constable had hardly been forgiving or understanding. And to be fair – as she unfailingly was – she had given him a whack which resulted in a weal which was still plainly visible on his left cheek. Word had it that the scar would never entirely heal.

At the Library she consulted every index of local solicitors specialising in allegations of misbehaviour against the police. And after reading the five-star reviews on the web she made an appointment to see the senior partner of the preferred firm.

'Very serious. Assaulting a police officer who was trying to alleviate a severe traffic obstruction, plus inflicting potentially lasting physical damage. You could be looking at a custodial sentence. My advice to you is to plead guilty and throw yourself on the mercy of the Court. If you plead not guilty and are found guilty you will forfeit the right to have your sentence reduced by a third which you would otherwise enjoy.'

'Could I really go inside?' asked Mildred to herself. Me! Mildred Grayson! Who has never so much as disposed of an apple core in the street? Deep in her thoughts on the way to the Library she met Bill Manners. He was working as a brickie on the next-door building. He too had received a summons.

'Let's discuss it after work,' he said.

And so, over a cup of coffee in the Almond Tree tea rooms, they talked. Bill had been charged with obstructing a police officer in the execution of his duty. He told Mildred that, with his experience, he had no confidence in these big firms of lawyers. 'All bluster and cockiness, if you ask me. Huge fucking fees and no concern for the poor client – excuse my French. I tell you what. I'll ask around my connections and see what I can come up with.'

They met the following day. 'Word has it that there's a brand newly qualified solicitor – Anthony Harrison – in the High Street who is very keen, very conscientious and pretty clever. He hasn't yet appeared in court but was apparently a star at his university debating society. Also, he says he needs experience and would represent us for nothing – "*pro bono*" I think they call it.'

'Well – I've got nothing to lose, so I'm willing to meet him,' replied Mildred.

'Me too,' said Bill.

'Not guilty,' said Mildred in court in as confident a tone as she could muster in the circumstances.

'Mr. Harrison. Has your client seen the reporting police officer's face?' the Judge asked in an incredulous tone.

'She has, Madam. Thank you for asking.'

'Very well,' said the Judge, oblivious of the sarcastic innuendo. 'Mr. Robson [the prosecuting counsel]. Call your first witness.'

PC Dave Richards gave his evidence like the seasoned pro that he was. Clear. Confident. Concise. Would not have it that he was doing anything beyond his prescribed duty. Consulting his notebook. 'Need to restore traffic movement to normal. The assault had been entirely unprovoked and uncalled for.'

Harrison rose. 'Mr. Richards – or may I call you Dave?'

'I don't mind if that makes your job any easier,' quipped the Officer who was aware that this was his first case.

'Thank you. Now Dave. Do you have any children?'

'Where's the relevance?' interrupted the Judge.

'Answer the question please,' said Harrison betraying a confidence which had the Judge metaphorically rocking in her seat.

'I do as a matter of fact. Two. A boy and a girl. Ten and eight.'

'Well brought up I presume. No problems with either of them? Normal, fun-loving kids?'

'I'd say so definitely.'

'You and your wife are excellent parents then.'

'Nice of you to say so.'

'Your children like animals, do they?'

'Not half. My wife's a fair one for pets and we've got three cats and two dogs at this moment. God knows how they'd feel if anything happened to any of them.'

'I suppose, Dave, it's fair to say that any child of yours would do anything for your animals if they were at any kind of risk?'

'They sure would,' said Dave proudly. 'Anything at all; regardless.'

'Thank you,' said Harrison and sat down.

The Judge sternly told the public to keep their opinions to themselves.

'That all sounds very clear and obvious to me,' said the Judge. 'Since that is all the – if I may say so – very cogent evidence of the Prosecution, it is now your turn Mr. Harrison.'

Mildred took the stand. Consumed with concern and compassion for the injured dog and believing that PC Richards was about to move the dog with lethal consequences, she lashed out to protect the dog.

'Do you make a habit of hitting police officers?' asked the Judge unable to resist a cheap dig.

'If you allow me, Madam, I will ask my client whether she regards your question as a serious attempt to ascertain the essential truth in this case before she answers,' interrupted Harrison, unable to resist the opportunity to embarrass the Judge. Tittering this time from the public went entirely over the Judge's head.

Under cross examination by Mr. Robson, Mildred gave as good as she got. Rejecting any suggestion that her reaction was disproportionate, she said, it was the natural behaviour of a bystander. When asked whether she was glorying in the publicity which the case had attracted, she told the Court that she had not even set eyes on the dog since it left in the ambulance.

Harrison called Bill as his second witness who corroborated Mildred's evidence. Unsurprisingly Mr. Robson managed to extract nothing which would damage Mildred's case. In a nutshell Harrison would submit that a person accused of assault is entitled to land a pre-emptive strike in the belief that such action was reasonable for the defence of himself or another. The 'another' in this case being the dog. A legitimate variation on the theme of 'Self-defence'.

'Is that it? No further evidence for the defence I assume.'

'It's not it I'm afraid to say, Madam. I will now read out the written evidence of Sarah Johnston, the vet who saved the dog's life. It describes the grave risk of death resulting from any amateur third party intervention. The Prosecution has told me that it accepts it in its entirety.' Harrison read out the statement and Mr. Robson confirmed that he did not propose to challenge it.

'Thank you,' said the Judge. 'I will now hear closing arguments.'

'May it please you, Madam,' said Harrison, 'but I do have one more witness.'

'Really!' huffed Judge. 'As far as we have been told nobody else was closely present at the scene when the assault was perpetrated.'

'I presume you mean "alleged assault" Judge. And you are wrong. I will now, if I may, with your kind indulgence, call my fourth witness.'

'What's his or her name?' asked the Judge.

'Stavely, Judge.'

'Stavely? Stavely who?' asked the Judge with more than a hint of irritation.'

'I regret that I am unable to tell you, Judge, because I don't know. Moreover there is a distinct possibility that he has no surname.'

'What!' shouted the Judge this time. 'Don't play games with me, Mr. Harrison.'

Those in the public gallery were becoming more than a little concerned. Harrison was playing a very dangerous game.

'I will call him now. Stavely please.'

And with those words the doors of the Court opened and in, proudly, but with a slight limp, walked a beautiful, short haired German Shepherd whom the usher shepherded towards the witness-box. One glance at Dave Richards and he bared his teeth with a menacing growl. Dave recoiled. Harrison, meanwhile, introduced him as the dog whose life Mildred had saved. Stavely sat still. Good as gold.

The Judge's curiosity had been aroused. 'This is very entertaining, but where does the presence of this dog get us?'

'I am gambling, Judge. May I ask the accused to stand?'

The dock was ten yards or so across the Court from the witness box. Mildred stood. Stavely looked. Stared. Sniffed. Pricked his ears. And then launched himself with a ferocity of purpose towards Mildred which had everybody in the Court open mouthed. On reaching the dock, he began to whimper. Mildred returned his stare. Stavely took one further look and hurtled straight into Mildred's open arms, nearly sending her flying. Whining. This time not with pain but with the exquisite pleasure of re-acquaintance with his saviour. She cuddled him and began to weep. He licked her face. He would not desist. All efforts to separate him were hopelessly inadequate. A greater expression of love, of gratitude, was beyond one's imagination. The Court was silent. Not a murmur. Everybody, including the Judge, paralysed by the enormity of the moment.

After ten minutes the dog calmed down and was returned to the witness box where he sat on a hastily procured highchair to observe the proceedings.

'Mr. Harrison,' said the Judge, 'may I give you a word of advice after 30 years on the Bench. It is not the prerogative of an accused's counsel to gamble. Such behaviour is contrary to all recognised principles of advocacy. The consequences for the defendant can be catastrophic as you will no doubt appreciate. To have gambled, as you have so notably done in this case, first, by your subtle questioning, in an attempt to enlist the sympathy of the main prosecution witness – when you could not have conceivably known how he might react – was unwise to say the least and potentially as lethal for the prospects of your client's acquittal as were the risks inherent of moving the dog – as you submit. And then, with the production of the first canine witness in trial history, a histrionic display of its characteristics constituted behaviour so outrageous as to justify a complaint to the Solicitors Regulation Authority. It is as serious as it gets. It is fortunate for you and even more fortunate for your client that your gamble has paid off. Mildred Grayson. I am satisfied that your admitted striking of PC David Richards was more than justified in the circumstances in which you found yourself. Even the victim conceded that his children might very well have done the same thing, The notion that you should be convicted for what was, in effect an act of self-defence in protecting the wellbeing of such a beautiful grateful creature is inimical to the interests of justice. Accordingly, I find you not guilty. You are free to go.'

'Mr. Robson. I imagine you will not wish to proceed with the case against Mr. Manners.'

'Quite so, Madam, I formally offer no evidence against him.'

Stavely looked at the Judge (who for the first time in her life when sitting in Court – and who knows maybe anywhere – smiled), wagged his tail, and left the Court.

Pro Bono

Mark Truscott was born sucking a silver spoon. A large trust fund to mature into his control on reaching the age of 21. On top he had a brain invested with Einsteinian DNA and he looked terrific. He had what you might under describe as auspicious prospects. And no siblings, so all the family wealth was destined for his pocket.

Robert Fielding was less charmed. He was born in the same year into a family of modest means and brought up in a two bedroomed council house in Nottingham. His face was not especially attractive. His miner father died at the age of 44 from lung cancer leaving his mother to undertake the Herculean task of rearing three children. To make ends meet she had to do two day jobs as a morning waitress for four hours, and an afternoon high street florist's assistant for four hours. She also had a zero hours night-time contract cleaning offices which gave her a further ten hours a week on such low pay as her employers could get away with. Hardship characterized the household but never despair. His mother's iron will and refusal to submit to circumstances ensured that the children grew up with a deep appreciation of values and obligation to those even less fortunate than they were.

Putting theory into practice, Robert proved himself. At the local comprehensive his academic results got him into law school, qualify as a solicitor and join a local firm which specialised in providing redress for the impecunious underdog. No riches for him. But ambition for financial wealth was never on his agenda.

By contrast Mark's progress was spectacular. He flew through his law exams with the facility of a Usain Bolt, joined a commercial law practice in the City, became a partner at the age of 25 and introduced to the firm commercial transactions of great complexity which he would resolve to the satisfaction of those whom he represented. Often it required every ounce of devious ruthlessness which he developed in achieving his client's end – and his client's triumph meant defeat for his opponent's client.

His sadistic pleasure on one notable occasion, was made all the sweeter when his client gave him two cases of Louis Roederer Cristal 1947 champagne, one case of Château Palmer 1989, and a bottle of Balvenie 50-year-old malt whisky. Not that he expected anything less. 'It's no big deal,' he boasted to the raised eyebrows of his colleagues with the blasé of a serial seducer, 'he can afford it.'

His stellar career was stopped dead soon afterwards. The same client had prevailed upon him to act in a scheme which involved the dubious transfer of substantial funds into and out of his firm's client account. The client was charged with, and convicted of, money-laundering offences; he blamed Mark for failing to advise on the legality of the arrangements. But that was only the half of it. A lawsuit against the firm followed, the client alleging negligent advice leading to huge losses. Its professional indemnity insurers threw in the towel settling the claim with little resistance, but only after requiring Mark to stump up £15 million by way of contribution in accordance with a term of the policy which allowed that in the event of the taint of criminality. Mark could not pay and was compelled to file for bankruptcy – his career foundering on the rocks of his own hubris.

Despair and depression followed, accompanied, as it was, with suspension of his practising certificate. He could still work in the solicitor's profession, but under severely restrictive limitations, and only under the close supervision of another solicitor. A daily internet search for other employment failed hopelessly. His despair deepened.

Then, an advertisement in the *Law Society Gazette* for a position in a newly formed firm specializing in assisting those whose previous entitlement to legal aid had recently been removed by the myopia of the Ministry of Justice's program of austerity, caught his eye. The pay was derisorily low but with no other prospects in view, he lodged a none too hopeful application for the post. At his interview he learned that the venture was being funded by a Nottingham philanthropist whose own fight against a miscarriage of justice had been fought on a shoestring by the firm's founder – Robert Fielding. The job was his if he wanted it. Was it his sort of thing? It was a big comedown but faced with destitution he accepted – but not without misgivings.

Robert was the archetypal poor man's lawyer. He had an unquenchable thirst for justice and redress of wrong was his raison d'être. The charging of fees was beyond his vocabulary. *Pro Bono Publica* – for the public good – were his bywords and he would try to take on any case where an impecunious victim could convince him that he/she had suffered a miscarriage of justice.

Mark was given, as his first case, Sharon. A divorced, well-educated mother of 31 years, who, having fallen on hard times following a bitter and protracted divorce had been living on benefits from hand to mouth, with two children aged four and two. Her hitherto impeccable reputation for honesty had been impugned by an allegation that she had been dealing drugs, two packages of cocaine having been found in her shopping bag after a tip off. She faced criminal charges. Worse, social workers recommended removal of her children from her on the obscenely premature grounds that she lacked the moral fitness to look after them. And – to make matters even worse – they had been seized and taken into care by local authority social services after a Court hearing, notice of which Sharon had only received that same morning. She vigorously denied knowing anything about the cocaine and was desperate for help.

With all the ruthlessness and enthusiasm which had served him so well in his previous role, Mark got to work. He applied to the shop in question for disclosure of its cctv images of that day, a claim which it refused on data protection grounds. An emergency court application was filed which sought preservation and disclosure of the digital tape which was due to be erased the following day. Failure would have meant inevitable disaster. But failure was not on Mark's agenda.

Summoning every ingredient of persuasive skill, he succeeded. Tellingly, the images revealed a man surreptitiously introducing two packages into the shopping bag. Further exhaustive enquiries led to the discovery of his identity. When he was caught, he confessed to having planted the evidence at the behest of Sharon's embittered ex-husband. Dismissal of the criminal charges followed swiftly. But even in the face of overwhelming evidence social services declined to reconsider on the baseless and shameful grounds that Sharon might well have been in cahoots with the drugs planter as part of a conspiracy to discredit the ex-husband. The next day Mark succeeded in his emergency application to the High Court to review the original decision, which the Judge had little hesitation in reversing.

'Let this admirable, tenacious, wronged, impoverished, dedicated mother be in no doubt that this Court regards her character as wholly untainted – as opposed to that of each of those working for Social Services who have shamefully attempted to discredit it,' were his closing words.

When Mark got to his office the next day, he opened a note which had been left for him. It read:

Dear Mark,

I will forever be indebted to you for the selfless and unremitting dedication which you applied in the pursuit of my claims to clear my name and to have my beloved children restored to my custody. To have achieved, against all odds, the delivery of justice in the face of the most serious allegations made against me with the devastating consequences which I and my children suffered as a result of the wicked refusal of the

Local Authority to recognize the possibility of my innocence, has restored my faith in humanity. It may surprise you to know that before my case was allocated to you, Robert told me about your professional history and asked my consent for you to act. I have thanked God a million times for giving me the insight to have made what was a momentous decision. You are a remarkable person. Here is a small gift which I hope you will enjoy.
In deepest gratitude
Sharon

As Mark removed the re-used brown paper packaging to reveal a half bottle of inexpensive whisky a teardrop no bigger than a spot of rain oozed down his right cheek. *Pro Bono Publica* became *Pro Bono Privatus.*

The Right Decision

When Melanie James announced her retirement from M J Holdings plc at close of business on Friday 28th October 2016, colleagues, family and the press were all shocked. She was one of the most successful hedge fund managers of recent times, she had smashed the glass ceiling of City discrimination and, was hanging up her commercial boots at the height of her career.

She had graduated at Harvard Business School and formed her own Hedge Fund in 2003 after apprenticeships with three major US commercial banks and a stint in the risk management department of a major UK financial institution.

She was steely sure of her ability to predict currency catastrophes. In March 2004, she exposed her company to the risk of insolvency by adopting a highly precarious short euro/sterling position. So, unless the euro's value to the pound declined by at least five per cent by the end of June of that year she was done for.

By 17th June, the euro's value had dropped by more than 10%, her faith translated into one billion pounds sterling. Stellar for her reputation for fearlessness combined with nerve and an unflinching resolve to resist weaker counsels. A similar currency coup in 2007 cemented her reputation. Within the City hedge fund culture, she sat on the throne.

Melanie James did not believe wealth should not enjoy the trappings. A pied à terre in Belgravia, a six bedroomed mini mansion in Beaconsfield, holiday homes in Florida, St. Barts and St. Tropez, all proof that money can buy pleasure. She had married a prominent sports journalist. They had twins at university. Family, success, money – the total package.

And yet…

The truth was that she was bored. Bored stiff. Up to the eyeballs. Her uncanny ability to create personal wealth no longer excited. How many bottles of Krug 64 can one drink? How many lobster thermidors can one eat before baked beans on toast proved more satisfying? Enough was enough. She needed a change of direction.

During the reign of Queen Victoria reformers established Boards of Visitors for prisons, a statutory body of citizens with a duty to report on the conditions suffered by prisoners in British jails – in which violence, bullying, exploitation and intimidation have always been rife. Members of the Independent Board can make a real difference to the abject lives 'enjoyed' by inmates. Not that it's easy. Far from it. Challenges it presents. But just occasionally IMB members can find the means to redress wrongs and to shine a ray of light into the darkness suffered by those with no hope. The weak. The vulnerable. The unintelligent. The uneducated.

Melanie James, bored and restless, read an advertisement online for IMB vacancies at a prison in Hertfordshire, which attracted her interest. But would her decision to apply turn out to be the right one? Or would it, even if it was successful, constitute a huge disappointment?

Once on the Board, Melanie could not wait to get started. First, she bought a Primark collection of clothes – no City power dressing from now on – which allowed her to experience a welcome feeling of comfort. Several weeks on and she was entrusted with the freedom she felt needed. She passed the test of knowledge of the appropriate prison procedures and was authorised to carry keys.

She now could roam, pass through locked gates, speak freely to prisoners and staff, investigate, redress injustices. She was impatient to make the difference. She was used to crude talk in the boardroom but there was always ambition in the boardroom. Greed is good. Behind bars there was little hope.

'You lot are a fucking waste of space', or similar, was something frequently uttered by hard bitten, cynical inmates to whom she attempted to offer help. 'Sorry Miss, but I've been doing time for 15 years, and you IMBs are all a load of bleeding useless rubbish'.

Melanie was not one to submit, to be deterred, even if there was more than a grain of truth in the criticisms. She soon learned that to get anything done required monumental tenacity in the face of monumental frustration. When – as an illustration – hours of fruitless time spent on pursuing a prisoner's fantasy of mistreatment – would be wasted with no apology from the prisoner on being confronted with the truth. Not a 'sorry miss'. Was her time of so little value?

It was on one Monday late afternoon, after a particularly trying six hours during the first two of which she had spent trying to convince Jackson Merritt, a particularly belligerent prisoner whose television set had been confiscated as a punishment for a rules infraction, to accept that the enjoyment of Sky Television was not a human right that could be challenged in the European Court of Human Rights, that Melanie seriously began to question whether her time was being productively spent. 'What exactly am I doing in this god forsaken hell hole?' she asked herself.

Passing Bury Wing, she literally walked into Vincent. 'Excuse me, Miss. Sorry for the inconvenience, Miss. Have you got a moment?'

Melanie raised her head and looked at Vincent. A mild, reticent, diffident sort of man of 40 years or so, with apparent mild learning difficulties – a prime target for the bullies.

'How can I help you?' she asked with a barely disguised absence of enthusiasm.

Vincent was incensed. He had ordered, and paid £1.76, for four oranges which had been delivered from the prison warehouse where such produce is stored, but which had never reached him. There had been a big problem in tracing the oranges' journey, with a confusion of various signatures along the way. All Vincent's efforts to prove he had never received them had failed. He had exhausted the exhausting, bureaucratic, prison complaints procedure. Fobbed off every step of the way. He was left with no oranges and £1.76 out of pocket.

Everyone had laughed at him. Taken the piss. Staff, prisoners.

'Leave it with me,' said Melanie, 'I'll see what I can do.'

In her City life decisions had to be made fast. Prison time was utterly different. It took her three tenacious weeks to uncover the oranges' trail and to prove that a corrupt member of staff had nicked them. In her former occupation three weeks' work might have yielded a return of £1.76 billion. But to Vincent the yield of £1.76 was equally, if not more, important.

Wandering round Bury Wing four weeks later Vincent accosted her. He was excited as a nine-year-old child about to drive his first fairground dodgem.

'Excuse me, Miss, could you come to my cell?'

'I'm a bit busy.'

'Please, Miss.'

'Very well.' Melanie followed.

'Wait here a minute, Miss.' And true to his word, a minute later Vincent emerged, a paper bag in his hand. 'For you, Miss.'

When Melanie returned to her office, she opened the bag. A note read:

Dear Miss,

Because of what you done for me, I not only got me for oringes but also got an extra two as compensashun. I wood like to thank you Miss by giving you those two extra oringes and here they are Miss. You've been fucking fantastic Miss, you really have. Bless you Miss.

Vincent Shardworth.

If there was one moment when all doubts about her decision to join the IMB were exploded, it was then. 'Bless you, Vincent Shardworth,' she said to herself. 'Bless you.'

Herd Community

If any institution in the United Kingdom wished to compete for the mythical prize awarded for embodiment of English values, it would need much to better Durham Park Golf Club. Founded in 1966, a clubhouse created out of a 26-room Palladian mansion, a 6700-yard golf course of unparalleled beauty, challenge, serenity and peacefulness, which boasted a super-liberal membership policy. Unlike some, where wealth or position were prerequisites for acceptance. Issues of race, religion, lack of wealth or background, did not matter – as long as the relatively modest subscriptions were paid. Recognition of the statutory obligations not to discriminate on anti-diversity grounds, shone through the decision making of the membership subcommittee. Once in, behaviour determined one's re-non-election for the next year.

Good behaviour was rewarded with re-election. Conversely the infraction of any section of the club disciplinary code of conduct, however trivial, constituted grounds for a 'Disciplinary', a kind of mini trial before six committee members plus a chairman with no vote save a casting one. An adverse finding might result in any punishment ranging from immediate expulsion to a warning as to future behaviour. Such was the power of the disciplinary committee members. A power rarely exercised, as it happened, as the members nearly always behaved well.

When Gerry Maddison's application to join arose for consideration, Howard Jeffries, the chairman of the club as well as of the membership sub-committee, was faced with a test of tolerance and open mind which was novel in the history of the club. Bodily abuse of a minor – in all its forms – is generally regarded as anything from anti-social to downright evil, vile, unforgivable, repellent – depending on the ages of perpetrator and victim, the severity of the offending acts, and the impact upon the alleged victim. An 18-year-old girl convicted of fondling the backside of a boy of 17 who she might fancy like crazy hardly compares with a man of 35 plying a date rape drug to a 14-year-old girl as a prelude to grooming her for prostitution. And it was an offence involving a particularly brutal rape of a15-year-old girl of which Gerry – now 35 years old – had been convicted ten years previously that he was amongst the baggage he had put on his CV. But with one crucial qualification. He maintained that he hadn't done it. Moreover, after he had served ten years, the Court of Appeal found his conviction unsafe and set it aside. So Gerry was free to resume his life. To get a job. To go to the pub, To join a golf club.

'I don't know,' mused Howard, 'the Court did not exactly pronounce his innocence as such. An 'unsafe' finding means nothing more than that the jury might have got it wrong. Not that he didn't do it exactly. We need to think long and hard before accepting his application. Heaven knows what our members might think about having a convicted rapist among our throng.'

'But,' said James Curtis to his chairman, 'what about the presumption of innocence? An unsafe verdict may not necessarily mean that it was wrong, but it can't mean that he definitely – or even probably for that matter – did it. We have a reputation at this club for fairness, don't forget.'

The other four members of the subcommittee were equally split. The chairman's casting vote would decide.

It was not without a supreme effort that the members of Durham Park were finally persuaded to welcome Gerry Maddison into their ranks. Word of his recent ten-year history had spread. There were a good number of initial misgivings. Requests to make up a fourball – the usual golf format at Durham – as with many clubs – were hardly plentiful. The atmosphere when he entered the bar where games were conventionally made up was tense. A collective clearing of throats. But if there is one thing which the prison experience gives its inmates if they are to survive the ordeal, it is the capacity to exercise patience and understanding. It is the route to acceptance by your peers. So Gerry was able to overcome, and to gain a measure of respect, albeit accompanied by an equal measure of circumspection. A certain undercurrent would be present, however friendly his playing partners might appear. An elephant in the room which nobody was anxious to expose. But compared to the Scrubs at Wormwood, this was paradise.

'Get your hands off me,' screamed a hysterical junior member – 16-year-old Louise Abrahams. 'Let me go for god's sake.'

'Shut up and get in the car,' Gerry Maddison said as he forcefully bundled her into the front seat of his Mercedes saloon before speeding away from the car park of Durham Park Golf Club that Saturday afternoon. It was seven months after Gerry had joined. But not before an astute and observant Harry Bowden, a club member for the past 33 years, had filmed the episode on his smart phone.

'Bloody hell,' said Harry to himself. 'Don't tell me he has been fooling us for all this time.' Wasting no time, he sought out, and found in the bar, the club chairman.

'Just as well you were around at the time, Harry,' said Howard. 'To be honest I've never really liked the man. How I was persuaded to vote for his admission as member I'll never know. I'll have to convene a meeting of the disciplinary panel without delay. How we're going to keep this secret heaven above knows.'

Howard conspicuously failed to achieve that. Within the day there was barely any member of Durham Park Golf Club who was not obsessed with condemning not only the original admission, but also the acts of which he had been accused. 'An utter disgrace'. 'Made us all a laughing stock'. 'Talk about bringing the club into disrepute'. And 'The man deserves to be hung drawn and quartered', were four of the more moderate opinions. The club had worked itself up into a collective frenzy of hysteria. Not one member was prepared to suggest any scintilla of doubt of his guilt of whatever he might be accused of.

Meanwhile Gerry kept his distance. He sensed the reaction which his appearance might have provoked. Especially since he had failed to provide any explanation for his graphically recorded conduct.

'You can think whatever you like, but I am not prepared to say anything. It's none of your business,' he told Howard.

Words which served only to infuriate. Words which when broadcast to the membership. provoked a clamour to hold the disciplinary hearing 'in public', before the lot of them. A demand to which Howard readily acceded.

'Let the members vent their fury,' he said to James Curtis. 'As long as we make sure we have sufficient security to keep Gerry safe.'

'And for the safety of Anthony Harrison,' added James. Just about the only club member prepared to undertake the unenviable task of representing Gerry before the panel.

Harrison had been a club member and a solicitor who felt that a refusal to accept a *pro bono* retainer from Gerry would betray the principles of his profession. He incurred the wrath, as well as the odium, of those who hitherto he had regarded as his friends, for daring to act for Gerry.

'You've taken leave of your fucking senses,' said Martin Black, a member with whom Anthony had regularly played in a fourball for 22 years.

A full reception area was converted into a giant courtroom. Gerry was led in, flanked by two burly security guards, followed closely by Anthony. They sat together at a small table at the side of the wide table occupied by the panel members. Booing morphed into a baying of wolves. At the far end of the room Howard Jeffries was flanked by his six panel members – three on either side and called for decorum. Once the crowd had been persuaded to calm down, Howard said that all attempts to contact Louise Abrahams had failed. She had answered no emails nor had she responded to the many texts and what's app messages imploring her to get in touch. Her father had, however, indicated that she was so sedated that she would not be able to provide any coherent testimony. Mutterings of disgust. 'See what that rapist bastard has done.'

The charge eventually was read out: 'That on the sixth July this year you, Gerry Maddison, assaulted and abducted Louise Abrahams without reasonable excuse and with excessive force – acts which constitute injurious conduct within the meaning of paragraph 46 of the Constitution of Durham Park Golf Club.'

When Gerry was asked whether or not he admitted the allegations, Anthony stood. 'My client makes no such admission.' Provoking a gasp of disbelief which itself defied belief.

'Very well,' said a disbelieving Howard, 'let's proceed with the evidence.'

By means of some extraordinary display technology, Harry Bowden's recorded video of the events of that afternoon which one might be forgiven for thinking constituted incontrovertible evidence of the assault and abduction, was shown on a giant screen accompanied by Louise's piercing screams. The spectators shuddered.

'I'll show it once more,' said Howard. 'Just so that there's no doubt as to what happened.'

The mood was vicious. The unsavoury herd community in full voice. A lynch mob in embryo. The security guards twitched.

'Shoot the fucking bastard,' shouted the otherwise impeccably respectable Lady Marjorie Manners. Sir Robin Goodweather – Clerk to the Lord Chancellor agreed. 'Tear his fucking balls out.'

'I think that that's perhaps enough,' was Howard's half hearted, weak attempt to calm the mood. 'Now – Mr. Harrison – forgive the formality – do you have any questions of the witness?'

'None.'

'Would you like to call your client to testify then?'

'The strict answer to that question is "yes" – I would. But in the circumstances, I regret that my client refuses to testify. He thinks it would be the wrong thing to do.'

'No doubt,' said Howard. 'I can't think of anything which he might say that wouldn't make things even worse for him. In which case – and unless you wish to call any witnesses to speak on your client's behalf – we will retire to consider our findings.'

'I was rather hoping against hope,' Anthony said, 'that a witness might turn up, but it doesn't look like it, so I suggest you retire and do what you have to do.'

'I doubt we'll be longer than three minutes, so everybody please stay where you are,' Howard said.

It was two minutes and 43 seconds precisely before the door to the hall opened and in trooped the panel. All grim faced. None deigning to look at Gerry.

'Members of Durham Park Golf Club,' said Howard in tones that did not lack for pomposity. 'We have reached our decision.' Silence. Not a sound. 'We, the panel convened for the purpose of determining the allegations made against Gerald Maddison find…'

A sudden, violent jolting opening of the hall double doors, through which a distinguished, middle aged, mildly agitated gentleman appeared. Heads turned. The man approached the panel.

'Forgive me, gentlemen. I hope that I am in time. Let me introduce myself. My name is Freedland, Archibald Freedland, Senior Consultant Psychiatrist at Charter Nightingale Hospital.'

'If you are here to testify as to Gerry Maddison's mental state, I am afraid to tell you that you are too late. Our findings are complete.'

'No sir, I am not here for that purpose. As far as I know Mr. Maddison suffers from no abnormality of mind. On the contrary his thought processes are a model, both as an example of logic, but also courage and a respect for confidence.

'Continue please,' said an intrigued Howard.

'Thank you,' said the doctor. 'It's like this. Saturday two weeks ago a young lady, Louise Abrahams, was brought into my hospital by a man who introduced himself as Mr. Maddison. She was hysterical. Evincing suicidal thoughts which, in my professional opinion, were more than simple cries for help. But for the timely intervention of Mr. Maddison who had overheard her confiding on her mobile to a friend that she would "do away with herself once and for all", there is every reason to believe that she may well have carried out her threat to self-harm. His extreme actions literally saved her life. She was sedated soon after arrival and has remained semi-comatose ever since while we consider how best to treat her. Meanwhile Mr. Maddison was forcefully reminded of his responsibility not to disclose to anybody what he knew about Louise's mental state which was to remain a matter of confidentiality.'

'Go on,' said Howard.

'After being approached by Mr. Harrison to testify in these proceedings on behalf of Mr. Maddison, I was compelled to take my own professional ethical advice which, you will gather from my presence here, allows me to disclose the condition of a patient in these exceptional and unusual circumstances. The committee which decides such matters only reached its decision an hour ago. Hence my late arrival.'

A pause while everybody tried to assimilate what the doctor had said.

'If I may add one thing. Mr. Maddison is a remarkable human being. You are very fortunate to have him as a member of your golf club.'

After a stunned period of 11 minutes of complete silence an embarrassed Howard announced a finding of no misconduct. Whereupon Anthony suggested a formal apology.

Whereupon Gerry asked, that rather than have an apology, would anybody be available to partner him the following weekend.

Whereupon – almost as one – the whole room raised their hands, accompanied by an 'I will'. Once again herd community. This time to applaud.

A Matter of Disguise

A first glance at Johnny Bardini and one would be transported into the world of Damon Runyon. A second glance would conjure up visions of Frank Sinatra and Marlon Brando. As if a member of the cast of 'Guys and Dolls' had walked off the screen straight into Dean Street, one of Soho's less salubrious areas in the late fifties.

He was of Sicilian descent, brylcreemed, sleek, swept back black hair, bright blue eyes he hid most of the time behind perpetual dark glasses, clean shaven, sharp suited, black shirted, white tied, Hermes jacketed, Gucci shoed, exuding the scent of French aftershave – he was the archetypal hood. Intelligence was not his forte. Birds – of the human variety – were. His trade in fact. None of the noxious, destructive heroin which provided the source of wealth for the suppliers at the expense of the ultimate misery of the users. His was good, clean, respectable prostitution. No coercion. Willing providers matched with willing buyers; he took a 25% handling fee – as he liked to term it. The local hotel concierges were only too happy to provide clandestine suitable accommodation for a small reward. That's how it worked in the fifties.

Johnny prospered. One of those who believed that he could do no wrong. And he couldn't. Until the day when, with all the ruthlessness associated with his heritage, he beat up a punter who defaulted on payment of the fee and wishing to escape the scene before he could be identified, he drove away down Wardour Street with such ferocity that it attracted the attention of a passing police patrol car. An arrest followed by a charge of dangerous driving.

He needed the services of a solicitor. Not the ordinary,

conventional, play by the book, kind. No. A specialist creative defence lawyer. Who better than Harvey Barker? Fifty-five years of age, a man, in comparison to whom the imagination of Ernest Hemingway was that of a mere copywriter. His ability to dismiss the obvious in favour of the ingenious, was legion. A history of spectacular acquittals in the face of overwhelming evidence, made him a continuing thorn in the side of the police. Maltese Mick, Corsican Christo, and Turkish Tony were a representative sample of his clientèle. But there was no denying his charm, sense of humour and generosity, as well as an unimpeachable integrity within the demi mondiale culture in which he operated.

'Not a problem,' explained Harvey to Johnny during their first meeting. 'Leave it to me and come back in three weeks. And bring me £5000 in readies.'

At the second appointment Johnny met Maud Williams. A lady in her sixties with a distinguished professional history in theatrical costume and creative makeup. 'Well, what do you suggest?' asked Harvey after explaining all the circumstances.

'All taken care of,' Maud said, after no more than five minutes thinking, 'just make sure that Johnny gets to my studio by 7 o'clock on the morning of the trial.'

And so he did. And at 9.30 on that morning, he presented himself to the custody clerk at the Old Bailey. The clerk saw a bald headed man cutting a pathetic figure, with his authentic looking false beard and moustache, crumpled nylon unwashed white shirt, brown, ill fitting, holes in sleeves jacket, and ill matching green baggy trousers. His black shoes had not been cleaned for weeks.

His case was called at 11.30. The jury was sworn in. In answer to the Court Clerk, he acknowledged his name as Johnny Bardini and entered a plea of not guilty.

Prosecuting Counsel, Rufus Slade, opened by describing in graphic detail to the jury the degree of danger caused by the defendant's 'wholly irresponsible, reckless and dangerous driving'. The two patrol car policemen also gave graphic descriptions.

Police Sergeant William Burnside, was the first witness. 'Tell the jury in your own words, officer, what you saw in the afternoon of 26th June this year.'

Burnside was immaculate. Clear. Concise. Descriptive to a fault. Certain beyond any shadow of doubt of what he witnessed that afternoon. A car driven by Johnny Bardini at 65 miles per hour down Wardour Street at 4.37 pm causing other vehicles to swerve violently and all but colliding with innocent pedestrians.

'Thank you,' said Counsel. 'I just have one further question. For the record, and for the jury: could I trouble you to identify the defendant? Would you be good enough to point him out?' Burnside peered up. Looked towards the dock. Blinked and looked again. Then shook his head.

'Yes?' asked Counsel. 'Do you have a problem?'

Clearing his throat and taking a deep breath Officer Burnside explained that he did indeed have a problem. And no small one at that. Whoever was in the dock was not the man he had arrested at the scene. Counsel was baffled. He asked the officer whether he was sure.

'Yes,' came the reply. 'The man in the dock doesn't look anything like the driver of the car who we apprehended. In fact, he couldn't look less like him.'

The jury began to titter. The Judge was irritated.

'Mr. Slade. It seems to me that this may well be a case of mistaken identity. Are you sure that you really wish to proceed?'

After a hasty conversation with the lawyers sitting behind him Rufus Slade rose.

'Your Honour. I am instructed to offer no further evidence in this case.'

'Very well,' said the Judge, 'case dismissed.'

The trick had worked. Maud's brilliant creation of Johnny's disguise had succeeded. He emerged from Court elated. Ecstatic. So much so that with all the impulse of a man possessed with untouchability while on the steps outside Court he ripped off his false bald head, moustache and beard and threw them straight up in the air shouting, 'Brilliant Mr. Barker. Thanks a million. Worth every pound of that five grand.'

It was unfortunate for him, and Harvey, that the beard landed in the hands of the passing Officer Burnside who had little difficulty in recognizing Johnny. 'Got him now,' thought Burnside. But those days preceded the change in the law which allowed a person to be tried more than once for the same offence. That was it. He was free.

Or so he thought. The police were livid. They had been humiliated; made to look a laughing stock. Something had to be done. Urgent consultations with the Director of Public Prosecutions resulted in a trial of Johnny and Harvey for conspiracy to pervert the cause of justice. The allegation was that he had altered his appearance to give the impression that he was somebody other than the alleged culprit. This time there was to be no disguise. Nor a sympathetic Judge whose summing up could not be criticized for showing too much accommodation to the defendants, neither of whom gave evidence, relying instead on submissions that the prosecution had failed to establish its case beyond reasonable doubt – arguments which received short shrift from the intemperate Judge.

'Guilty' was the unanimous verdict in each case. Followed by a conditional discharge for 'brainless' Johnny, and a sentence of one year's imprisonment for Harvey.

In the Judge's words 'the prime instigator of an outrageous scheme of deception wholly unworthy of a member of the legal profession.'

But there was yet another turn of events. Harvey's barrister marched straight down the road to the Court of Appeal who granted Harvey bail pending a full appeal hearing. The grounds were simple. At no time had Johnny ever denied who he was. On the contrary, the only words which he had spoken at the trial, apart from pleading not guilty to the charge of dangerous driving, were to confirm his name. How, could it be maintained that he was pretending to be somebody other than who he was? There is no law which – without transgressing the rules of decency – prevents a defendant from adopting in Court such mode of dress and appearance as he or she might choose.

Grounds which the Court of Appeal felt unable to resist. Unscrupulous? Maybe. Ingenious? Certainly. Illegal? No case to answer. Conviction quashed.

PS. This is a story based on truth. The names of the *dramatis personae* have been changed.

A Higher Duty

It all started in the bar in the magnificent turreted Wentworth Clubhouse. The host to that select band of golfing enthusiasts lucky enough to enjoy the outstanding golfing facilities comprising three golf courses. The Edinburgh, The East, and The – iconic – West. Each posing its own challenge to the users who, regardless of their level of competence, would, if they took the time to reflect on their fortune, thank the Lord for the opportunities presented by the experience.

Wentworth – a quintessential Surrey piece of life enhancing real estate – was an experience to savour – to appreciate for the most aspiring high handicapper to the seasoned pro. And all the more special if the weather – and the putter – obliged. The taste of the 19th hole Cobra beer would be all the sweeter.

Charlie Fairhaven on that Saturday afternoon in June halved his match with co-member Chuck Ainsley thanks to a wickedly curling left to right putt of 23 feet which, after hesitating for a good five seconds, decided to drop in the hole just when it seemed to have run out of steam.

'Well played, buddy. Well played! Great putt. Let me buy you a drink,' said a genuinely delighted Chuck.

They both enjoyed their drinks at the 19th hole.

'Wow. That's good,' Chuck beamed as he took his first gulp of the ice-cold liquid. 'Beautiful. Simply beautiful. Cheers.'

'Great match,' replied Charlie. 'We must do it again sometime.'

'Agreed,' said Chuck. 'Now! When I fixed the game with you I must confess to an ulterior motive. You're a lawyer – are you not – with a firm of City Solicitors.

'Correct,' replied Charlie. 'One of ten partners in Woodfields. A splinter rim from a much larger City Magic Circle firm. Been going now for three years. If you were to ask me how things are going, I'd reply "pretty good". But always on the lookout for new business of course.'

'What's your speciality, if I might ask?' said Chuck.

'Corporate,' replied Charlie. 'Acquisitions, mergers. That sort of thing.'

'Great. I'll let you into another secret. I googled you before fixing up and checked on your expertise. I've got a proposition to put to you,' said Chuck. 'Let me know what you think.'

At 6pm the following Monday the ten partners of Woodfields were all seated in the boardroom to await the start of the monthly partners meeting to be chaired by Robert Harding, the firm's practice manager.

'Good afternoon, Gentlemen. I hope we are all well. Let's start, as usual, with the monthly figures. Everybody seems to be doing pretty well. All on your billing targets. Except – I have to say – you Charlie. Your billings are, on average, 35 per cent below everyone else's. Also, it's my duty to remind everyone that for the last six months your generated income has been 26.38 per cent below the other nine partners' average.'

Charlie was fixed with a resentful collective glare from his colleagues, all of whom, together with Charlie, enjoyed an equal 10% share of the practice profits. The activities of different clients yielded different returns and that some hours worked were, inevitably, effectively unbillable, but generally things would tend to even out over a six-month period.

Nobody said a word. The very silence increased the temperature.

'True, gentlemen,' replied Charlie eventually. 'I can't deny it. But I'm not entirely sure that one's contribution to the success of this practice is exclusively down to fees billed.'

Three gasps of incredulity to that.

'It's fees what pay our bills,' retorted Martin Gates, the partner heading the ultra-lucrative high worth matrimonial division. 'And I, for one, am prepared to speak my mind and say that if this state of affairs continues there should be a reallocation of profits which recognises the disparity.'

'Hear hear,' echoed four or five others.

'Now, now, brothers,' said Roy Brown, the senior member. 'Let's all calm down. We've all had a good run. We get on well. We have a thriving practice. Maybe there is something in what Charlie says. Now, Robert, what's next on the agenda.'

'Ah. Before moving on you might be interested in hearing something I have to say,' Charlie put in and proceeded to recount the gist of his conversation in the Wentworth bar with Chuck Ainsley. Would the firm be prepared to act for Cox Pharmaceuticals plc, a newly formed UK subsidiary of an expanding Vietnamese group, in its proposed takeover of SS Pharma Inc, an American company with sole, patented, rights to the production of a new drug, Perigot, an SSRI – Selective Serotonin Reuptake Inhibitor – specially modified for the treatment of pregnant mothers. Perigot had recently acquired US Federal Drug Agency approval. UK regulatory approval was expected to be granted shortly. The deal would be exceptionally complex.

Chuck was the drugs expert advising Cox and was ready to instruct Woodfields to act on its behalf. The retainer fee would be calculated not on hours expended but on a percentage of the purchase price, 3%.

Martin Jones was quick to intervene. 'We don't charge like that,' he said snootily. 'We're not commission agents.'

'The purchase price is $700 million,' said Charlie, unperturbedly. Followed by a stunned silence.

'Do we need a vote?' asked Roy Brown, to which there was no answer. 'Right then. Go ahead Charlie. A fee of £15 million, or thereabouts, depending on the exchange rate, is not to be sneezed at.'

Charlie, on a winning streak, added: 'By the way. There's more than likely more to come. Cox has lined up buyers to take them out after one year. As long as an agreed sales target is achieved, they will buy the company for $800 million. We will be instructed on the same percentage retainer. That OK with everyone?'

It was all systems go at Woodfields. In an atmosphere of anticipation at the prospect of their largest – by a mile – single fee of all time. Charlie being treated as a bit of a hero.

'Everything alright, Charlie?' asked Martin. 'If you need any help on anything that my department can provide, you'll let me know of course. Don't hesitate for one second.'

After 13 meetings over five weeks with the solicitors for SS Pharma, all outstanding matters had been resolved. All 18 draft documents agreed. The warranties, the terms of payment, the add on sums having constituted some of the contentious matters. Everything was finally ready for completion of the deal, the funds for which would be available from the lending bank on seven days' notice. A date was set. 30th June, the purchase funds to be lodged in an escrow account to be released to the sellers on the publication UK regulatory approval. A special meeting of the partners of Woodfields had been convened to hear first-hand of the deal's progress.

Charlie assured everybody that all outstanding problems had been ironed out. Nothing, bar a happening which no one involved could foresee, could go wrong. Every eventuality had been covered. The meeting ended with 'good luck Charlies' being offered by everyone.

The wait for the completion meeting made all the partners very tense. It was a matter of keeping calm.

Poor old Charlie was becoming exhausted at having to deal with the increasing number of partners 'everything OK, Charlie?' enquiries which would interrupt his own increasingly stressful days.

At 3.17pm on 28th June an email pinged into Charlie's computer.

With no inbox message he opened spam. From a 'Ibkurv 236@ nobler'. Charlie hesitated before opening it. His computer had been sabotaged two years earlier when he had inadvertently opened a virus ridden website. This was not the same thing but for some reason he felt nervous. Nevertheless, he felt compelled to open it. Eschewing his misgivings, he clicked.

'Dear Charlie Fairhaven,' it read. 'My identity must remain secret. I am aware that you are acting on a takeover of the manufacturers of Perigot. Your clients need to know that there have been 29 cases in the USA in which the birth of the second child of the mother taking Perigot for anxiety, has resulted in death of the baby within 48 hours of birth. These cases have been kept secret from the public and payments totalling several million dollars have been paid to the mothers to buy their silence. On a betrayal of which the sums will become repayable. While the evidence is not conclusive that death has resulted from the drug, questions need to be raised – and answered. Your clients should think twice before proceeding.'

To suggest that Charlie faced a dilemma would be a huge understatement. Was the email authentic? Who was the author and what would he/she have to gain? And assuming it was genuine, was it his duty to pass on to his client and his client's lender something from an anonymous purported whistle-blower who might turn out to have sent a false, damaging and mischievous message, motivated by any one of a million reasons? Might he or she be a crank? And in any event if the transaction went ahead the buyers could always sue for compensation under the warranties if the drug was to become prohibited. On the other hand, if he were to remain silent the takeover would proceed, subject to the expected imminent grant of regulatory approval, when Cox would be free to distribute the drug for administration to mothers, with a risk of death to babies. He was also conscious of his duty to his partners. No deal. No fee. How could he let them down without compelling evidence?

Charlie's attempts to communicate with the sender were utterly frustrated, his emails being returned as undelivered and undeliverable. It was beginning to look as if there might have been some kind of conspiracy, for whatever reason, to hoax Charlie into a monumentally disastrous interference. One thing was for sure. He would have to make up his mind one way or another. Either act and take the consequences, or not act and live with what might turn out to be the indescribably horrendous consequences – blood on his hands.

He briefly considered whether or not to pursue some kind of investigation in the USA but decided that it would be too complex an exercise beyond his resources.

He chose to act and that led to trouble. The complaint against him issued by the Solicitors Disciplinary Tribunal read as follows:

That in breach of your duty to your clients, Cox Pharmaceutical plc, and in further breach of your duty of good faith to your partners in Woodfields, you did intentionally and without justifiable cause disseminate to your clients Cox Pharmaceuticals plc and their proposed lenders, the contents of an unauthenticated email from one Ibkurv 236@nobler with the intention of causing your clients to break the terms of their contract to acquire the issued share capital in SS Pharma Inc. Your febrile actions having caused substantial loss and damage to your said clients, and loss of potential substantial fees which would have become payable to Woodfields, you are required to answer the charge of serious professional misconduct.

Delivered by email on 13th July and by post on the following day.

At a specially convened meeting of the partners in Woodfields on 2nd July, to which Charlie had not been invited, a decision was taken to report his conduct to the Solicitors Regulatory Authority and to suspend him pending its findings. Meanwhile he was to be placed on gardening leave. He was barred from attending the firm's offices but would be paid as if he were free to work.

It was to Anthony Harrison, a solicitor practising in the West End to whom he turned for help.

'It might be pretty expensive,' said Anthony at their preliminary meeting. 'If you get done, I'll do it for nothing, of course. I'll regard myself as having failed and would not want to incur a charge for a fellow solicitor. It'll be different if we succeed in getting the charge thrown out. My usual charges will then apply and we'll hope to recover them from the SRA. But there will definitely be outsiders' fees. If you use the best – as I do – they don't come cheap.'

The hearing of the disciplinary panel of the SRA was scheduled to take place at its offices in Farringdon Street on 16th August.

'It gives me little time,' said Anthony to his client. 'Should I apply for an adjournment, do you think?'

'I'd rather get it over if we can,' Charlie said.

'It means I'll have to ask them to act double quick. They're good chaps and will do their best,' Anthony replied.

The hearing opened on its due date. The panel consisted of three members. In the Chair Paul Gates, a solicitor of 15 years' standing with a reputation for upholding the strict principles governing the conduct of solicitors.

He was not widely known for leniency. He sat with two lay members. Audrey Masterson, a retired prison governor, and George Miller, an ex army veteran. Given their respective backgrounds neither was likely to be any kind of soft touch. If Charlie were to escape a striking off or a suspension, Anthony would have to produce the goods and be on top form.

The SRA was represented by Mary Goodfellow, QC. After outlining the facts – the instructions of Cox to Charlie to act on the acquisition, the terms of the retainer of Woodfields, the content of the email and its disclosure to Cox and its bankers, their withdrawal from their commitment to advance the purchase price, the consequent breakdown of the deal, and the reporting of Charlie to the SRA, the case for the SRA was established.

Charlie had got cold feet. Had failed to properly exercise his professional judgement and thereby breached his duty to act in the best interests of his clients and his partners. He had, in reality, acted out of fear at the expense of evidence. He was accordingly unfit to practise as a solicitor.

'It's your turn now, Mr. Harrison. May I have your list of witnesses and documents please,' Paul Gates said.

'I regret I am unable to give you any such list,' replied Anthony. 'It will all depend.'

'On what precisely?' asked the Chairman.

'I can't tell you I'm afraid,' said Anthony. 'To be honest I'm not exactly sure myself.'

'Well, that's not good enough,' said the Chairman. 'No list means no testimony, documentary or in person – strictly according to the rules. Now I presume you will want to call your client.'

At which point Charlie went into the witness box and repeated a prepared written statement of his reasons for acting as he did. He had regarded the risks of silence as against the consequences of disclosure as too great.

'You were unable to establish contact with this anonymous whistle-blower, is that correct?' asked Mary Goodfellow.

'Correct,' replied Charlie.

'So, you had not a shred of evidence to support the truth of his/her allegations?'

'Correct.'

'And you were prepared to make a decision detrimental to the interests of your clients and your partners, on the word of a possible malicious crank?'

'I made the decision in what I regarded might have been in my client's interests – as well as the interests of the population at large – and not against them.'

'With no supporting evidence? Do you really believe that to be acceptable behaviour of a competent commercial solicitor?'

Charlie remained silent.

The Chairman intervened. 'We are waiting, Mr. Fairhaven.'

Still no answer. Anthony tried to rescue the situation by asking Charlie to explain in detail why he acted as he did, but Charlie appeared broken by the intensity of the interrogation. He left the witness box a forlorn figure.

As he walked back to his seat his emotion got the better of him. He stopped and turned towards the Chairman. 'I'd like to know what you would have fucking well done in my situation. You talk about duties to my clients and my partners. What about my duties to humanity? To all those potential victims?' And muttered just about audibly under his breath 'supercilious bastard'.

'We will adjourn for 15 minutes,' said the Chairman, 'during which you may wish to give some further advice to your client. An admission of responsibility is something you may wish to bear in mind.'

The panel members retired. Anthony reminded Charlie that a recognition of unprofessional conduct coupled with an expression of regret and remorse might avoid a striking off.

'No way,' said Charlie. 'I did what I thought was right.'

At which point Anthony's mobile tinged. A text message. Resulting in an enigmatic smile.

The panel returned. 'Yes, Mr. Harrison? You have something helpful to tell us I hope,' said the Chairman.

'I hope so,' said Anthony. 'If you would be good enough to indulge me ten minutes.'

'Very well,' said the Chairman.

Anthony left for the foyer of the building. After an agonising wait of 15 minutes his expected visitor arrived.

'Here are the documents,' he said. 'The owners are on their way.'

'Thanks a million, Victor,' said Anthony. 'You're a star.'

'If I may,' Anthony said to the panel, 'I would like to produce these documents in evidence.'

'Too late,' said the Chairman. 'You've had your opportunity. It's passed.'

'You have a discretion to admit them,' retorted Anthony, 'and since they are crucial to the interests of justice, I suggest that you allow me to produce them before I pop round the corner to the Court of Appeal where the Master of the Rolls is ready to hear an application to overrule your ruling.'

The Chairman froze in his seat. Stared at Anthony stunned by his impertinence. Considered his options. 'Very well. What do you wish to produce?'

Anthony opened an A4 envelope and removed 19 documents. All from one or other coroner's office in one or other state of the USA. Each a death certificate.

'I will save you the burden of reading,' said Anthony. 'This is one of 19 similar death certificates issued by a State Coroner of the USA. It records the death of a child. Richard Parsons. Born 17th October last year. Died 19th October two days later. The cause of death is recorded as unknown. A separate signed coroner's note is attached. It records his suspicions that death was caused by the administration of the SSRI drug Perigot over five months to the mother, Eileen Parsons.'

Brandishing a second certificate Anthony proceeded to read its content. Similar in wording. Name of child Mildred Chase. Date of death two days after birth and a similar accompanying note. Mother – Nancy Chase.

'I have 17 further similar certificates. I assume that you do not wish me to read them all out,' Anthony said.

'I am not convinced,' said Paul Gates. 'Where is the evidence of their authenticity? None as far as I can see.'

The other two panel members nodded in agreement.

'Are you seriously suggesting a conspiracy to deceive the Panel?' asked Anthony.

'We will draw our own conclusions as to their genuineness,' Gates replied. 'Now we will retire to consider our decision.'

Anthony removed his mobile from his pocket and texted a rapid message. The reply pinged back. 'Ready and waiting.' One further text from Anthony and the rear double doors of the room opened to let in a dignified and solemn procession of 19 women, whose ages ranged between something like 20 and 40. They stood. Still as an oak tree.

'What is this unannounced intervention?' asked Paul Gates.

The first lady to have entered was the first to speak. 'My name, Sir, is Eileen Parsons. Like my 18 friends here, I was prescribed Perigot which I took daily for five months before the birth of my second child, Richard. He lived for two days.'

'My name is Nancy Chase' said the second lady. 'My daughter Mildred survived for two days before she died unexpectedly. I had been taking Perigot to treat depression and anxiety for three months before the birth of Mildred, my second child.'

Visibly moved Paul Gates took a handkerchief from his jacket pocket and dabbed his eye.

'Would you care to hear the testimony of these further 17 brave ladies?' asked Anthony. 'They have all come over from America to testify in support of my client in breach of their respective non-disclosure obligations. Hunted down, if that is not too an offensive expression, by Victor Hardacre, a private detective employed at my client's expense to trace the whereabouts of some of the unfortunate victims of this lethal drug, the potential damage from which would have been kept secret but for the actions of my client. Something that you may regard as material in considering your decision.'

'Mr. Fairhaven,' said Paul Gates after a retirement of three minutes, 'perhaps you would be good enough to stand while I address you. It is the panel's unanimous decision that your conduct, far from being unprofessional, was a quintessential illustration of the highest standards of the solicitor's profession your membership of which it is honoured to respect. You have discharged an unwritten duty. A duty beyond the mere respect for one's client. A higher duty altogether. One directed to the protection of universal health of humanity. All allegations of misconduct are hereby rejected. This application accordingly fails. You leave this hearing with our most profound admiration and respect. And, in anticipation of an application by your solicitor, we hereby order the SRA to pay all your legal and other expenses incurred in connection with this enquiry.'

A hastily convened ad hoc meeting of the partners of Woodfields was held later that day at 6pm. This time Charlie was invited. The proceedings were so confidential that it was decided not to minute them.

'See you tomorrow, Charlie,' said Roy Brown. Adding, as he turned to leave, 'And it will be an honour.'

A Higher Duty – the Sequel

'Look at this, Roy. What do you reckon?'

Peering over Charlie Fairhaven's shoulder at the computer screen on the Monday morning eight days after Charlie's 'acquittal', Charlie's senior partner was looking at an email from an important sounding James Bernard Huntley-Jones, CEO of Huntley-Jones Associates, Recruitment Agents. It was an invitation to attend their offices at 6pm the following day for a preliminary chat concerning an exciting new global venture, whose sponsors would be seeking legal representation at the highest level.

'Your name has been supplied to us in strict confidence by a confidential source. All that I am at liberty to say is that you come highly recommended. Please be good enough to email your acceptance or rejection by close of business today.'

'Hm,' grunted Roy. 'Sounds a bit mysterious to me but I suppose you have nothing to lose. After what you've recently been through you ought to be pretty circumspect and battle hardened to avoid being duped by any sophisticated hoax or other. You ask me what I reckon. Give it a go, I say. Even if only to satisfy your – and my – curiosity.'

Charlie walked into the imposing Mayfair building in Curzon Street through the polished oak front door which clicked free of its electrically operated lock once his arrival had been approved. He was greeted by a tall, beautifully manicured, Hermes suit, Philip Starc spectacles. Hair swept back. Discreet pink lipstick and a faint aroma of Ma Griffe perfume.

'Mr. Fairhaven, I presume. Do follow me please,' the receptionist smiled.

Charlie was led to the first floor up a wide, impressively constructed spiral staircase with yew bannisters. At the top of the stairs, a door opened and Charlie was shown into a breathtaking imitation of what could have passed for the National Gallery, with impressionist paintings of Monet, Degas, Millais, Seurat and others, which Charlie was unable to identify but none less spectacular for that.

'Nice, huh,' said the figure standing by the side of the open door observing Charlie struggling to absorb what he was seeing. 'I believe you know Chuck Ainsley.'

For the second time in 30 seconds, Charlie opened his mouth in disbelief.

'Hi, pal,' said Chuck. 'Good to see you again. Let me introduce you to James Huntley-Jones.'

After exchanging 'good to meet you's', Charlie was invited to sit on one of three leather sedan chairs, while James and Chuck occupied the other two. James set the ball rolling.

'Let me tell you what this is about. You must be intrigued I daresay. Now it's all highly secret and hush hush so what may be said in this room stays here. Understood I hope.'

'Take it as read,' replied Charlie.

'Good,' replied James. 'I'll begin. We represent some exceptionally powerful and influential interests who have combined to form a global taskforce to address the problems posed by what is commonly accepted by governments to constitute the most serious and pressing issue facing humanity. Animality and reptility as well, come to that. That is to say climate change. Secret talks between leading, and not so leading, nations have been held over the past three years. A political alliance is underway, involving, in addition to the recognised obligations to conduct green energy research, questions of financing, provision and allocation of resources, employment of personnel, the sharing of data and ideas – and so on. As well as national governments on board the project, are private corporations like Microsoft, Amazon, Apple, Facebook, Sony, Barclays, Deutschebank, Coca–Cola – to mention a few of the more celebrated names.

'A non-profit making umbrella organisation – let's call it CC Holdings – has been established to oversee the project. Its name is top secret. Those on its board recognise the importance of setting up the necessary legal structures under which the different operations will be governed. The engagement of a set of lawyers with impeccable credentials is critical. Not just of ability and expertise. But also of integrity befitting the ethical objectives of the entire operation. A sub-committee has deputed me to find a lawyer who has the qualities and qualifications to form a professional team dedicated to handling all the commercial legal work.

'The reason why you are sitting here is Chuck's recommendation. To suggest that he speaks highly of you is to grossly understate the extent of his admiration. He has told me that never in his career has he encountered a more moral, unselfish, self-sacrificing individual than you. You will obviously have to think about it. From what I understand you have a distinguished collection of partners well qualified to handle the work.

'Before I forget; a small matter of remuneration. The fee arrangement would not be governed by actual hours worked. I have always considered that to be a recipe for overcharging. Instead, an annual retainer would be paid and calculated on the basis of a projected 40 hours working week per lawyer at a rate of £2000 per hour for senior grade, £1500 middle grade and £1000 for junior grade. A charging scale which should let you easily recruit top quality staff.

'Chuck will see you out. Let me know your thoughts when you have had a chance to discuss it with your partners – assuming, that is – that you may be interested in exploring the possibilities. Take your time. Seven days, I would hope, ought to be sufficient. By all means speak to Chuck in the meantime if there are questions to be asked or anything might be troubling you.'

'I'm not sure whether this is real or I'm dreaming, to be honest,' said Charlie. 'It's almost too much to take in.'

James held out his hand to be shaken. 'It's real enough. Charlie. Take it from me. You're not dreaming.'

They went for a Starbucks coffee, Charlie and Chuck.

'There is something troubling me and it's what you're not telling me, Chuck,' said Charlie once they had sat down and ordered. 'I would have thought that after Cox missing out on a likely profit of $100 million – all because I blew the gaffe – that I would be your worst enemy. It doesn't make any sense.'

Chuck gave Charlie a quizzical look.

'Would you really like to know? First, I am not, as I held myself out to you, a drugs expert. I know no more about the subject than the next person. I work for Huntley-Jones Associates. Have done for 23 years. They deal with recruitment to positions of the highest nature. Financial directors of FTSE 100 companies, that sort of thing. Four months ago, we were instructed to look for an exceptionally qualified solicitor meeting all the criteria which James has just described to you. Integrity being key. Alongside competence, skill and vision. Your name was on our radar.

'The question was: would you pass the cornerstone test? How could we find out? Be sure? Both Cox and SS Pharma are clients of James. With their permission we contrived to fabricate an imaginary takeover with a false story of a prospective sale on for a $100 million profit. The drug Perigot was a fiction. The whole scenario concocted. The whistle-blower emails a perfect device to present you with the opportunity to show your true colours. Pursue your own, your partners' and your client's interests at the expense of wider interests of society, or do the noble thing and risk your career? And what did you do? Exactly what we hoped. And expected.'

'But what about the Solicitors Disciplinary proceedings?' asked Charlie. How you could have been sure about the outcome?'

'A risk we had to take,' said Chuck, 'when we reported you, but one which we were confident of minimising. The fake death certificates. The budding actresses hired from RADA to play the roles of the bereaved mothers. It was all meticulously calculated to be nothing short of authentic and likely to melt even the hardest heart. Following our hunch that you would more than likely be inclined to instruct someone like the "go to" Anthony Harrison, we guessed rightly that he would instruct the legendary Victor Hardacre, your private detective. So, we brought him in on the plan. Instructing him to pretend to Anthony that he was "on the case" and finally to produce, at the last moment, the phoney documents and the troop of students in that dramatic, impact maximising manner.'

'Thanks a million,' replied Charlie. 'I'm glad you were so confident. Gambling with my career like that.'

'Ah. But we had insurance. You don't honestly think that you would have been left high and dry in the unemployment pile, do you? With our resources we had a more than appetising menu of employment choices at our disposal.'

'If you say so,' said Charlie.

'So that's it. Now you know the whole story. And now you've got an opportunity of a lifetime. Talk to your partners about it and if, as we hope, there is more than a flicker of interest, don't hesitate to come back to me with what I guess would be a catalogue of questions. How about a further conversation on Saturday? Tee off say 11.30 OK for you? I can think of worse environments than the fairways of the West course. Good weather forecast. I've already checked.'

Almost Sold Down the River

As UK boarding schools at the start of the 21st century went, Greyfields was among the more traditional. Single sex. Boys between the ages of seven and 18. Slavish to the Church of England ethos of its founding fathers, there was a rigorous insistence on pre-assembly morning chapel. An equally rigorous regard for discipline as well as respect for one's fellow man. Academic achievement was recognised by the award of end of year prizes for excellence. Sporting prowess was recognised too but to a far lower degree.

The school had produced distinguished mathematicians, chemists and scientists, as well as authors and musicians. Its Governors had to maintain its reputation for eminence in learning and artistic merit. Failure was treated with a certain disdain. Demoralising for some. But inspiring determination in others. Some pupils could not cope and left which occasionally might place some strain on the school's finances. On the other hand, survival of the fittest made for keen competition and improved prospects of excellence. Greyfields was no place for the complacent.

As an experiment in incentive, a weekly points system had been instituted. Good points conferred several privileges consisting principally of recreational visits to the local town of Berkhamsted, a 20-minute bus ride away. The greater the number of points the longer the permitted absence after 5pm with the latest return time of 10.30 at night. If pupils were late, they incurred a penalty calculated according to some convoluted formula which nobody even purported to understand. By 2012 the system had had its day. Not only unfathomable but counterproductive and effectively unenforceable. More important, the age of technology was rapidly beginning to influence. Search engines – rather than the obsolescent school library – would be the preferred option to gain knowledge. Broadcast entertainment would be available at the touch of a screen. The only problem at Greyfields was its reluctance to embrace 21st century technology.

The start of 2012 produced a bombshell. Dr. Fishman, the headmaster for the previous 24 years, announced he had a terminal illness. His health would allow a maximum of six weeks further attendance before he would have to sit his final examination at the pearly gate.

The school needed a new head urgently who had to be appointed through the accepted formal processes. The Governors conferred. Applications for new students had been in steady decline. Was this not the time for a review of direction? To abandon antiquated practices. Adapt to the modern world. Jettison the worst and retain the best. Seek a leader who would implement the new approach. By a majority of five to four – and after a thorough and robust exchange of opinions – it was resolved to change tack.

'Let's go for it,' said the Chairman of the Board, Sir Hartley Robinson. 'No holds barred. We've been waiting too long for this moment.'

Applications were invited both from the current teaching staff and from outside. The advertisement specified the primary requirement – for change. A vision through which rapidly evolving technology would be harnessed to the school's cultural tradition to create a vibrant, modern environment in which creative expression, as well as the basic educational repertoire, would flourish. Candidates would be invited to give a short speech on their proposals to revolutionise. Down to a short list of five, including the one surviving member of staff – 42-year-old bachelor Barry Pritchard, a maths teacher for the past 17 years and the last ten as the senior tutor. He had secretly considered himself to be the natural successor to Dr. Fishman. The process of selection had been continuing in earnest when, with two weeks before the prospective departure of the headmaster, fate intervened. On suffering a debilitating stroke Dr. Fishman had to stop work. Barry was asked to the fill the gap on an interim basis. He rose to the challenge with admirable skill and attention. At his desk at 7 o'clock every morning. Retiring never before 8 in the evening. Not a foot wrong. Reliable as the chimes of Big Ben.

The Governors extended their profuse thanks just before the announcement of the new appointment on the last day of term.

Miles Richardson was 37 years old. On leaving school with three GCSEs and one D grade A level in geography, he had gone on a year's round the world trip with his guitar. After a cannabis filled year stretching between the spiritual heights of Nepal, the hippy community of Los Angeles and the cultural excitement of Florence, he returned to England convinced of the educational merits of a non-regimented curriculum. The exclusive study of traditional subjects – arithmetic, geography, Latin for example – constituted an anachronistic waste of human resource. How much better to study philosophy – even Sartre – law, pop music, the media for example. Not to the exclusion of basic subjects, but as additional options.

After his round the world tour Miles had qualified as a teacher and had taken various jobs in various schools over the past 15 years, and none for longer than three. As he changed from private to state, from junior to senior roles, he got experience of many types of teaching and student.

He was never able though to practise his philosophy of education. His interview with the five governors was a not just a breath of fresh air, but rather a tornado of modern thinking. Here was a candidate with the experience, breadth of experimental vision and ambition, to revolutionise Greyfields. An opportunity to restore its eminence. Risky perhaps. But a worthwhile gamble in the panel's view. He would start at the beginning of the Easter term.

All the school staff and students felt excited when the announcement was made. The exception being Barry. He appeared stoical but he had an all-consuming, seething, obsessional, jealousy. His birthright stolen from under his nose. His dreams shattered by this unconventional, untried, untested ex-nomadic non-achiever. He resolved that his opportunity would come – somehow or other. And so, it did. And sooner rather than later. But not before the advent of the first of the sweeping changes introduced by the new Head. The window on the world. An Ipad on loan – and free – for every pupil.

The summer A level examinations would start at the end of May. Barry was particularly excited. One of his pupils, Richard Brogan, was about to make history by taking the senior exams at his tender age of 13. A boy whose genius had shone since excelling in maths GCSE when he was only ten, earning the nickname Einstein. He was almost exclusively focused on numbers. Some might have placed him on the outer edge of the autistic spectrum, but that would have ignored his ability to socialise with his peers. But there was no denying his burning desire to succeed in these exams and to create what would be a major bit of history. Oxbridge for Einstein at the age of 15 beckoned.

Forty-eight pupils sat down to be examined. Each one had been subjected to an external body search to ensure they had not hidden electronic devices which could be called upon to help them. Twenty minutes remained when Einstein held up his hand. 'Desperate to go to the loo,' he said.

'Not on your own,' Barry, one of the invigilators said. 'If you really can't control your bowels until the end of the sitting, I will take the exceptional step of accompanying you and will wait while you evacuate.'

Einstein hurried for the lavatories along the corridor – Barry in pursuit. Entering the third cubicle in the row he finally was heard to pull the chain after three minutes. Barry was waiting for him in the body of the facilities and hurried him to return to the examination hall. Excusing himself Barry returned to the lavatories. And entered the third cubicle where he discovered above the cistern, and out of view from below, an Ipad.

'One moment, Einstein. Would you mind joining me in my study?' asked Barry as the exam ending bell rang out. 'There's something we need to discuss.'

As they sat down Einstein saw an expression of deep concern on his teacher's face. And when Barry produced the Ipad from his briefcase, Einstein collapsed in an uncontrolled heap of tears.

Barry locked the door to his study.

'How could you? I assume that this must belong to you. You know where I have recovered it from.'

Einstein stopped snivelling. Blew his nose. And sat in silence. Barry allowed him to suffer. Just sat staring at him. Eventually Einstein spoke. 'What are you going to do with me, sir? I'm so sorry. There was an answer that needed checking and that's why I made the enquiry. I admit it. I attempted to cheat even though the information which I got only merely confirmed that the answer which I had written was correct. I can't deny it.'

Looking a tearful Einstein in the eye Barry spoke in a grave and menacing tone. 'If you play ball with me the answer is "nothing". If you don't then I will have no choice but to report your actions to the authorities.'

'Anything, sir. Anything you say.'

'Right,' said Barry. 'This is what you will do. Listen to me. You will go to the headmaster's study and knock on the door. I am assuming that he will ask you to enter which is exactly what you will do. You will suggest to him that you believe that I – that is to say Mr. Pritchard – deserve some kind of recognition of 17 years faithful service to the school. And that perhaps a suitable embossed plaque should be presented to me on prize day which nobody will know about until it happens. Confidentiality will be something about which the headmaster will feel very strongly. Be sure to ensure that as you are leaving via his open study door you say in suitably audible tones that he should not worry and that the secret is safe with you. After that you will go and see Mr. Jeffries, the deputy headmaster, and tell him that you have been a victim of an indecent assault by Mr. Richardson who took his trousers down after inviting you into his study and required you to touch him. To add credibility to your story, say, if asked to describe his genitals, that you noticed that he had only one testicle. Something I happened to learn during my last, and Mr. Richardson's first, term at the same school when he suffered a terrible rugby injury. It was everybody's talking point.'

'You're asking a lot of me,' replied Einstein.

'It's your choice,' said Barry.

'Can I think about it?' said the boy.

'I'm afraid not,' said Barry.

'Which is the way to the headmaster's study?' asked Einstein.

The speed of events after Einstein's complaint had been made to Mr. Jeffries was fast. Within 15 minutes two police cars arrived. Miles was arrested on suspicion of indecent assault. The governors consulted. Miles was suspended on full pay pending further investigation. A comprehensive statement taken from Einstein in which he described Miles' anatomical deficiency. A statement from Jonathan Swallow, a biology teacher who had been passing the Head's study as Einstein was leaving, and who he remembered distinctly saying that the secret was safe with him. The interview with the Detective Inspector where allegations were put and met, on the advice of Miles' solicitor, Ralph Goodfellow, a member of the panel of solicitors appointed by the National Union of Teachers, with a 'no comment'. A consultation arranged by Ralph Goodfellow with leading counsel who advised that Einstein's was so 'compelling' that a plea of guilty was the only sensible step. All within three days.

'I'm not even going to ask you whether there is any truth in the allegations,' said Sarah, the librarian at Berkhamsted library for the past seven years and Miles' fiancée of eight months. 'Miles, my darling. I know in my heart that you would be incapable of such behaviour. As far as I am concerned you are the personification of Jesus Christ. So, if you want me to stand by you, you will fight these allegations tooth and nail. Get rid of your pusillanimous lawyers. There's only one guy for you. He's a solicitor with rights to advocate in the Crown Court. Anthony Harrison is his name. With an office in the High Street. Go and see him as soon as you can get an appointment.'

Which he did.

After asking a number of searching questions about Miles, the school, its staff in general, and Barry Pritchard in particular, Anthony agreed to represent Miles.

'About your fees,' said Miles.

'You've no need to worry,' said Anthony. 'If you lose it will be my fault, so I won't charge a penny. If you win, I'll make bloody sure that the school pays. Either way it's not your problem. Leave matters to me. I'm going to Greyfields to make my own enquiries. Just remind me. When did you suffer the rugby injury which caused the removal of the damaged testicle, and what was the name of your school again?'

Anthony was allowed to visit three days later.

'I'd appreciate a sight of your staff records please,' he said to the deputy head. 'Nothing of a personal nature. Just background, education and the like.'

'With pleasure' was the reply. 'But details of schools attended are out of bounds. Something to do with data protection.'

The case came to St. Albans Crown Court on 2nd November before the Honourable Judge Mortimer Matthews. Master of all he surveyed within the precincts of the Court building where he had presided for the past 31 years. Matthews was known for his irascibility and impatience but he had never had even one case overturned by the Court of Appeal. A record of which he was justly proud especially since, in the eyes of most observers, it defeated all the odds.

At 10.30 am on Monday 12th November 2012, Court One had assembled. In the dock Miles Richardson. Representing the defendant Anthony Harrison. Counsel for the prosecution Sir Raymond Feniston QC. As His Honour Judge Mortimer Matthews entered the courtroom all those present were commanded by his clerk to rise. When he sat they were permitted to do likewise. The charge was read. The plea of not guilty entered. The jury was six men, six women.

Sir Raymond outlined the case for the Crown. How Einstein, lacking any conceivable motive to lie, would testify in graphic detail, how the accused had invited him to touch his private parts. An act which, if proved, would constitute an assault in law. How a teacher, Mr. Swallow, who had been passing the headmaster's study, would testify that he distinctly heard the complainant tell the accused not to worry that the secret could get out. And how, during police interrogation, the accused merely replied, 'no comment', rather than issue a strong denial which one might reasonably have expected from an innocent man. Sir Raymond went on to call his first witness, Jonathan Swallow, who testified exactly according to his written statement.

'You're absolutely sure that Einstein – as he is known and referred to throughout these proceedings – was keen to tell the accused that he would keep the secret?' asked Anthony.

'I am,' said Swallow.

'No doubt? Not even the smallest whiff of uncertainty?'

'None whatsoever.'

'How can you be so certain? Was there no general noise in the vicinity which might have made his words inaudible?'

'Well, to be honest, he said them in such a way that that the headmaster could not have been in any doubt. The way he spoke was both emphatic and unmistakeably loud and clear.'

'Too loud and clear if you ask me,' muttered Anthony under his breath.

'We do not need your private musings in my Court,' said the Judge. 'So, keep them to yourself if you don't mind.'

It was to be the first of what might be described as antagonistic exchanges between the Judge and Anthony Harrison.

Next it was Einstein's turn. As he took the oath the Judge smiled at him. 'You have nothing to be scared of,' he said to the boy. 'How do you like to be addressed? By your real name or, as people seem to refer to you as, Einstein?'

'Einstein, please sir.'

'Very well then. Einstein it is. Now just relax and tell the jury the truth just as you have been with your bravery and honesty with the police. I'm sure it must have been very hard for you.'

Anthony glanced at the jury. At least two were, by their facial expressions, indicating mild concern.

Einstein gave his answers in a careful, deliberate and confident manner. He repeated his original account. Sticking word for word to the script of his written statement.

'Are you sure that you wouldn't like a short break before Mr. Harrison subjects you to his questioning?' asked the Judge.

'No thanks, your Honour.'

'And don't forget. If you believe that his questions are at all unfair do not hesitate to ask me for my help.'

'I hadn't realised that you had undertaken the role of witness assistant,' Anthony complained. 'Is this the consequence of some new directive issued by the Lord Chief Justice in the case of under18-year-old witnesses?'

'Enough of sarcasm and proceed with your cross examination,' said the Judge testily.

'I will call you Einstein, if that's alright with you,' was Anthony's opening remark which was partly designed to put the witness at his ease.

'Einstein is fine by me.'

'You have been a pupil at Greyfields for six years, is that right?'

'That's correct.'

'And you have acquired the reputation of being something of a genius when it comes to mathematics?'

'That's correct,' he replied without a shred of conceit.

'Your teacher throughout this period has been Mr. Pritchard?'

'That's correct.'

'And since you achieved a starred A in GCSE maths at the age of ten you have been – what is fair to describe you as – the apple of his eye.'

'I can't disagree.'

'And would it be fair to say that at the same time, as your relationship has developed, you have acquired a high regard – bordering on reverence – for Mr Pritchard?'

'Mr. Harrison,' said the Judge intemperately. 'Where are you going with this line of questioning?'

'I'm going to wherever it it's leads me, your Honour.'

'And pray where might that be?'

'To be honest I'm not entirely sure, your Honour, but I'll do my best to put you out of your misery without undue delay.'

The Judge's beetroot-red face betrayed his growing anger but he did not rise to the bait.

'Einstein,' said Anthony, 'might you possibly be scared of Mr. Pritchard?'

'Really!' interjected the Judge. 'This is quite enough. I will not allow you to pursue questions of this perplexed young witness which constitute, as far as I can see, nothing more than an intimidating fishing exercise. If that is all I must ask you to sit down.'

'And I will remind your Honour, that whilst the Court of Appeal has yet to interfere with any one of your cases, there is always a first time for everything.'

Sir Raymond could not resist a surreptitious grin. At least five jurors were beginning to betray their sense of unease at the Judge's apparent bias.

The Judge, himself, simply exploded. 'I will see Sir Raymond in my chambers directly. You, Mr. Harrington' – 'Harrison' interjected Anthony – 'Mr Harrison, will remain in Court while I consult.'

It was the turn of Sir Raymond to intervene. 'I'm sorry your Honour. Do forgive me, but your attempt to see me in the absence of my learned friend merely perpetuates any appearance of bias on your Honour's part. Perhaps I might suggest that you grant Mr. Harrison a little latitude in his efforts to cross examine the witness.'

'Very well,' said a suitably chastened his Honour, 'continue as you wish.'

'I repeat the question, Einstein. Are you ever scared of Mr. Pritchard?'

'He's always treated me fairly if that's what you are asking.'

'He is a good teacher, is he not?'

'Absolutely brilliant.'

'Do you believe that he would have made a brilliant headmaster?'

'I do, as a matter of fact.'

'And you know that he applied for the post?'

'Yes.'

'And that he was disappointed to have been passed over in favour of a man five years younger than him and who had only been at the same school for one term.'

'Yes. I believe that was the case, but he managed to disguise his feelings.'

'How did you know that he had attended the same school?'

Einstein paused. A faint light was beginning to dawn. 'It was common knowledge, I believe.'

'When I tell you that nobody at Greyfields to whom I have spoken was aware that they shared the same school, even if only for one term, would you like to reconsider your answer?'

No reply.

'Let me come to your loo episode.' Einstein began to fidget. To look distinctly uncomfortable. 'After you had taken time out to evacuate, accompanied to the loo by Mr. Pritchard, you returned to finish the exam. And immediately after the bell rang you had a conversation with Mr. Pritchard, did you not?'

Einstein was beginning to show signs of becoming rattled.

'Tell the jury what was said between you.'

'I don't recall exactly,' Einstein said, unsure as to whether Anthony knew that a conversation had taken place or whether he might have been bluffing.

'Let me jog your memory for you. Was there perhaps some suggestion that a plaque be presented to him in recognition of his years of service to Greyfields. Or was that solely your idea?'

'You're quite right. We did discuss the plaque.'

'And whose idea was it to tell the head to ensure that the presentation was to remain a closely guarded secret between you and the head?'

'I don't recall.'

'Suppose that I were to suggest to you that it was Mr. Pritchard who told you that the new headmaster had only one testicle. Something that he would have known from being at the same school when Mr. Richardson suffered his distressing rugby injury. And that you submitted to Mr. Pritchard's pressure to frame Mr. Richardson of whom he was insanely jealous. And before you answer remember that you are under oath.'

Einstein looked up. He momentarily encountered the glance of Barry Pritchard sitting in the public gallery. He had had enough. The lies. The deception. The cheating. He was better than that. 'I prefer not to answer,' he answered.

Anthony looked at the Judge who was about to intervene. 'I have no further questions of this witness.'

It was Sir Raymond who rose. 'May it please your Honour. The Prosecution formally requests that the evidence against this defendant be withdrawn.'

'My pleasure to grant it,' said a suitably contrite Judge. 'I presume, Mr. Harrison, that you have no objection.'

'Tell me, Anthony,' said Miles when they had an alcoholic celebration at the Alford Arms, 'how did you know that Barry had put young Einstein up to it?'

'Let me explain what my thinking was when you first consulted me,' Anthony said. 'Other than your spirited denial – which I unconditionally accepted – I had absolutely no means of challenging Einstein's story. No inconsistencies in his evidence which I could find. I was starting with a blank sheet of paper. So, what was the first thing which I did – or rather considered? Motive. What reason, I asked myself, could Einstein have possibly had to fabricate such a wicked tale? I racked my brains. And concluded that there was only one way to find out. Make enquiries. Go to the school. Explain to the staff who I was and what I was doing there. My task was made infinitely easier because there was an equally infinite fund of goodwill towards me. Not a hint of evasiveness in the answers to my questions. By the time I had finished my third visit I reckon that I had found out just about everything there was to know about you, Miles – your strengths, your weaknesses, your legendary kindness and tolerance. I became more and more convinced of your innocence. But my sheet of paper remained blank. You appeared to have not an enemy in the whole world, let alone at the school. Nobody remotely eligible to qualify as a grudge holder as far as I could make out. One question however continued to trouble me. If Einstein was lying, how could it be that he knew that you had one testicle? Somebody must have told him. The answer had to contain the clue to the conundrum.

It was a matter of pure chance that George Potter, the HR administrator, happened to mention in passing that he had been completing a recent Education Survey concerning the schools which each schoolteacher had attended, and had found, to his utter amazement, that Barry's final term at Newcastle Grammar had coincided with your first term there. Almost certainly you had never been aware of it.

'After thanking George enthusiastically, I was totally convinced that the answer to my quest was to be found in Barry Pritchard. Further discreet enquiries elicited what all the staff seemed to know, but what none of them was keen openly to talk about. Barry's profound disappointment at missing out on the headship. So, I was able to deduce at a stroke that Barry had a credible motive for the frame up, evil though it would turn out to be. My next task was to establish a connection between Barry and Einstein in the conception of the plan. It was by a further coincidence that I made the discovery while talking to another teacher – Jenny Marshall – who had been invigilating the A level maths exam with Barry on the day.

'"I don't like to criticise",' she had said, "but when Barry allowed Einstein to take that so called comfort break towards the end, I did raise my eyebrows somewhat."

'That was all I needed to set my juices flowing. When was the break? How long had it lasted? Could it have been for reasons other than the stated ones? How soon after the end of the exam had Einstein had the incriminating conversation with Barry? My answers to myself to all these questions had led me to one conclusion. Barry had exerted some sort of hold over the boy who had been up to some kind of no good. Theories washed around in my head, as a result of one of which I arranged for a forensic interrogation of Einstein's Ipad. The result confirmed my worst suspicions, its startling revelations constituting the coup de grâce. I had hit the jackpot. The audibly stage-managed remark by Einstein on leaving your study was a mere piece of icing on the cake. So – you see – what may have appeared to everyone, including the Judge, as a speculative piece of fishing cross examination was really nothing of the kind. Fortunately, I had struck gold.'

'You're a star Anthony. Another large Glenfiddich 18?'

'I've a request to make of you,' said Anthony in a telephone call to Miles. 'Barry has asked me to represent him in his trial on a charge of conspiracy to pervert the course of justice. First, I need to know whether you have any objection. And second what the attitude of Greyfields might be towards him once his trial is over and his current suspension terminates. I can tell you that I have advised that anything but a guilty plea is unimaginable. It is to present a powerful plea in mitigation that my services would be required.'

'You'll have my answer within 24 hours,' replied Miles.

The trial of Barry Pritchard charged with conspiracy to pervert the course of justice was short. He pleaded guilty before His Honour, Judge Mortimer Matthews and Anthony was on his feet to try to persuade him to avoid giving a custodial sentence.

'I have the permission of the victim in this case to represent the defendant, your Honour,' said Anthony, 'and of course your Honour is fully conversant with all the relevant facts. I am instructed to tell you that my client is full of remorse for his actions, motivated as they were by obsessional jealousy. It is also my happy duty to inform you that the victim, Miles Richardson, instructs me to say openly that he unconditionally forgives Mr. Pritchard for his actions and fully recognises the reasons which motivated his behaviour which so graphically characterise the sins of greed, envy and jealousy. Who among us, I ask rhetorically, can boast a vice free existence?'

'Quite so, Mr. Harrison. I am very grateful for your eloquent address. A case like this would conventionally attract a long custodial sentence. But I wonder what good it would do. The defendant has presumably learned his lesson. No lasting harm has been caused to anybody. If I could hear one argument to suggest that to allow Mr. Pritchard free access to society would be of greater benefit than confinement as a guest of Her Majesty, I would be more than ready to consider community service.'

'Fortunately, your Honour, I have read your mind. Would you like to read this. It is a letter from the Chair of the Governors of Greyfields to say that Mr. Pritchard's position of senior mathematics master remains open with the blessing of Miles Richardson, so long as he is at large to resume it.'

'In which case,' said the Judge, 'I impose a sentence of 200 hours unpaid community service. Let the defendant be released.'

'And now, Mr. Harrison, there is one thing which I need to say to you.'

Anthony momentarily froze but summoned the courage to ask what it might be.

'It's a pity there aren't more like you around these days. Everybody is so conformist. But you. Thank you.'

Destino

There are just three buses a day to Morwell Jail – arriving at 11am, 2pm and 5pm. One can also get there by road through the bleak countryside where there are far more cows than people. Eight hundred inmates are in the prison doing time for a cocktail of offences ranging from the most serious to the relatively trivial; their risk of escape is deemed to be high enough to live in conditions of high – but not the highest – security, it is a frightening environment in which to live and to work. All the less attractive ingredients of human nature appear in one form or another. Prison reflects the otherwise respectable, but exploitative commercial world – with a public regime of enforcement for the conventional transgression and a parallel self-administered regime of enforcing private morality.

'You grass at your peril' … is the unwritten law.

Most prison officers, not unlike those in different employment, work to pay the mortgage. But not all. A small, but significant, minority see it as a vocation with a calling to alleviate the suffering of those in custody. A helping hand, even for the most vicious and hard-bitten offender.

Kevin was one such. Married with two young children, wife a teaching assistant, of medium stature with a will of iron and a heart of gold. A sense of right and wrong which drove him to apply his principles in the pursuit of his duties. Keep the prison safe – number one – and keep the prisoners happy – number two – a practice which itself would help in realising number one.

Kevin noticed the misery of getting the 'Dear John' letter, the bereavement caused by the loss of a close relative, the knock back after a parole hearing, and he gave them undiluted and compassionate attention. His only 'failing', if one could call it that, was a pathological intolerance of illicit drugs and he would go to great lengths to deter their supply and consumption.

It was perhaps ironic that he was stationed on Beta Wing, a particularly unsettled and volatile area, where Vince was encelled. Not a word to be confused with excelled!

Like most closed prisons in the UK, Morwell enjoyed a reputation for the easy availability of a huge spectrum of drugs, ranging from the most potent crack cocaine to the relatively harmless cannabis. Add on to the menu the highly dangerous ex-legal highs – the auto psychotics known as spice, potentially the most potent of all. Two gangs controlled the supply, and the dominant player of the most dominant gang was Vince, which made him the most powerful and influential inmate.

Gangs are criminal but often behave just like businesses in the so-called legit world. The gangs had reached an accommodation where the dominant would dictate the distribution, with sufficient pickings for the other to enjoy substantial, though inferior, rewards. Administered with all the efficiency of a German car manufacturer, and with the enforcement of drug debt rigid, ruthless and rigorous, they flourished; the prison authorities did not have either the will and or the means to control them. So, although the arrangement was unequal it survived because both parties saw that confrontation would be in the interests of neither party.

Until the arrival of Danny, that is.

The new boy on the block was swarthy, of South Italian heritage and had a degree in Cosa Nostraism. He wanted, needed to prove to his outside family that he was someone – 'a contender'. A challenge to the authority of his own boss launched with the dexterity and subtlety worthy of the most distinguished magic circle member succeeded seamlessly. The aspirant had arrived. Danny, now himself a big fish, had bigger fish to fry. To negotiate an equal share of the spoils.

Vince had little, if anything, to commend his character. His father never even knew of his existence; his mother's affair with the bottle was matched only by a series of unsatisfactory brief affairs with married men. Vince was put into care at the age of eight where being casually abused by a succession of influential local politicians and dignitaries, his lifestyle choices were not exactly middle class. He would be an excellent case study for a sociologist to suggest that his criminal activities were destined to happen. He had no choice.

Midway through a 20-year stretch for gangland murder, GBH (involving torture of the most unspeakable nature), Class A drug importation, the control of prostitutes and conspiracy to commit armed robbery, he was impregnable. Other inmates who could be described as granite, were, by comparison plasticine. He was merciless with it, driven by a subconscious desire for control with a need to enforce absolute loyalty of his team who in turn had to enforce a steel like regime of debt recovery, with interest rates for late payment which the greediest high street lender would envy.

The atmosphere on Friday afternoons, when prisoners collect what is called their canteen – things such as tobacco and personal items which they buy within the prison – is routinely charged, one reason being that delivery of merchandise provides a ready currency for the settlement of debts between prisoners. A kind of debt clearing house. On that particular Friday it was a different Beta Wing. Normally violence free, calm and regulated. Not that day. Nervous, prickly, agitated. Whispers of a Danny inspired challenge were rife, supported by intelligence – in the form of secret prisoner disclosures to staff. A frisson – of fear, anticipation and excitement – lurked under the surface.

Vince was advised to watch himself, but he believed he was inviolable, so he took no special precautions. A heightened prison officer presence, with Kevin watching. And then it happened. Out of the blue. As Vince was exacting payment in kind for the price of drugs supplied, another prisoner raised his arm ready to hurl a jug of napalm at Vince's face – napalm being prisoner speak for hot water laced with sugar intended to cause maximum skin injury. With an instinct worthy of a meerkat on sentry duty, Kevin threw himself in front of Vince at the very instant the napalm was launched – and caught it full in the face. Pandemonium followed. Alarm bells, prison officers rushed everywhere, an ambulance arrived and everyone scattered.

The perpetrator was not identified, but everyone knew who was behind it. Kevin was hospitalized on five different occasions for cosmetic surgery operations which only partially succeeded in disguising the worst of his injuries, and left him permanently disfigured.

He returned to Beta Wing to the delight of many living there. The first prisoner to speak to him was Vince. 'Tell me,' said Vince, 'my role in the drug culture is an open secret as is the fact you hated what I do. How is it possible that you should intervene to protect me at such a heavy price to you?'

'I'll tell you, son,' he replied. 'I know more about you and your upbringing than you may think. Believe me when I say that I didn't hesitate for one second in doing what I believed was necessary to prevent damage to your face.'

Stunned hardly describes Vince's reaction. In his 38-year existence he had never enjoyed a modicum of kindness, let alone an act of self-sacrifice such as that which Kevin had committed.

I would like to have gone on to say that Kevin's selfless heroism had a marked effect on Vince's behaviour. But it did not. The environmental influences of his past had long extinguished any flicker of sensibility he might have been born with though his heredity was poor. If anything, he hardened, determined to face down any potential threat from Danny's whose operation he had squeezed dry.

With the ground cut from under his feet Danny had lost not only a handsome income but, more importantly for him, self-respect.

His spectacular fall from grace was the subject of surreptitious sneer throughout the jail. He was finished, humiliated, a failure and a disgrace to his omerta culture. Thoughts of revenge festered until the opportunity to exact arose. A small, out of cctv range corner of Beta Wing was where it happened. A matador would have admired the artistic skill with which the stiletto was plunged precisely into Vince's back between the minute gaps in the ribs. It was over in a trice. This time there had been no Kevin like saviour. Dear sweet Kevin's selfless sacrifice, had been in vain. Vince – the unreformable victim of circumstance. Destino.

Truth or Lies?

Fate dictated the fate of Bentley with Sir John Padgett QC. He had lost his wife five years earlier and was bringing up three teenage girls. At the age of 47 Sir John cut a pathetic figure, at least when he was not advocating in court, or advising in chambers. The prospect of a new partner was not only unappealing; it was positively repellent and offensive to his sense of honour. If loneliness was the price, he had to pay to avoid any charge of betrayal, it was worth the cost. 'Never', he had vowed to himself, 'would he allow himself to transfer his affections to another'. His Sarah, to whom he would forever acknowledge an irredeemable debt of love and gratitude, especially for her unrelenting, steadfast support when he had been faced with a malicious charge of infidelity with one of his pupils, deserved what he regarded as undying, unswerving, loyalty viewed, as he liked to believe, from the witness box on high.

It was no easy ride. You could not but feel sorry for Sir John who had to bring up three children semi orphaned at the respective ages of 10, 11, and 12. Girls at that. For whom the absence of a mother made the growing pains of adolescence worse as they struggled with more than the usual doses of anxiety, insecurity, isolation. Sir John was quite unfit to cope with those. He did not have any empathetic intelligence to understand the tribulations of female teenagers overwhelmed with frustrated hormonal urges. So he resorted to the imposition of discipline, to curb any aberrant behaviour. He was certainly inspired subconsciously by his experiences of prosecuting in the criminal courts. But the result was that his daughters deceived to avoid the discovery of dubious activities which he was highly unlikely to approve. Much as he was ripe to be duped even Sir John had to admit to himself that there was only a finite number of minicabs which would break down at two o'clock in the morning.

'I tell you what you need,' said Arthur Prince to Sir John over the first cup of coffee of the day which, as senior clerk to the barristers in 2 Madrigal Court Chambers, he would habitually offer to counsel. Arthur Prince had been a fixture at Number 2 for 31 years. He had mastered many roles, everything from business procurer – was there a solicitor worth knowing to provide briefs that Arthur had not cultivated? – to father figure. The one to whom counsel would be more than happy to confide their darkest secrets. 'A nice dog,' he suggested. 'Nothing too exacting mind, or too wild, too highly bred, too destructive. None of your labradors who will eat anything from the kitchen table to the curtains. Something like a nice little dachsie. Easy like. Cheap to run and all that.'

'Food for thought, I suppose,' replied Sir John. 'Meanwhile I've got my final speech to polish off in this damned boring murder trial. No jury will ever acquit but I've got to go through the motions, Maybe there's something more interesting on the horizon.'

It was love at first sight. One look at Bentley and Sir John's heart melted faster than a snowball doused with hot water. A pat on the head got the kindest, warmest, of responses. The animal stared at Sir John. Then gently buried his head between his prospective master's jaw and chest. So grateful for the meagre attention. A mini sob. As if to say thank you. Even Jessie, the Dog's Trust handler, was visibly moved. 'I think he might just like you, sir.'

Bentley was a two-year-old crossbreed – Alsatian/Retriever with a bit of springer spaniel thrown in somewhere. Cruelly abandoned on the Grand Union Canal towpath at Rickmansworth and found close to death ten weeks earlier. Rescued by the RSPCA and taken to Dogs Trust in Harefield. Patiently nurtured back to health. A big, browny, greyey, short(ish) haired dog.

'He's a bit special, sir,' said Jessie. 'You'll not regret having him if you decide to go ahead.'

'Special in what way?' asked Sir John.

'I'll leave you to find that out sir.'

Like a child with his first scooter Sir John bundled Bentley in the back of his Bentley whistling with joy. 'We'll have a ball old boy. I can feel it in my bones,' Sir John said to the dog. Who replied with a lick on the cheek.

'Uncanny' is the word to describe the 'speciality' to which Jessie had referred. The dog had an extraordinary ability, presumed to derive from the exceptionally sensitive nose of his breed to detect whether a person was telling the truth or lying. This ability first surfaced when Sir John decided to confront his eldest daughter Joanne about her reported non-attendance at school that day.

'Sorry, Dad, but I felt ill, so I stayed at the library instead.' Bentley sidled up to her, leaned heavily and refused to move.

'What's wrong boy?' asked Sir John? The dog remained glued to Joanne's legs. A thought occurred to Sir John. The drug dogs – those who can detect illicit drugs on a person – act in precisely the same way. Rather than bark or become agitated, they simply sit next to the guilty. 'Now tell me the truth, Jo,' said Sir John. Backing his hunch.

The truth emerged without too much protest. Joanne had spent the day in the company of her friend Zac, a drummer with a rock band, with whom she had struck up a relationship some way south of heavy petting. Recovering rapidly from his shock at her lies, Sir John was astute enough to recognise Bentley's potential genius. Or was it a one off? Laying a trap for Susanna, his second daughter, who arrived home at 01.45 on the next Tuesday morning, he calmly chose to ask her, in Bentley's presence, why so late when she had school later that morning. She gave the familiar car breakdown excuse.

Bentley camped by her leg. Sir John questioned the girl and she admitted she had lied. Two out of two became seven out of seven in just three weeks. What the girls could not understand was the equanimity, even pleasure, with which their father received the revelations of their fibs. Additional testing was conceived to ascertain Bentley's reaction when any of the girls was patently telling the truth. Wonderful! Rather than sidle Bentley would give a little bark. As if to complain that his presence was useless. Some companion!

'You'll never guess, Arthur. I've got this amazing dog,' explained Sir John to his clerk. He went on to elaborate on the wonders of Bentley's extra sense. 'It is a very rare trait present in some dogs who have the capacity to detect, through their highly developed olfactory senses, an otherwise undetectable effusion of some mysterious odour which is secreted when the subject suffers some kind of subconscious, uncontrolled, agitation caused by lying. Simple in a way. But because there is nothing tangible, impossible to prove. It just happens every time – or so it seems. And he's such a lovely – and loving – dog. To be honest I can't wait to get home to cuddle him.'

'I'm very happy for you, Sir John. Meanwhile there's this McArthur sexual assault case which you're prosecuting starting in two hours. We can talk dogs after court if you like. May I respectfully suggest that you put your dog on one side and concentrate on the job at hand.'

Harry McArthur was a happy go lucky investment banker. Thirty years old. Real Jack the laddish. A shoulder driven gait. Cocky might be the word for it. Married for two years to Sophie whose father owned the bank for which Harry had worked for the past seven years. It was at the firm's Christmas do that he had met Sophie Harcourt. The whirlwind romance had been born while smooching to Ella Fitzgerald's 'Dancing Cheek to Cheek' and rapidly developed into something more significant. A honeymoon in the Maldives. A four bedroomed house in The Boltons. Harry was well away. At the same time Sophie was not happy about his increasingly frequent late evenings home – sometimes at one in the morning. She tolerated that but could not help being suspicious.

'Could meetings really be going on that late?' she asked herself. She needed to find out.

'Ladies and gentlemen of the jury,' the hallowed opening words of Sir John Padgett used by every prosecuting counsel in a criminal case in the United Kingdom. He told the jury, 'This is a case which will involve, to a large extent, your intuition. You will hear the evidence of Jill Harrison, a co-employee of the defendant in Harcourt Bank. She will say that without any provocation, let alone consent, the accused confronted her in her flat on the evening of June 23rd at about 9.20pm, removed his trousers and underpants and forced her to perform – as they delicately say – a sexual act upon him. Having done so, he politely said thank you and left. She immediately called the police who collected his semen.

On the other hand, it is fair to say that the accused has always denied all knowledge of the alleged incident. He remembers going to the flat with the complainant, enjoying a very large whisky, feeling unwell, feeling a bit dizzy and passing out. When first interviewed by the police he admitted having taken the complainant home from work because she had said that she had felt unwell and did not wish to go alone. Once he had awoken, he stayed for a short time before leaving with a mutual peck on the cheek. There you have it members of the jury. Somebody is lying. Somebody is being truthful. Ultimately it is for you to try to be sure which of them is doing which. If you are to convict you must be satisfied that the complainant is telling the truth. Which necessarily means that the accused is telling lies. If you are not sure about the complainant's version, then you must acquit even if you are doubtful about the account of the accused. The burden of proof is squarely on the prosecution. Any reasonable doubt and the case collapses. It is, as his Honour will remind you, for you to try to reach a unanimous verdict and be as satisfied as you can be that it will serve the interests of justice.'

'Call your first witness,' said Judge Warner to Sir John after hearing

Sir Raymond Warmington QC, counsel for Harry, make an opening address to the jury which more or less mirrored that of Sir John.

The principal witnesses, Jill Harrison – Complainant – and Harry McArthur – Defendant – stuck to their respective scripts like actors on the first night of a play. Two members of Harcourt bank staff who had seen the pair leaving work together, the Police Inspector who had taken statements from both protagonists, and the written evidence from the science laboratory which confirmed that the semen was indeed that of the accused. The first chink in the armour of Jill Harrison was an admission, cleverly and subtly extracted by Sir Raymond in cross examination, that she had known Sophie McArthur for at least five years and was, she frankly conceded, a tad envious when she had become engaged to Harry.

'You fancied him, did you?' asked Sir Raymond.

'Possibly just a bit.'

'What is just a bit?'

'I wouldn't really like to say. It wouldn't be fair on Sophie, would it.' She then denied any current feelings for Harry.

'You're sure about that, are you?' Sir Raymond just got a blush. Evasive would be an accurate way of putting it.

Warming to his task the aptly named Sir Raymond Warmington tried another tack. He asked Jill when she last met Sophie. Almost telepathically as if he knew something was being hidden.

'We had lunch together in the week before Harry got me to suck him off,' came the bombshell reply. One of the jurors, an ageing spinster in tweeds, recoiling in disgust. They had talked about nothing in particular she said. Just a casual get together. Harry might have been mentioned. She couldn't remember exactly.

Harry took a few deep breaths before Sir John rose to cross examine. 'Tell the jury why you are so nervous,' were his disconcerting opening words. Harry spluttered some sort of unintelligible reply. 'Can you think of any reason why the complainant should lie about this whole matter and accuse you of behaviour which hardly commends itself to a man of your standing in Harcourt Bank. Son-in-law of its owner.'

'To be honest I can't,' replied a bemused looking Harry. 'I've really no idea. Maybe she has an unrequited crush or something.'

'So, you're accusing her of fabricating a story about an attack which never took place out of some sort of jealousy because she couldn't have you?' Sir John went on.

'Not exactly,' replied Harry, without too much conviction.

'Inexactly then' was the sarcastic rejoinder.

The jury seemed more than unimpressed. As if they were condemning Harry from insinuating, without a shred of evidence, that Jill had planned the whole thing to set Harry up. Further questioning revealed that relations between Harry and Sophie were strained, providing a possible reason why Harry might want to stray.

If this had been a boxing match one could argue for a draw. Six rounds each. No devastating punches by either side, no knock downs let alone any suggestion of a knockout. But one of them had to be lying. And although juries are directed to convict only if they are sure of guilt, in practice they often will do so as long as they simply merely prefer the evidence of the complainant even if it falls short of the 'sure' test. In a juror's mind to acquit might imply an unfair stain on the character of a quite possibly honest complainant. It came down to simple propositions. Who was lying? Who was telling the truth?

Before the jury retired to consider its verdict Sir Raymond rose. 'Your Honour. If it please you. I have an application to make following my short conference with my client. Would you please direct that the complainant produces her mobile phone for interrogation. We have reason to believe that it may hold the key to what happened on the evening in question.'

'I cannot oppose,' said Sir John, anxious as anybody to ascertain the truth.

It took only 37 minutes before an excited Sir Raymond was brandishing a hastily prepared report on the mobile. All texts had been deleted. But many of those had been recovered. The following sent to the mobile phone of Sophie McArthur at 9.27pm on 23rd June. It read: 'Mission accomplished. You were one hundred per cent right about him. Please delete this message after reading.'

Jill Harrison looked perplexed in the witness box as Sir Raymond rose to resume his cross examination. She was totally unable to explain the text which she denied having sent. The accused must have done it to discredit her by pretending that she had been its author. She could think of no other explanation. She admitted having Sophie's mobile details but insisted that there was nothing sinister to be read into that.

When Harry re-testified, he denied all knowledge of the text. He admitted that it would have been quite conceivable for his wife to have been complicit in setting him up into being alone with Jill Harrison to allow him scope to 'stray'. It was, he protested, a monstrous lie to suggest that he was trying to frame Jill Harrison by sending the incriminating text on her mobile; and thereby completely discrediting her evidence. When he had returned home his wife had acted very coldly towards him but refused to say why.

It was a stalemate. The Judge directed the jury on the law and the evidence. It was now 'A matter for you, members of the jury, to consider your verdict on what, I am constrained to admit, is not an easy case.' His words were to prove only too prophetic. After two full days of considering their verdict, and two directions from the Judge that a majority verdict of 10-2 either way would suffice, the jury returned to Court heads bowed.

'I'm afraid, your Honour,' said an apologetic jury foreman, Sister Maria O'Donovan, in resigned tones, 'we are hopelessly split 6-6. Even if we were to stay here until Christmas there would be no prospect of agreement.'

'In that case,' said the Judge, 'I'm minded to discharge the jury from giving a verdict. How do you feel about that Sir John?' No reply. 'Sir John. Are you with us?' asked the Judge.

'Indeed, I am, your Honour,' said Sir John, suddenly brimming with excitement. 'I am going to ask you to defer the jury discharge. With your leave I would like to introduce a further witness. I recognise it is unusual at this stage of a trial, but I have good reason to believe it will prove fruitful. I will tell all interested parties what is proposed.'

'Very well, Sir John, but you had better know what you are doing,' said the Judge.

They met in the Judge's Chambers. The Judge himself. Sir John. Sir Raymond. Jill Harrison. Harry McArthur. Sir John explained what, to most, would have appeared to be utterly outrageous. The curiosity of a plainly disorientated Judge got the better of him. Sir Raymond said that there would be nothing to lose if his client were telling the truth. Harry, on the other hand, argued that it would be like a mediaeval trial by ordeal. In the dim and distant past an accused was acquitted if, after being thrown in the river, he surfaced alive. Jill shrugged and said she was far from happy, but it would she supposed have to be alright by her.

First would be the reliability test. Followed by the real thing.

The next morning at 9.30, the Judge, with Sir Raymond, Jill Harrison and Harry, assembled in the jury room already occupied by all the jury members. Each juror was given a piece of paper on which two boxes were printed. One for guilty. The other for not guilty. Sir John then appeared accompanied by Bentley. In turn the Judge directed each juror to tick one of the boxes after one minute's contemplation. During that minute they would be required to consider how they wished to take part in an experiment designed to test a theory. 'If,' the Judge said, 'you want to tell a lie, tick the box which confirms the opposite of how you voted. If you want to tell the truth tick the correct box.'

'What's the point?' asked one of the jurors plainly anxious to get away.

'You will find out soon enough,' replied the Judge.

After one minute each juror ticked. Bentley proceeded by turns to sit for 30 seconds next to four of them. And completely ignored eight. Each of the four Bentley sat next down to had in fact lied about their vote! Each of the other eight had told the truth! Theory proved.

'Back to Court,' said the Judge, having explained to the jury the relevance of the procedure. 'We will hear further testimony from these two witnesses, this time in the presence of Bentley.'

Harry looked far from comfortable. Jill overwhelmingly composed.

Back in Court the Judge asked who would 'like to bat first.' Both Sir John and Sir Raymond were reluctant to put their client's toe in the water before the other the Judge tossed a coin. 'Heads or tails, Sir Raymond?'

Bentley sat nonchalantly two metres just below the witness box, looking as if he had not a care in the world. As the first witness testified Bentley appeared to take not a blind piece of notice. The second witness took the stand amidst an almost tangible atmosphere of apprehension. The first words following the confirmation of identity, resulted in a pricking of Bentley's ears – or was it imaginary? Almost immediately followed by a small fidget. Then after no more than 15 seconds he was up on his feet. Casually, but purposefully, Bentley placed himself as close to the witness box as he could. The jury were mesmerised.

The jury retired to consider its verdict and returned after 37 minutes after an unduly unnecessary delay in reaching it. 'I assume you are all agreed upon your verdict,' opined the Judge.

'We are, your Honour,' said a quivering Sister Maria.

'And how do you find the defendant. Guilty or not guilty?'

She looked at the dog who was seated nearby. The dog returned the look. She looked at the Judge.

'The Good Lord have mercy upon my soul,' she was heard to mutter under her breath before collecting herself and delivering the verdict she had been instructed to pronounce. A pause followed by the deepest of breaths. 'GUILTY.'

The Judge, as were both Counsel and the prime witnesses, was speechless. Sister Maria was on the verge of tears. It took just a few seconds before order was restored. In a display of physical dexterity which commanded the unanimous admiration of those present, Bentley sprang into action, vaulted over the front panel of the jury box and vigorously adhered himself to Sister Maria. Her prayers thus answered.

'I'm so sorry, your Honour. A slip of the tongue I'm afraid. I should have said "NOT GUILTY".'

The sigh of collective relief breathed by the remaining 11 jury members, was very loud. In passing the ultimate test the rescue dog had rescued the truth.

'Come on Bentle,' Sir John smiled, 'time to go home.'

The Pre-Nup

At the age of 38, with £550 million in the bank, give or take the odd few million, Regina – Gina for short – Huddlestone had at the same time everything – and nothing. Two years ago she had lost her husband George, a spectacularly successful dot com entrepreneur who had had the foresight to sell out one week before the bubble burst in 2001. She was childless, her parents were dead and with one brother living in Australia, she suffered the loneliness for which no amount of riches could compensate. Friends, of which she had a few – but only one whom she would term close – were one thing; the indefinable maternal bond quite another. She would have given everything to swap her wealth for the 'Goodnight, Mummy', 'Don't be late darling', and 'Don't worry sweetheart; there are plenty more fish in the sea'!

Gina was not unattractive though unlikely to be confused with any Ingrid Bergman lineage, maybe. A nose slightly too large, a forehead slightly too high, lips slightly too thin, and eyes slightly too close together, the combination of imperfections was sufficiently unusual to stimulate. Not that she was able to see it that way. 'Must be for the money,' she told herself when any man showed more than a passing interest. 'Be careful. You're a sitting duck – easy prey – for some conniving individual.'

So, she put the shutters up before any serious approach were remotely possible. This made her even more isolated. 'You really need to let yourself go sometimes' was the advice her closest friend Veronica Harding impressed on her at least once a week. Advice which was equally regularly rejected. 'To tell you the truth, Ron, I'm bloody terrified. You hear all these awful stories.' Veronica finally decided that dramatic measures were required.

At a dinner party for ten guests given at home in Lowndes Square by Veronica and her husband shortly after the third anniversary of George's death, Gina met Leo. Known to all as Leo Gradsky. He claimed to be the great nephew of the Russian Count Ivan Gradsky, and cut an imposing figure. He was strikingly handsome, tall with a noble bearing and aristocratic features, dark swept back hair, but with a kind of reticent charm. Gina's ice-cold reluctance instantly melted when they were introduced. Bearing no vestige of either conceit or aggression, and with an easy going, at ease putting manner, he posed no vestige of threat. On the contrary, save for a subtle compliment on her perfume, he appeared to show no interest in the physical or personal. Sitting next to each other over dinner, they effortlessly talked on subjects as diverse as Bruckner's ninth symphony, Serena Williams and the prospective decline of the Liberal Democrats. The party ended with a 'nice to have met you' handshake.

'Where did you find that gorgeous creature?' asked Gina when popping round to Veronica the next morning for coffee.

'Oh, yes?' retorted Veronica. 'Fancy him, do you?'

It took a lot to make Gina blush. But now her reddening cheeks said it all.

'I'll be perfectly honest with you, G, he is not all that he seems.'

Veronica proceeded to explain, with a word of warning, to be a bit careful. Born Lawrence Grimes in Bethnal Green, he first discovered his power over women at 16 when he was seduced by his schoolteacher who, when the affair was exposed, was sent to prison for two years. 'An unforgivable breach of trust,' the sentencing judge described it.

'Well, your Honour,', said Lawrence who was called – exceptionally – by the defence for an impact statement, 'I don't find much difficulty in extending the hand of forgiveness if truth were known. She taught me more in one night than I learned in a whole year's bleeding boring biology lessons meted out by that painful Miss Fogerty every bleeding Friday afternoon.'

That was the beginning of Lawrence Grimes' career. Women, older ones, fell under his spell. With a libido which would have put Casanova, Don Juan and Georges Simenon, to shame – Simenon claimed to have slept with 10,000 women which did not stop him writing over 200 books. Lawrence's almost supernatural powers of seduction exploited easy and rich pickings. Gullible and desperate women, often the victims of uninterested, semi-impotent husbands, were discarded like confetti. They would offer him the earth for one more naked tango 'for old times' sake'.

As he became bolder he became more reckless. Inducing, on one occasion, an unhappy wife of the local bank manager to 'lend him £25,000 to fund cancer care for his (so called, but non-existent) brother' in return for sexual favours. He was convicted of fraud and served his first sentence – eight months – at the age of 19. Further terms of imprisonment followed with the commission of more outrageous acts of deception. By the time he was 31 he had spent six years as a guest of Her Majesty. He needed to change his approach. He had served his apprenticeship.

His first act was to see a lawyer. The Deed Poll confirmed that Lawrence Grimes was no more; thenceforth Leo Gradsky. A new name, a new persona. Managing to insinuate himself into the society of hedge fund agents – those who, in return for a commission, seek out special situations in which speculators invest in ventures with the potential for huge returns (the more dangerous being the most remunerative) – it did not take him long to get rich and acquire respectability. The big time was coming. He had learned his lessons and was well placed to land his coup. Meeting Veronica Harding at the Cheltenham Racing Festival in March 2011 turned out to be a pivotal experience.

'I hope you don't mind, but Veronica gave me your telephone number. I am at a loose end this evening and wondered whether you might be available for dinner. Please don't take this the wrong way, but I really enjoyed your company the other evening and it would be a privilege to renew our acquaintance. How about dinner at the Ivy?' had been his opening words. A well-practised gambit which rarely failed. They enjoyed a bottle of Pol Roget 2008 pink champagne, oysters, followed by sole Veronique, and a gorgeous chocolate soufflé. Conversation flowed. They said their goodbyes at the restaurant. A peck on the cheek caused a minor frisson.

It does not require genius to predict what happened next. By degrees, and with a subtlety of the spider entrapping the fly, Leo's entry into Gina's bed was seamlessly achieved. With a power and stamina of gargantuan appetite, allied to a tenderness of sublime empathy, Leo had little difficulty in landing his catch. She was so needy that when he suggested that perhaps he might move in with her, she almost exploded with rapture. Resistance was gone. From an insecure, almost paranoid isolation, Gina had regained her former self confidence. Strong, stable, a sense of humour restored, the prospect of life with Leo was a fantasy transformed into reality. Leo's acceptance of her marriage proposal was accepted without too much hesitation.

'But, darling, I insist that we enter into a pre-nuptial agreement. The divorce laws being what they are I can't allow you to put half your wealth at risk especially since we have barely known each other for seven months.'

'If you insist,' said Gina.

Even Veronica was taken aback. 'Are you absolutely sure G? Is it just possible, do you not think, that he is doing this to get his hands on your money?'

Offended at the suggestion, Gina stressed it was Leo who had insisted that they enter into a pre-nup.

'Well – let me recommend a good lawyer,' said Veronica. 'My family has used Richard Wells for years. He is brilliant and will make sure that your interests are protected. I will introduce you.'

Richard Wells was as far removed from the stuffy image of staid lawyers as one could have imagined. Eminently talkable to, imaginative, impressive in his knowledge of matrimonial law, he assured Gina that since 2010 pre-nuptial agreements entered into in circumstances such as existed between her and Leo, were enforceable. They were designed to ensure that such assets as she owned at the date of the marriage and thereafter would, in the event of a divorce, remain her sole property to the extent that she would want to keep them. Without a pre-nup there would be a very real risk that Leo would be awarded half of everything she had, regardless of who might be to blame for any breakdown of the marriage.

'By the way,' he said, 'forgive my asking, but how much do you actually know about Leo?'

'As it happens, I know quite a lot. He is no angel. But I also know that he is a reformed character who I can't live without. He makes me so happy and fulfilled.'

'All the more reason to take extra care,' said Richard. 'What is it, if I may be so bold, that attracts you so much?'

When Gina confided her sexual obsession, Robert nodded. 'I get the picture. Leave the rest to me.'

On being put in touch with Leo's solicitor, Robert drafted the following clauses:

In the event that the husband shall unreasonably refuse or otherwise fail, on demand, to engage in the act of sexual intercourse with the wife on such occasions as the wife shall reasonably require within the first five years of the marriage, the husband shall, on the grant of a decree absolute of dissolution of the marriage following the institution of divorce proceedings by either party at any time before the expiry of the said period of five years, be entitled to the sum of £100,000 in full satisfaction of his claim for a share in the wife's assets held on the said date. And, for the avoidance of doubt, nothing else.

Any such refusal by the husband to comply with a demand for sexual intercourse as previously mentioned shall be deemed to constitute unreasonable behaviour and thus grounds for divorce.

In the event of a dissolution of the marriage following the institution of divorce proceedings by either party after five years of the marriage, one fifth of the assets, or their value, belonging to the wife on the date of the decree absolute shall, subject to allowance made for the value of assets then belonging to the husband, be transferred to the husband.

Leo would be put on very strict sexual terms for the first five years. To have prescribed any longer period would, in Robert's opinion, be unreasonable and risk annulling the arrangement. Robert reported to Gina that Leo's solicitor had readily – almost too readily – agreed the terms of the draft proposals. The pre-nup was signed.

The marriage was celebrated quietly at Marylebone Registry Office on 5th December 2011.

'I hope you'll both be very happy,' Veronica beamed, quietly congratulating herself on her achievement.

For the following five years Gina lived the dream – or at least believed that she did. Her newly discovered voracious sexual appetite was satisfied on demand – a knowing nod – a thumbs up. Leo's prodigious powers managed. She had a loving and attentive husband to boot. A surprise whisk away for a Venice weekend, a sudden flight to the delights of Barcelona, an unannounced trip to Peru and the Galapagos Islands, were just a few illustrations of his apparent devotion to Gina. She was, so she believed, living in paradise.

Seismic describes the shock with which Gina reacted to the

letter she received from a firm of lawyers representing Leo. Dated 5th December 2016 it read:

Dear Madam,

We are instructed by your husband, Leo Gradsky, to commence proceedings against you for divorce on the grounds of your unreasonable behaviour. In particular we understand that you have exploited our client's exposure to sexual exploitation by demanding an excessive number – on frequent occasions as often as five times a day – of sexual conjunctions against the background of financial discrimination in the event of his refusal. Please be good enough to arrange to instruct a firm of lawyers to represent you in these proceedings.

When Gina telephoned Leo's mobile, she heard the brush off message. His office told her he had gone abroad on business for a couple of weeks and could not be contacted. Distraught, she sought the advice of Veronica who could only suggest that Gina see Richard without delay. His advice was exactly what she had feared. She could contest the grounds for divorce but an unsympathetic judge might well regard her excessive demands for sexual gratification to constitute unreasonable behaviour. Her only realistic chance would be to allege that the marriage had been a sham from day one and that Leo had always intended to end it after five years and thus get his hands on a fifth of her estate.

'Do whatever you have to do,' Gina ordered.

Gradsky v Gradsky opened at the High Court on 6th March 2017. It was in two parts. The first – to determine whether grounds existed to support Leo's divorce petition; the second – to determine Gina's allegation of a set up. Her only argument being that while Leo had voluntarily submitted to the prospect of numerous sexual demands, the irresistible conclusion to be drawn from the timing of his petition was obvious – that from the outset he had not entertained the slightest intention of entering into a marriage for life. Rather for five years only.

After a day of examination and cross examination in the course of which Leo's barrister reduced Gina to a quivering wreck, mass of tears and desolation, the Judge, Mrs. Justice Speakman, rejected outright any suggestion that Gina's behaviour was reasonable. She had never heard anything like it, either on the bench or as a barrister. The decree nisi was pronounced. Leo nodded but not without a degree of discomfort. During legal argument on the second issue that there emerged a commotion in court.

'You bastard, Leo,' screamed a young woman who burst into court brandishing her mobile phone. 'After waiting all this time, you're chucking me aside for some woman who you say you love more than me. You promised me five years ago that once you got your divorce we would live together forever. And now I get this text from you saying it's all over; that there is somebody else who you love more than me.'

To cut a long story short Mrs. Justice Speakman, in total disregard of the rules of evidence and clearly impressed by the outburst, set the pre-nup aside on the grounds that it had been entered into by fraud and misrepresentation. When Leo's barrister, to try to save the day and without even taking instructions from his client, argued that he should be entitled to a share of Gina's assets in any event, she dismissed the submission on the grounds that his conduct was so gross and offensive, justice required that he got not a penny. His claim was dismissed with costs.

Gina was numb. How could she have been so stupid, so naïve, so gullible, so easily duped? She looked at Leo. Distraught would be an understatement. He had been reduced to ruin.

'Come on Gina,' said Veronica, 'leave him to it.'

Gina hesitated. 'Give me a moment.' She approached Leo. 'I'm sorry that things had to end like this,' she said. 'What a fool I've been.'

'I'm sorry too although unlike you, believe it or not, this is precisely how I wanted it to end.'

She gazed at him – puzzled.

'What do you mean?'

'It's all true. From the outset I conceived this plan with Moira – the girl who interrupted proceedings – to get hold of some of your estate. An easy target. To be too greedy would have been too obvious. So, I was prepared to settle for a fifth. To give you the confidence to marry me in the first place I had to pretend that I was looking after your interests by suggesting a pre-nup and was only too ready to agree the terms your lawyer proposed if that was what it would take for our plan to work. Five years of sex with you for £100 odd million pounds at the end of it was cheap at the price. And you fell for it. While all the time Moira was on my back to tell me not to let an unnecessary day go by before I could get my hands on your assets. As the case progressed, I was congratulating myself that I was nearly there. But then I saw you crumple in the witness box. And something happened. I think the word is epiphany. In a trice I hated myself. That you, who had been the only woman who had ever truly loved me, should suffer like that at my hands was unforgivable. I saw the light. You are worth fifty Moiras. I texted her to say that there was a woman who I loved more than her. That was a statement of fact. That woman is you.'

And with that Leo broke down uncontrollably. As did Gina. As did Veronica.

'Come on, Leo,' said Gina, dragging him from his seat, 'let's go home.'

A Matter of Sympathy

To all outward appearances Paul and Caroline Dobbs had it all. The five bedroomed, two acre gardened, house in Esher, Audi R8 – for him – and Mercedes 350 SE Convertible – for her – privately educated 17-year-old twins, Mark and Sarah, each with looks that made a career in modelling possible following in the footsteps of their mother, plus the obligatory Golden Retriever.

Paul was a partner in a magic circle firm of London solicitors, drawing profits at the rate of just over £1 million a year. Caroline, once a successful model for Karl Lagerfeld, had fallen on hard times following a cocaine addiction, and Paul rescued her 18 years earlier when, as a newly qualified assistant solicitor, he persuaded the Magistrate to dispense sympathy for his client. Caroline had been arrested dealing the drug on the steps of Fortissimos, a little-known night club in Conduit Street. Contrary to just about every precept of professional conduct, Paul succumbed to Caroline's pleas to be paid in kind. And contrary to every forecast made by just about every colleague and friend, the relationship flourished.

Paul brought the very best out of an abstinent Caroline, who brought the very best out of a stimulated Paul. They were the perfect couple – or so it seemed. No financial worries. No health worries. Paul had become the envy of most of his peers, even if there were those who regarded the prize as little compensation for his rather dull looks. 'It can't last' were some of the less spiteful predictions made discreetly by those who knew him best. 'With a personality as sparkling as a decomposing corpse, it's hard to be optimistic.'

But how wrong people appeared to be. Caroline was no great socialiser. The odd superficial friendship with the odd neighbour but she generally kept herself to herself. Like the reformed addict who won't risk a dram or a snort Caroline had become ultra responsible. When, recently in the past year, she had been seen to be sporting a heavily made-up black eye, she explained, without too much conviction, that she had had an argument with an open cupboard door, a rather feeble attempt to humourize, and thereby mask, the sinister questions were surreptitiously asked.

When about a month later she attended a party with Paul, she was heard to complain to him loudly that he was suffocating her, which he denied – alarm bells began to ring. Not that the institution of marriage is presumed to comprise uninterrupted utopia. But warning signs were flagged. Rumours began to circulate.

The sirens of three police cars as well as a screeching to a halt ambulance shattered the genteel silence of Esher on that Monday morning at 8.11 precisely. The front door of the Dobbs residence open. The dog barking. Caroline Dobbs weeping hysterically. 'He's in there,' she said to the uniformed officer first on the scene, pointing to the kitchen, the officer closely followed by two ambulance paramedics.

'In there', on the kitchen floor, lay Paul Dobbs, a serrated kitchen knife stuck in his upper chest. Almost certainly in the heart of the heart. In a pool of blood. A rapid examination revealed no pulse. Paul Dobbs was dead. Stabbed, according to Caroline Dobbs, by Caroline Dobbs. A few minutes after the children had left for school. Barely audibly she was heard to say 'enough was enough', 'control, control, control' and 'I snapped'.

On the morning of Monday 21st May 2018, in Court 1 of the Central Criminal Court, Old Bailey, the 12 members of the jury were sworn in before Mr. Justice Richard Margerrison. By a statistical quirk, 11 of those members were female. A gender bias which was as unwelcome to the prosecution as it was welcome to the defence.

Caroline had been advised to plead not guilty to the charge on the grounds that the coercive control exerted upon her by her husband meant that she could claim diminished responsibility for having 'snapped'. That would convert a charge of murder to the lesser one of manslaughter. A manslaughter conviction allows a sentencing judge considerable scope in assessing the minimum length of the tariff (time to be served inside) depending on the circumstances of the case and the leniency which might be exercisable, even to the point of allowing immediate release in exceptional cases. For reasons which are not exactly obscure, a jury comprising 91.666 recurring per cent female would be perceived as more likely to sympathise with a female defendant. Twenty-five percent would be enough to thwart any finding of murder guilt.

The prosecution, led by Sir Patrick Anderson QC, who lacked nothing in the way of hauteur, began by telling the jury that this was an open and shut case, with the accused's admission of what he explained were the principal components of many crimes – the *mens rea* – guilty intent – (unnecessary to prove in what is known as cases of strict liability – exceeding a speed limit being a classic example) – and the *actus reus* – physical act. Both were freely admitted by 'this wicked woman'. The burden of proving the 'so called coercive control', a relatively new legal proposition, lay squarely on her shoulders.

And with that he called his first witness, James Cunningham, the Home Office pathologist whose report on the deceased described the injuries which had led to 'the inevitable death' of the victim. A smug Sir Patrick sat down with a knowing look at the jury who were all seen to nod as if to accept without question the irresistible logic of a knife wound through the heart. This was followed by a theatrical rendition by Sir Patrick of the transcript of the defendant's confession/admission, in which she freely owned to having deliberately plunged 'with all the force at my command' the knife into her husband's heart. Another telling stare at the jury.

It was the turn of the defence in the form of John Reynolds, a barrister of only one year's call, but reputed to be destined for the top. His opening address to the jury would have brought tears to the eyes of Albert Pierrepoint, the celebrated/notorious – whichever way one wants to look at it – post war hangman. Reynolds described the 'Jekyll and Hyde' character of Paul Dobbs. To the outside world, he appeared civilised, meek even, but he was really a monster who controlled every modest desire that his long-suffering wife entertained. He had little difficulty in setting the scene for the maximum impact of her evidence. Which she gave in a fashion which was as convincing as it was riveting. A husband, who, from the very beginning of the marriage, had never forgotten to remind her how fortunate she had been to be rescued by his generosity. How insecurity flowing from his unattractive appearance contrasted with her striking beauty had led to paranoia and, an increasingly consuming suspicion of infidelity of which she was completely innocent. He impounded her car keys and stopped any attempt that she might make to form social relationships with others. In the last year he had, she said, physically assaulted her, but fearful of reprisal and out of a misplaced sense of shame, she had fabricated an ingenuous explanation of the cause of the injury on which others had commented.

On the morning in question, after a week effectively imprisoned at home, she had wanted to go to a lunch, which a new neighbour was giving for other residents nearby, but he had forbidden her. He accused her of pursuing an unfaithful relationship. At which she snapped. Saw red. Lost complete control. On an impulse picked up the knife from the kitchen table, delivered the one – clean, fatal – lunge and immediately regretted what she had done. As evidenced by the immediate call she made to the emergency services. A heart of stone would have been unable to resist the sympathy which her performance evoked.

Sir Patrick Anderson QC would himself admit later, that his cross examination was not sharp enough. Try as he did to discredit the accounts of Caroline Dobbs, he got nowhere. Her children, she said, could not testify, because Paul had been sufficiently cunning to ensure that they were not aware of his overbearingness. He took good care to play the loving husband when they were around. She had been unable to leave him because 'he controlled all the purse strings and I had nowhere to go'. And when Sir Patrick put to her that she was really a calculating, cold blooded killer, she asserted, with a long hard, stare at the jury, 'that any woman in my position could have been driven to commit such an irrational act which I will regret to my dying day'. At least two members opened their handbags to reach for their tissues.

Nothing engages the full attention of a spectator than a trial for murder. Especially one which has 'cause célèbre' written all over it. Over the three days so far, the public consisted of a fairly mixed bag, some of whom had attended every day. Representatives of J4 BW – short for justice for battered wives – were prominent. Two elderly and often tearful women had obviously been spellbound throughout. Were they perhaps reliving events of an earlier period in their lives? They sat next to a bespectacled, serious, attentive man in the front row, about 40 years old, perhaps a journalist. Another spectator was a female, young and looked every inch a law student. What, one wondered, did she make of the proceedings. Would they inspire her to join the legal profession?

After the closing speeches of counsel for the prosecution and the defence, and the barely disguised pro-defence summing up of the Judge, the jury retired. Mrs. Gladys Fortescue was appointed chairman, and they began to consider their verdict.

'To be honest,' said Daisy Harrison, a retired schoolmistress, 'I can't see that we have much to talk about. Poor woman. I reckon she should walk.'

Laura Venison, a librarian, whose own controlling ex-husband she had recently got rid of by the conventional means of a divorce petition agreed. The snowball was beginning to roll. Halted after ten minutes and hearing the concurring views of seven of the jury, by Gladys

Fortescue who reckoned that they should at least pay lip service to what the Judge had said.

'What's your opinion Brian?' asked Gladys.

Brian Fairbrother, London cabbie, had been sitting in silence. It was no exaggeration to suggest the label 'man of the world'. With little formal education after leaving school at 15, a succession of menial jobs had led him to being a cabbie. He had loved it from the word go. Forget the books, the exams, the lessons, the discipline. What he had learned since doing 'the knowledge' turned out to be more than the knowledge of London streets. He had become a keen observer of human weakness. When you transport the rabbi to and from an all faiths welcome brothel on a Saturday afternoon after conducting his local synagogue service, an exercise enjoyed by the vicar the following day after delivering his sermon of rectitude, perverse behaviour comes as little surprise, Brian was not easily fazed. He regarded his opportunities to transport the rich, the poor, the sick as well as the healthy, as a privilege. He saw the best and the worst of human society – often the product of circumstances beyond the control of the individual, and thus, over time, had developed an extreme reluctance to judge. Ironic perhaps that he found himself in the rare situation of having to do exactly that.

'I want to think about it overnight, if you don't mind,' he said. 'Another day shouldn't be too much for all of us. And I want to have another look at the pathologist's report. Just to be sure, you know.'

As close reading of the report did disclose something which had not attracted any comment. A small recently acquired bruise on the left thigh.

'Are we to disregard this observation?' asked Brian shortly after the jury had resumed deliberations. 'I wonder if it has any significance?'

'Too late now,' replied Gladys, in a display of what she regarded as the foreman's leadership. 'The evidence is finished.'

Brian shrugged. The others, clearly impatient, suggested that they 'get on with it'.

But Brian was not easily persuaded. 'Isn't it all a bit too convenient?' he asked. 'The knife just happening to be on the table. The story of the neighbour's lunch party. The children having left for school. Her injuries. I've just got this lingering suspicion that maybe our Caroline Dobbs had her own motives for killing.'

'You're talking a load of balderdash if I may say so,' said Gladys. 'A more convincing witness than Caroline would be difficult to contrive – poor woman. I bet that some of us here would have reacted in the same way faced with the behaviour of that evil minded controlling bastard of a husband and don't forget that any flaw in her case would doubtless have been lethally exposed by cross examination of Sir Patrick Anderson – "one of the leading barristers of our times",' she grandly added.

Not only in a gender minority of one but also an identical view-point minority, Brian de- and resisted. 'I'm still far from convinced,' he said.

The vote was 11-1. On the Judge's direction the jury retired again to attain unanimity.

'It would be best if you could all agree,' he said, 'but if this impossible I will accept a majority verdict of no less than 10-2. Off you go now.'

And they did. Brian remained unpersuaded. Perhaps it was his self-admitted reluctance to judge. To deliver the final blow to justice for the victim. Faced with uncharacteristically strong language from his co-jurors he nevertheless held firm.

'That's enough,' said Gladys just before lunchtime. 'One final vote. All those in favour of acquittal down to manslaughter?'

On returning to court the jury was told that the Judge had been called away urgently to see his wife who had been taken to hospital. But he would return in the morning. And that, in a step which was regarded as unusual, if not unique, he would allow the accused bail overnight to reside at her home in the company of her two children. And, in a gesture which confirmed the Judge's anticipation of a not guilty verdict, he allowed her to have her mobile phone which had been impounded to be returned. This phone had been forensically interrogated and found to contain no incriminating material. On the contrary. The number of her contacts was a mere six, including the children, the deceased, the local minicab company and the dentist. The tiny list did nothing to challenge Caroline's plea of isolation at the hands of her husband.

Order was restored at 10.30 the following morning. The Judge was quick to apologise for the inconvenience which he had caused by his absence in attending on his sick wife who had undergone successful surgery.

'Hopefully we can proceed without undue delay. Members of the jury, have you reached a verdict?'

'We have, your Lordship. By a majority of 11-1 we find the defendant, Caroline Dobbs…'

Then Brian Fairbrother said from the jury box – as the place where the jury members sit is quaintly termed – 'Hang on a second.'

Startled the Judge raised his spectacles and looked across. He politely and firmly advised Brian to keep his silence.

'I can't, my Lord. Allow me to address you in private. I beg you.'

The Judge, who was nothing if not broad minded and ever one to bend the rules to accommodate the dispensation of justice, felt an urge of sympathy for Brian. The thorn amongst the bed of roses. A minority of one could at least be accorded a degree of latitude.

'Very well. I'll see you in my chambers.'

Words which attracted a protest of an almost unseemly nature from John Reynolds acting for Caroline.

'You may well – as I am sure will have occurred to you Mr. Reynolds – have unassailable grounds of appeal,' said the Judge, 'if things go against your client as a result of this intervention. But this is my court, and I will do what I want if it will lead to a just verdict. Something which your client no doubt favours,' he added with a none too subtle hint of sarcasm.

Brian had scrawled on a piece of paper his thoughts for the Judge. One. No explanation, or even questioning, of the unexplained injury in the pathologist report. Maybe it was evidence of an earlier assault by the accused. Two. A failure by the prosecution to investigate whether the so-called lunch party which the victim had allegedly prohibited his wife from attending ever took place at all. Whose party was it? Three. The ease with which the lunge with the knife was delivered straight to the target, slashing the space between the ribs – something which an expert would not find easy. Four. The mobile phone. Was it not extraordinarily convenient that here was a phone which quite possibly listed fewer contacts than the phones of any of another 20 million or so users in the UK. So few might support the suggestions of coercive control by limiting social contact.

'I have an idea, Judge. A hunch.'

Whether or not the Judge's profound relief at his wife's recovery influenced his state of mind one will never know, but it certainly did not damage his willingness to comply. At, it need be said, enormous risk to his reputation.

As John Reynolds was to submit to the Judge on his return to the courtroom. 'Your conduct is a betrayal of your solemn duty to conduct a fair trial in the pursuit of a just verdict.'

'Thank you, Mr. Reynolds. Now I will proceed. This case has enjoyed a number of unusual features, as I am confident, we all – especially you Mr. Reynolds – will agree. I am about to introduce yet one more. I am ordering every person in this court to switch on his or her mobile phone' – an act which was ostensibly forbidden during criminal proceedings.

Turning off, not on, was the invariable order of the day. Looks of sheer perplexity from counsel, court officials and the public alike were followed by a flurry of activity. Phones out of pockets and handbags and all switched on. Even that of Caroline.

'Pass the defendant's phone to me please, usher.'

The implement was handed up. An IPhone 5 SE. The Judge scrolled. Contacts. Absolute silence in the Court. What was going on? The Judge was seen to tap. And then it happened. The unmistakeable sound of a phone ringing. Not answered and after seven rings stopped. The Judge looked around the Court.

'I heard a phone,' he said. 'It's now gone to an anonymous voice message: "The person you called is not available" … etc. I will now ring it again and I want it answered. I must warn that any person seen trying to put his or her phone on to "silent" will be apprehended.'

The Judge retapped. This time the recipient could not avoid detection.

At the Judge's direction the attentive journalist, otherwise described in Caroline's contact list as 'Dentist', took the stand. And relinquished his mobile to the usher who passed it to the Judge. After giving his name and address he attempted to explain his relationship with the defendant as one of confidant. Having little freedom to mix with others Caroline had taken the opportunity, on a recent dental appointment, to disclose her misery. He had felt sorry for her and tried to provide some platonic comfort.

'In which case,' asked the Judge, relishing his rediscovered opportunity to cross examine – an exercise the loss of which many judges have difficulty in coming to terms with – 'perhaps you would be good to explain the meaning of this text message "not long now darling", sent from the mobile of none other than the defendant not more than ten minutes before today's proceedings became underway?'

The game up, the jury was redirected to reconsider its verdict, returning no longer than 30 minutes later. It consisted of one word – not two. The Judge thanked the jury in general and Brian in particular, to whom he conveyed his 'unreserved appreciation'.

Addressing Sir Patrick immediately thereafter he was unable to resist the observation that this had not been his finest hour.

'Quite so, my Lord.'

'It is no thanks to you, Sir Patrick, that I am able to impose a minimum tariff of 17 years.'

Nec Vi, Nec Clam, Nec Precario

'Beautiful. Absolutely fucking gorgeous. There are no other words to describe it.'

Harold Wooderson's delightful portrayal of the credit entry on his Nat West bank statement of £2,550,000 to be precise.

The sum which he had screwed out of Burlington Golf Club with its lawyers, for access over his farmland from the ninth green to the tenth tee. A mere matter of 40 square metres of pathway which, without its connectivity properties, would have a value of zilch. But its unique property in affording egress from the ninth green to the tenth tee without having to travel 400 circular metres from the former to the latter, gave it a value for which its owner, Harold, could effectively name his price. The reason being a cock up of major significance by the firm of Magic Circle London City Solicitors whose negligent failure to notice an ownership gap between the plan on the 90 years' lease which Harold had granted to the club and the actual layout of the piece of land concerned, was unarguable. The access land had not been demised. It remained in the unencumbered ownership of Harold. Whatever may have been intended was unrecorded anywhere, so any suggestion of a mutual mistake, or rectification of the plan was out.

The amount of compensation was matter of discussion between the indemnity insurers of the lawyers acting for the golf club and the officers of the club who bore some limited responsibility on the one hand, and Harold on the other. When Harold's lawyers had suggested to him before the showdown meeting £100,000, he knew that they would be a pushover against the London heavyweights.

'You're a load of useless weaklings,' he had told them. 'Just think what that piece of land is worth to a golf club aspiring to reach top ranking in the county. They've already forked out millions to buy the land in the first place and to build the course. And you are seriously suggesting that I settle for a comparative song? What a load of wankers you lawyers are. Think you know it all. All that intellectual superiority. But when it comes to business, you're just hopeless.'

The 250-acre Burlington Farm had been owned by the Wooderson family for 72 years, having been acquired for a comparative song by Harold's paternal grandfather just after the end of the war in 1945 when he was the tenant farmer. By 2015 arable farming had lost its commercial appeal.

Harold had decided to exploit its non-farming value. Strategic discussions with Strattons, a major firm of local land agents, produced several alternatives. One of which, a 150-acre golf course plus clubhouse, would prove lucrative. The remaining 100 acres would remain fallow until her opportunities might present themselves. Residential development being one. But that could wait. Harold was in no rush.

Just seven months later the commercial sun was to shine once again on Harold Wooderson. Demand for housing was beginning to grow. A phone call from Strattons led to negotiations with James Reynolds plc, a firm of entrepreneurial up and coming residential property developers who, given the green light to proceed with negotiations to buy, applied for planning consent to build 125 housing units on the land between the golf course and its northern boundary bordered by a private road which had been owned by the Miller family for the past 90 years together with further farmland to the north. Planning consent was granted despite some raised eyebrows at the presence on the council planning committee of Charlie Winters whose long-standing friendship with Harold Wooderson was well known. Lawyers for both seller and buyer were instructed. Contracts finally exchanged. Harold was licking his lips at the prospect of £5 million in his Nat West account.

'There's a potentially major problem, Mr. Wooderson,' said Christopher Parkin, the senior partner of Parkin and Parkin who had summoned his client to his office. 'As you are aware access to your plot is gained via the private road to its north owned by the Miller family. The contract requires you to prove title to the means of access, failing which the buyers can withdraw and sue for damages. Unfortunately, there does not appear to be with the deeds any evidence, that a binding right of way has ever been granted.'

'You lawyers are all the same,' replied Harold. 'I've been using that road for the past 40 years or even more and nobody has objected. Surely, I must have acquired some rights of way. Isn't there some kind of doctrine on adverse possession or prescriptive right of way? I'm sure I've read about such things somewhere.'

'You're quite right, Mr. Wooderson. There is. But in the absence of what is called a binding grant of a deed of easement, any such doctrine – as you call it – is subject to the quaintly described principle that the use of the land has been enjoyed – as the Romans would have said – *"nec vi, nec clam, nec precario"*.'

'Well,' said Harold, 'I've little doubt what *precario* must mean. It's pretty obvious. But what about the other two. I've never heard the words.'

'Very simple,' said Christopher Parkin. '"*Vi*" means force. And "*clam*" means secretly.'

Harold thought for a moment. 'Nothing to worry about then. There has never been any suggestion that we have ever used the road clandestinely or other than in full view or that we have ever used any force.'

'And *precario*?' asked Christopher.

'Leave that with me,' replied Harold.

'Are you sure?' asked the lawyer.

'Absolutely,' Harold said.

'You had better be,' said Mr. Parkin. 'They are currently refusing to complete and are threatening to sue for damages. I'm not at all confident that you will win. Best to try to settle now.'

'I can't believe you said that. I'm fed up with you defeatist lawyers. I'll handle the case myself.'

'This should not take long, Judge,' Harold said confidently to his Honour Judge Peters in the Norwich County Court in the case of James Reynolds plc v Harold Wooderson. 'It's a very simple issue. The Miller family concedes that neither I nor my predecessors in title have ever used force or behaved secretly when using the claimant's land to gain access to my land. And only a fantasist would contend that my use of the land, or its prospective use by the owners of the houses to be erected on it, could conceivably cause the road owner any concern that it might be put at any risk by such use. Nothing precarious about it whatsoever. I go even further, your Honour. I cannot resist a modicum of satisfaction when I brandish the piece of paper in my right hand. Something I recently discovered. A letter addressed to my grandfather, Peter Wooderson, from Ian Miller, dated 3rd July 1945, in which he specifically grants permission for my grandfather and any future owners of our family farm to always use the private road for access to it. Here it is, your Honour. I invite you to read it.'

'Are you sure about that, Mr. Wooderson? I note that you are unrepresented in this case and perhaps it might be in your interests to take legal advice.'

'Unnecessary,' retorted Harold.

'In which case, Mr. Wooderson, so is any further argument in this case,' replied the Judge.

Judgement for the claimant for rescission of the sale contract and damages of £3 million. Plus costs to be taxed if not agreed.

'I don't understand, your Honour,' said a plainly shaken Harold. 'Can you explain?'

'Willingly,' said the Judge. '"A little knowledge is a dangerous thing" is a saying well known in English folklore. So, otherwise than among practising lawyers, is the entirety of the words as translated by Lord Hoffman, of the Latin *tag nec vi, nec clam, nec precario*: "not by force" – you got that right – "nor stealth" – you got that right too – "nor the licence of the owner" – you got that wrong. Let me put it another way. The grant of permission otherwise than by a binding legal easement nullifies the underlying concept of adverse possession – of acquiring a right over land behind the back of the owner. If you hadn't, by some magic or other, discovered the letter, you might have stood a chance. As it is, I'm afraid…' His voice tailed off.

'Chastened' would describe the mood of Harold Wooderson at that moment. Maybe lawyers were not such a waste of space as he thought.

On the Other Hand

Helen Russell's circumstances suggested inevitability. A life beyond the normal boundaries of control. Born of an Irish father who disappeared minutes after his drunken impregnation of an equally drunken English mother, Helen had been taken into Local Authority care by the London Borough of Haringey. By the time she was ten Helen had enjoyed – if that is the correct verb – no fewer than four different foster mothers. The first three failed to discharge the burden of quasi parental responsibility which they had signed up to. On Helen's tenth birthday the fourth of these, Marie Sanderson, a kindly, single, retired 55-year-old nurse, had inherited a wild, damaged, unruly child, who could not be disciplined.

But Marie refused to succumb to frustration. She recognised that any kind of punishment only made matters worse. So, she adopted a different philosophy. Ignore the misbehaviour. Reward good behaviour. Rely on the child to work out for herself that sociability brings its own benefits. Anti-sociability leads up a blind alley. How much better to go to bed on a full stomach after helping to peel the potatoes. Within no longer than six months temper tantrums had become a thing of the past. Helen had made substantial progress from the disagreeable to the likeable, the antagonistic to the compliant.

Tragedy struck after two and a half years. Marie was diagnosed with terminal cancer. No worse time for a pre-pubertal teenager for whom Marie was a rock of security and affection. When she died after three months a devastated Helen was moved to a children's home in Tottenham. It was the beginning of a slow decline. She found herself progressively isolated. All the good which had flowed from her relationship with Marie was gradually disappearing. In short, she was becoming a rebel. She often failed to return to the home by the stipulated time in the evening, instead mixing with every local undesirable while dabbling with drugs.

At 16 she became pregnant, giving birth to a son, Danny, when she was barely 17. The birth certificate recorded the father as 'unknown' – as indeed he was, with a potential list of nine equally exploitative, qualified candidates.

Helen fiercely resisted all attempts to have the child adopted. He was to become the focus of her stability. Placed in Council accommodation with three other single mothers, Helen mentally grew five years in a matter of six months. She thrived. The child thrived. After two years she was allocated a two bedroomed council flat and, qualifying for free childcare, she found work at the local hospital in the admin department.

Everything in the garden was rosy until the day when she was hauled before a kangaroo tribunal accused of dealing drugs by her immediate boss whose advances she had been steadfastly refusing. Protestations of innocence fell on deaf ears. Gross misconduct they called it. Summary dismissal. And that was when she really went off the rails. It began with drink, then cannabis, then opiates. She paid for these by shoplifting. Her luck had to run out. As it did when caught red handed in the jewellers, Ernest Jones, with a £50,000 diamond ring secreted in the inside pocket of her jacket. She was given a three-year prison sentence by the Crown Court Judge.

Danny, now four years old, was taken into temporary Local Authority care while she served 18 months in HMP Bronzefield, a gleaming new jail whose inmates included the killer Rose West.

Back in the outside world Helen was persuaded by a fellow ex-convict to attend a Sunday church service. Which was where she met Jackson Edwards. Thirty-one years old, a lay preacher, secretary of the Wood Green Temperance Society who managed a health food shop for a living. An unlikely relationship was kindled. Jacksons' suppressed carnal desires somehow fused with Helen's desperate need for comfort and security and a father for Danny. How could she resist his proposal of marriage?

The matrimonial home was a four bedroomed detached in Palmers Green which Jackson shared with his widowed mother, Maisie. Danny was now six years old. Jackson was the cat that swallowed the cream, with whom she 'enjoyed' – in the sense of 'participated in' rather than 'obtained pleasure from'– sex every Saturday night. Sunday was church.

Helen found work as a medical receptionist in the local surgery. Where her life's journey was to change. She met the Armani jeansed Jake. Collecting a prescription for his father. One smile sealed it. They both knew. A drink after work was followed by two hours of ecstasy made more passionate by three lines of cocaine. Jackson's curiosity had been satisfied by a lying excuse that she was needed for the evening shift owing to staff sickness.

True to her chaotic lifestyle Helen succumbed to disaster. A tip-off inspired police raid on Jake's flat led to charges of possession with intent to supply. It was Helen's luck to be arrested in mid sexual stream when on her cocaine fuelled high. She was told to get dressed, escorted to the local nick and duly charged with Jake. She had to confess all to Jackson whose charitable Christian principles did not, in this instance, embrace those of forgiveness. When she got a two-year jail sentence, Jackson did not hesitate to file for divorce. 'I'm also going to claim custody of Danny.'

'Over my dead body,' Helen retorted.

'We'll see,' replied Jackson. 'Meanwhile I presume you have no objection to his remaining with me and mother while you are otherwise located. Remember I did adopt him when we got married.'

The divorce petition was served on Helen while in Bronzefield. Arrangements had been made for her to occupy a council flat on her release by which time the decree nisi had been issued. Jackson refused to allow Danny to live with Helen.

'I don't rate your chances at more than 20 per cent,' said Giles Worthington, the sympathetic legal aid barrister acting for her on her custody application. 'In fact, I regret to say that after reading the social enquiry reports, there is precious little going for you. Your son appears perfectly content living with his adoptive father and grandmother. He's nearly nine years old and his view will count for a lot before the Judge. We'll have to hope that we get someone enlightened. One of those modern school, progressive judges who can think imaginatively.'

The Notice on the doors Court 17 at the Royal Courts of Justice stated that the hearing was in camera. No members of the public allowed. This was a family custody application before Judge Archibald O'Connor.

'A more unfortunate choice of judge is hard to imagine,' Helen's counsel told her. 'It's like he was born in the 19th century. As severe and old school as anyone who sits on the Bench, the only thing in his favour being a man known for applying scrupulous reason and logic, with not one successful appeal to dent his reputation. We're stuck with him I'm afraid. My estimate of 20 per cent is looking more than optimistic now. I'm so sorry. Five per cent is nearer the mark.'

The parties and their legal representatives were all seated in Court. The child social worker was also present. She was a severe looking woman in her forties who plainly had not been receptive to any notion that the boy should live within a hundred miles of this depraved, delinquent mother. Danny had to wait outside in the corridor with Maisie looking after him, until the evidence had concluded lest either claimant should be unnecessarily disparaging about the other with damaging effects upon the boy. The Judge entered Court, all stood, and when he sat down so did they.

Everything was proceeding predictably. Jackson explained how his Christian principles required him to oversee the upbringing of this unfortunate boy. The Judge's head nodded so vigorously it almost came apart from the neck.

It was Giles' turn to call his client to testify and explain why she felt that she was best qualified to have custody of Danny.

'He's my son,' she said. 'We have an unbreakable bond. We understand each other. Moreover, I don't want him to have to endure the sanctimonious, stifling rectitude of my ex-husband. It's enough to kill any sense of joy and adventure in a boy of his age.'

'Let's now hear what Danny has to say,' said the Judge. 'Bring him in, usher.'

When Danny entered the Court Helen made an instinctive movement towards him. To hug him. To kiss him.

'Stay where you are,' said the Judge. 'No physical contact if you please.'

Danny looked at the floor, with no eye contact either. Helen was reassured by her counsel that he would have been told not to look at her, so not to worry.

The Judge conducted the questioning. 'Of course, you love your mother, Danny. It's only natural. But Jackson who is your father by adoption, is kind is he not? And you adore his mother I understand.'

Jackson nodded.

'If I may,' said Giles, 'just one or two questions.'

'Very well,' said the Judge, 'but be discreet.'

It was all too much for Helen. 'Why can't I speak to my boy? My son. The only thing in my life that's worthwhile,' she screamed. 'Don't you all recognise what he means to me?'

Giles tried in vain to pacify his client. 'It's the procedure,' he told her. 'You have to leave the questioning to me.'

Helen ignored the advice. 'What's wrong with all of you? she shouted. 'You won't even let him look at me. What the fuck are you all afraid of? That he might betray his feelings, and tell the unpalatable truth about that nauseating, sanctimonious prick of a father for whom virtue trumps vice every time. Go to church on Sunday and you're fucking wonderful. Have a dram of whisky and you're the devil. You're all a load of heartless thugs.' At which she collapsed in a flood of tears.

Danny rushed over to where his mother was sitting, flinging his arms around her. 'Please don't cry mummy. I will always love you mummy, to the end of time,' he blurted out with a maturity beyond his age.

Giles saw no point now in questioning the boy. The Judge announced an adjournment for 30 minutes while he prepared his judgement.

'I would normally not have needed to give more than cursory consideration to this case,' the Judge began. 'The despicable, unruly behaviour and language of the mother in front of her son earlier in this Court being sufficiently powerful so as to decide my judgement for me.'

'You're a fucking wanker, Judge,' screamed Helen. 'A fucking disgrace.'

'I will ignore this unseemly outburst. Do try to keep your client under control, Mr. Worthington. Otherwise, I shall have her removed.'

Helen was not for restraining. 'Don't you understand, you stupid prick, the life which I have endured since birth. No parents. The one sympathetic carer dying so prematurely. The cruel exploitation which I have suffered. And despite everything my refusal to abdicate my responsibilities to care for my precious boy.'

Giles was quick to intervene. Placing his arm around her shoulder he told her to keep her thoughts to herself. 'You're playing into Jackson's hands,' he told her. 'Think of Danny before opening your mouth.'

The Judge continued. 'However, I recognised that to make a judgement on the future of this delightful young boy against the hysterical reaction of a distraught young single mother would have constituted grounds of appeal for the losing party. So, in the last 35 minutes while I retired to consider my decision, my thoughts followed the following pattern. On the one hand we have an adoptive father. A man whose behaviour towards his wife and adopted son has always been of the highest order in accordance with the standards which he sets himself. Kind. Considerate. Loving. And God fearing. A virtue which Mrs. Edwards seeks to decry as being harmful to the interests of her son. I disagree.'

An intuitive Giles managed to squeeze Helen's shoulder sufficiently tightly just in time to restrain an impending outburst.

The Judge continued. 'On the other hand, I cannot ignore the factors which Mrs. Edwards has so bravely, if crudely. enunciated before me. Her views on alcohol consumption are by no means unique and do not, in my view, imperil the welfare of her child. The observance of religion and Sunday worship are matters which, even for a child as young as nine, are perhaps better left for Danny to decide. Who can know what is best for him? So, I am left to weigh the competing and diametrically opposed interests. To balance the risks attendant on custody granted to the mother with her aberrant behaviour compared to the risks of custody granted to the safe bet of this adoptive father which deprive the boy of his mother's close love. How do I decide? It took me ten seconds of further thought. A light shone upon my decision-making process with the words of Danny ringing loud and clear. "I will always love you mummy till the end of time." How – I asked myself – could I deprive a son of the exercise of the permanent custodial responsibility by the one person who he plainly adores or deprive the mother of the opportunity to exercise that responsibility towards the son who appears to be her raison d'être. The answer was clear. How lucky they are to have each other. I therefore award custody of Danny Russell to his mother, Helen Edwards.'

As the Judge rose Helen shouted to him: 'Thank you, Judge. Thank you so much.'

'Don't thank me,' he replied. 'Danny's the one you should be thanking.'

Lex Talionis

'Well, ladies and gentlemen. You have been ensconced now in your jury room for nigh on 17 hours stretching over a period of two days. The time has arrived when either you deliver a majority verdict, or I will have to discharge you and invite the prosecution to decide whether they wish to proceed with a further trial before a different set of 12. So may I ask you, Mr. Foreman. Has the jury reached a verdict?'

'You will be gratified to learn, your Honour, that we have,' replied the jury foreman.

'In which case,' replied His Honour, Judge Peregrine Crabtree, 'would you put us all, that is to say me, Counsel and Solicitor, the public, the press, and – forgive me, I almost forgot – the defendants, out of our respective miseries, and be good enough to tell us what it is.'

Everyone was sure what the verdict would be in the case of R v Pardew and Barton prior to the announcement of the defendants' universally predicted fate. The time: 3.55pm on Tuesday, the 16th day of the month.

Jason Pardew and Percy Barton had each been accused of committing grievous bodily harm involving vicious acts of violence to Billy Walters and Jonathan Mates. If convicted, it would be at least seven years for each. An acquittal would constitute a triumph of forensic persuasion for their young advocate/solicitor Anthony Harrison. He had qualified to practice not more than four years earlier with an idealistic, burning ambition to achieve justice. For the oppressed. For the underdog. For the financially outgunned who were unlikely to get high class legal representation. For Anthony the legal profession conferred a privilege which allowed him opportunities to redress. Anthony Harrison was physically unremarkable, a shade under 6 foot tall, fair haired and blue eyed. He wore spectacles. He looked – and was – approachable. His smile was friendly, sometimes even when he was asking a very sharp question.

He would not reject an invitation to take on a case which seemed hopeless in the face of what at first sight exhibited overwhelming evidence of guilt. He would find that a challenge deserving preliminary investigation at least. Consideration. Appraisal. What were the chances of success? The tougher the challenge the greater the risk of failure. But success against all odds would bring its own unique sense of achievement. He was also demanding of himself. However exciting the challenge might be, it would have to satisfy his own ethical standards of behaviour. A case bursting with the promise of a David v Goliath success, but with no moral integrity, would fail the Harrison test.

By contrast Anthony might be tempted to represent a person accused of a crime even if he believed that the only defence lay in the moral justification for the acts complained of. He had never had to face that until the knock on his office front door one Tuesday afternoon. His original, trusted, percipient, faithful and, loyal Mrs. Johnson, the receptionist, the gatekeeper, who had responded to the advertisement in the *Law Society's Gazette* situations vacant section, when he opened his practice four years previously. 'Salary negotiable, but not beyond modest levels' it concluded.

'When would you like me to start?' she asked after the first minute of the interview.

'Yesterday' had been the reply.

'I'm sorry to interrupt you, Anthony,' said Mrs. Johnson, 'but there are two gentlemen who wonder if it might be possible to see you for five minutes. They say that they are in a spot of trouble and that you might be able to help. I told them that you are a very busy man who does not make a habit of seeing cold callers off the street, but they asked if you could possibly make an exception in their case. They were very polite about it.'

Recognising Mrs. Johnson's remark as a hint to depart from his usual practice not to see strangers without an appointment, Anthony agreed to meet them. One was Jason Pardew. The other Percy Barton. Each late thirties or so. Fit as gym instructors. Similar height – 5 feet 9 inches. Short back and sides schoolboy haircuts. Inexpensively dressed. Serious and nervous expressions on each face.

'Sit down, gentlemen, and tell me what I can do for you,' said Anthony in a manner calculated to put his guests at ease.

Visibly relaxing Jason was the first to speak. 'If I am to tell you everything I apologise, but it's going to take considerably longer than the five minutes which I told your receptionist, Mr. Harrison,' Jason said.

'It's Anthony. And take as long as you need.'

They had both been soldiers in the same regiment with stints of service in Afghanistan where they had witnessed appalling, and in some cases unspeakable, acts of violence. To this day the memories remained etched. Each of them had recently completed 15 years in the field and had left the armed services for civilian jobs in the security sector. They lived together in rented accommodation in Pinner. Nine weeks earlier, on a Saturday morning, after leaving Tesco they had witnessed from a distance what could only be described as an assault of the most cowardly nature. Two balaclava'd young men attacked an elderly woman from behind with a baton. The woman screamed. But clutched her handbag tightly. She was not letting go. The attackers persisted. One crack on the head and she collapsed. They made off with the bag.

By instinct Jason and Percy gave chase. But the attackers were too fast and made off towards North Harrow. Getting into their Mini Cooper Jason and Percy decided to search for the attackers, using their military skills of search and find. It paid off when they observed the perpetrators gratefully entering a house two miles away from where the incident had taken place. Jason looked at Percy. Nodded. They were of the same mind. Call the police and they would have relinquished control of the outcome. Time to exact their own brand of justice. They rang the doorbell.

Answered by one of the assaulters who let out a piercing scream as Jason grabbed him by the throat. Percy similarly grabbed his accomplice. Each was given what could objectively be described as a going over which neither would ever likely forget. Fingers smashed; kneecaps expertly cracked. Ten minutes of continuous, relentless retribution for the victim. Then came the sound of a police siren. Followed by arrest, escort to South Harrow Police Station. After vigorous police interrogation, both Jason and Percy gave written statements in which they admitted a beating which were to lead inevitably to charges of GBH.

They were bailed to appear at Brent Magistrates Court the following morning. From where the proceedings were transferred to the Crown Court. The story in a nutshell. Was this something that Anthony might be prepared to handle?

'What happened to the old lady?' asked Anthony.

'I wish we knew,' replied Percy, 'but nobody will tell us anything.'

'OK,' said Anthony. 'Leave it with me and I'll be in touch.'

'So does that mean that you'll represent us?' asked Jason.

'If your account of the Pinner incident stacks up you can take my answer as a yes.'

The prosecution evidence which was served on Anthony did not materially depart from the account which Jason had given to him. It consisted of victim statements and medical reports on the injured men, as well as the written admissions of Jason and Percy. And consistent with the prosecution's duty of fairness it disclosed bystander evidence of the Pinner attack, the dreadful impact on the physical and mental health of the elderly victim. The two perpetrators had been arrested and granted bail – and had bailed off somewhere abroad where they remained at large. The prosecution also profiled the respective service records of Jason and Percy which included two gallantry awards citing 'exceptional bravery in the course of an attack on civilians many of whose lives were saved as a result'.

'I have to warn you,' Anthony told his clients at their second meeting, 'that your chances of an acquittal are close to zero. I can see only the tiniest chink of light, and you may well feel that an early plea of guilty, with a one third reduction in sentence, would be in your best interests.'

'And give up all future prospects of work in the security industry?' asked Percy rhetorically. 'I'd rather take my chances.'

'Me too,' added Jason. 'I reckon that if we could emerge intact after what we went through in the Middle East, we can do the same here.'

'Hardly the same,' said Anthony.

'We needed a miracle then and we need a miracle now, so let's go for it. I know you'll do your best.'

The trial had opened amid a fanfare of publicity at Harrow Crown Court, not two miles from the scene of the Jason/Percy offences. Local interest was high and there was no vacant seat to be had in the public galleries. Sympathy for the accused had been running at a high level.

Conscious of the requirement for objectivity Judge Crabtree had begun his opening address to the jury by reminding them they must ignore any comment or news information which might have come to their attention before the trial. The jury was every shade of the human rainbow – six men and six women. Five white, three black, three Asian and one Oriental. One priest, one rabbi, one retired lawyer. A boxer, a postman, a nurse, a dog walker, a teacher, and four unemployed. As broad a selection as was ideally recommended to make up a broad-minded tribunal. Although Anthony did inwardly flinch at the sight of the religious men. The odds had lengthened by a further sixth.

'Tell me, Sergeant,' said Anthony to officer Burgess, who had taken the statements in the police station, 'would you say that during their interviews after their arrest, my clients were truthful or evasive?'

'Absolutely truthful as George Washington, sir.'

'Angry or calm?'

'Absolutely livid, sir, with what they had witnessed had happened to that poor old lady in Pinner?'

'And finally, officer, would you characterise the defendants as a force for good or evil?' At which prosecuting counsel jumped up to object.

'Your Honour,' he said. 'What is the relevance of this officer's opinion?'

'I agree,' said the Judge.

'In which case,' said Anthony, 'it cannot harm the prosecution case if he gives it. So please, officer, let us all hear from you.'

'Salt of the earth, if you ask me,' he replied.

Anthony looked at the jury for signs of approval. Other than the boxer, they remained inscrutable.

Anthony had decided that little was to be gained by calling either of his clients to testify. It had been accepted by the prosecution that their actions had been motivated by a humane desire to exact justice for the victim in the form of retribution against the perpetrators. For whom – they had said in their statements – prison would be a cop out. Their respective military records would speak for themselves.

Anthony had to overcome the mountain of legal authority which afforded no grounds on which to engineer an acquittal. Violence against another might be justified if committed while defending the perpetrator or his property or of another person or his property, so long as it was proportionate – whatever that may mean. But certainly not by way of reprisal or punishment.

This was to be the most important closing speech of Anthony's

career to date. Get it wrong and heaven help Jason Pardew and Percy
Barton. Get it right and the miracle might happen.

'Members of the jury I address you in all humility on behalf of
my clients Jason Pardew and Percy Barton. Two upright citizens who
have fought to protect innocent citizens of a foreign country against
the ravages of war. You have heard of the exceptional bravery for which
these two salts of the earth – if I may quote the opinion of Sergeant
Burgess – have earned official recognition. You have heard how angry
they each were to have witnessed behaviour redolent of the attacks
with which they were confronted on their tour of duty. You have heard
how two vicious thugs committed the most cowardly attack on an
elderly lady who continues to this day to suffer physically and mentally.
Thugs who have managed to evade justice by escaping to a foreign
country. Is there not some irony in the proposition that in return for
the only punishment inflicted on these two criminals – the reward
is a possible career destroying conviction and substantial sentence of
imprisonment?'

Anthony paused to assess the reaction of the jury. Nothing
positively encouraging. But they were plainly listening to every word.

'So,' he continued with eyes fixed upon the religious teachers, 'let
us consider what Hammurabi might have thought about it. The man
who nearly four thousand years ago in Babylon, developed the theory
of presumption of innocence until proven guilty. The cornerstone of
almost every progressive legal system in every continent. The man whose
religious philosophy embraced the notion that a wrongdoing should
be redressed by the perpetration of the identical wrongdoing on the
wrongdoer. *Lex Talionis*. Forgive the mouthful, ladies and gentlemen,
but I cannot put it any other way. And who among you would believe
it right, or fair, or sensible, or just, to discriminate against the righter of
that wrong? Particularly in this tragic case. Where two brave soldiers,
acting on the most commendable professional instinct, each suffering
the awful post traumatic effects of warfare, have put themselves at risk

for the sake of a defenceless pensioner. Follow your consciences. Be bold. And give these two brave men the acquittal that they so richly and humanely deserve.'

The Judge had made short shrift. 'Members of the jury. The evidence in this case is clear, unambiguous, and unequivocal. Each defendant has frankly admitted the offence with which he has been charged. Do not be persuaded by the silky tones of their advocate. Unless you wish to discredit the legal system in this country you will disregard Mr. Harrison's plea to apply the law of Hammurabi and instead apply the law of England. So I invite you to retire to consider your verdict in each case.' As short a summing up as could ever have been provided in the history of jury trials in the UK.

The jury had retired at 11.30am. By 3.45pm they had not given any indication of an imminent verdict. A note had been delivered to the Judge who read it out to both advocates.

'Given your Honour's stern rebuke of Anthony Harrison's arguments, if we were to return a verdict of not guilty would we be guilty of some sort of contempt of court?'

The Judge told the advocates that he would simply tell the jury to return verdicts which the law required.

'With respect your Honour, that is avoiding the question,' said Anthony.

'On the contrary, Mr. Harrison, I am reminding the jury to do its sworn duty,' replied the Judge. And with that sent his own note back to the jury.

At 11.20 the following morning after a further 50 minutes in the jury room, the 12 fate holders were summoned back by the Judge to give them a majority direction. He would accept a verdict of at least ten jurors if they could not all agree.

'Go away ladies and gentlemen and see if you can reach a verdict.'

An hour later came another note. It read: 'If we convict will the defendants go to prison and if so for how long?'

This time the Judge returned a terse reply. 'Your question lacks legitimacy and I strongly urge and remind you to do your sworn duty.'

The jury had certainly been given something to think about. While there was life there was hope for the defendants. The hours dragged on. Until the jury had returned. As they were taking their seats Anthony had tried to infer some clue as to what the agreed verdict was. But nothing. Each juror studiously avoided eye contact. Usually a bad sign. The tension was palpable. Anthony nervously fiddled with his watch. 3.56pm.

The defendants stood at the command of the Judge. The foreman held the piece of paper on which the verdict had been written. And spoke. 'The verdict is unanimous, your Honour. "Not guilty".' Followed by an explosion of clapping from the public gallery. The rabbi and the priest embraced. Tears streamed down the boxer's cheeks. Jason and Percy stood open mouthed. As did the Judge.

Anthony gathered up his papers and mouthed a thank you to the jury. Justice had been done. *Lex Talionis* was still alive.

Last Throw of the Dice

HMP Wednesbury, built in 1987, was a Category C – low risk of escape – ten wing jail in Hertfordshire. Once the top performing jail in the country it was heading towards its death throes. With 1000 inmates whose offences embraced the whole panoply of antisocial behaviour, it was undergoing a staff crisis of hitherto inexperienced proportions. Uniformed prison officers, disillusioned with pay and conditions, were leaving in droves. Failure to attract new recruits meant that safety of prisoners, as well as of staff, was at severe risk. There was a rapidly increasing rate of serious assaults by prisoner on prisoner and prisoner on staff. Drug supply and use were rife. Prison officers, scared of reprisal, were allowing inmates to break the rules at will. A culture of fear, bullying and insecurity pervaded the atmosphere. Neither the weak inmate nor any but the strongest willed prison officer, stood a chance.

Governor Julie Bradley joined Wednesbury in June 2017, replacing the outgoing Governor who had retired prematurely suffering from acute stress. Bradley had 12 months left to serve before she retired with a nice pension. She had wanted to round off her service with a cushy number, having survived a career not without controversy, but no such luck. Those that decide such things allocated her the poisoned chalice. Succeed and be a hero. Fail and 30 distinguished years would end in ignominy. The staff shortages had prompted her predecessor to lock down – or lock up in a prison cell – depending on which expression you prefer – every prisoner for 22 hours per day for four days a week. The aim was to ensure a modicum of safety by isolating the inmates while depriving them of basic freedoms of association, let alone in the open air. Such draconian action was bound to provoke unrest. Riot would be inevitable unless there was a change of policy. It needed an action plan of radical imagination.

Would Bradley be up to the task? Having once been rapped over the knuckles for allowing inmates to present their own monthly entertainment shows contrary to prison rules, she was wary about being bitten for a second time.

'Fuck it,' she said to herself, 'something's got to be done and they can't touch me now, so I'll do what I think is best.'

'Radical' is an over used word but Julie's idea made 'radical' seem like a mere tweak. She conceived a brand-new approach. Prisoners basically prefer order to chaos, justice to injustice, safety to peril, occupation to boredom, an ability to get on with their miserable existence with a degree of hope, the formation of friendships, the chance to prepare constructively for life on the outside. A dark tunnel with no shafts of light amid a sea of bullying and rife uncontrolled drug taking is not the preferred option. So how to attain the objective amid the dire conditions of Wednesbury. A declining, failing, hell hole of an institution.

On Monday 24th July the new dawn surfaced. The eight wings Alpha to Harry were back to normal. Fully staffed. Prisoners out of cells and unlocked on time to be on their way to places of work and education classes. Jaunty and glad to be back on the standard regime. Staff smiling and relaxed. Who would ever have sniffed a crisis? For the prisoners on the interconnecting Wings India and Jordan things were not quite the same. Not a prison officer in sight. Cell doors had been open all night. A new hierarchy had been created. A kind of civilian army run by prisoners appointed by prisoners for the benefit of prisoners which freed the usual 16 India and Jordan Wing staff for other duties. The 'Generals' consisted of two armed robbers and a bent copper in charge of discipline. A struck off lawyer to adjudicate on law and order and arbitrate on disputes. A chef to control the food supply and preparation, never mind that he had committed arson. An accountant and a businessman convicted of a joint VAT fraud to control expenditure of the budget provided by the prison to buy supplies for recreational activities – table tennis, snooker, musical instruments, card tables, playing cards and chess sets.

Most important two rival drug gang barons joined to regulate the supply of drugs on a strictly moderate and controlled basis, which would avoid all the bullying and violence. The lawyer drafted a strict disciplinarian code. Any infringement would lead to physical punishment which was to be administered by Mick – an inmate known as 'the executioner' who had convictions for violence involving exceptional depravity. Two months of unblemished behaviour was to be rewarded with a one-hour conjugal visit twice a month in cells specially fitted out for purpose.

The improvement over the next six months in just about every aspect of prison life was spectacular. Any fears that wings managed according to democratic egalitarian principles would lead to chaos were effectively stillborn. All hopes that the project might prove but a mere qualified success were exceeded beyond calculation. The Wednesbury Warrior Prison Jazz Band was so successful it was booked for a monthly evening performance at the local village hall. Purposeful activity statistics went off the scale, the prison workshops were full up. One satisfied wife of a Jordan Wing prisoner was heard to exclaim that if her husband could be inspired to perform as he did, she prayed that he would never be released; he never had managed so much for so long before. An unqualified success.

Or so it seemed until Julie Bradley received a summons to attend the offices of the Justice Minister 'on a matter of some urgency'.

What did they want? She prayed that her innovation would not be squashed in its infancy. On her return she remained nervous and tight lipped and refused to disclose what had passed. All she would say was that she was asked something in the strictest confidence.

When Julie Bradley stood up in the Ballroom at Buckingham Palace following the dabbing by Her Majesty The Queen of the ceremonial damehood conferring sword, she was asked how she had managed to succeed in restoring the prison to its former glory.

'Ma'am,' she said, 'it wasn't difficult for someone like me. I had nothing to lose. The prison was suffering heart failure. All previous treatments had failed. I decided that drastic times demanded drastic measures. A bit of imagination. The prison was in the last chance saloon, and this was the last roll of the dice.'

'Well,' replied the Queen, 'I won't detain you. Off you get to Ascot before I get there.'

A note from the publisher. I made a film about Broadmoor. One inmate sent the Queen Mother roses for her birthday for years. When he was released, she invited him to join her at Ascot.

A Matter of Justice

'Members of the jury. Are you all agreed upon your verdict?'

'We are now, my Lord.'

'Thank goodness for that. And do you find the defendants guilty or not guilty?' Mr. Justice Warren asked the three women and nine men whose decision it was.

A case in which questions of reason clashed with considerations of fairness and sympathy. A case in which disagreements in the jury room had, let us be poetic, been inflamed in a cauldron of boiling passions. Between those who had great difficulty in reconciling their duties to convict or acquit strictly according to the evidence rather than to their own sense of right and wrong, and those who felt able to disregard emotion at the expense of logic. When the foreman had told the Judge the jury was hopelessly split, he told them to think more and think again. The 12 members conferred for a further three days before achieving unanimity – the resolve of the initial minority finally prevailing.

Charlie Harris, chief executive officer, and majority shareholder in Harris Homes PLC, a company which, with an inheritance from Uncle Dickie of £520,000, he had founded in 2009 to specialise in building of homes at the cheaper end of the market in the high winds of the recession. He had luck which not only gave him the opportunities to succeed where others failed but stifled any compassion. Half a dozen half developed sites unloaded on to the market by a dodgy liquidator desperate to realise some cash were snaffled for a fraction of the costs incurred to date, the obligatory backhander being a mere drop in the ocean. Four separate building plots with planning consent for a combined total of 375 units, financed in part by bank loans on which the borrowers defaulted, were snapped up at a price barely enough to discharge the impatient bank's indebtedness – the equity effectively being gifted following a lavish lunch at Le Gavroche with a senior bank employee. Almost overnight the surplus showing on the balance sheet of Harris Holmes PLC had upped from a modest £482,000 to one of £2,600,000.

However dubious Charlie's business practices might have been, they were but mere amuse-bouches compared to his building practices, or malpractices. Where a corner could be cut in the quality of installation of anything, from a light switch to a drain cover, from a sink unit to a boiler, no opportunity was lost. Part of a classic selection of hors d'oeuvres. The main course, and major cost saving enterprise, was using sub-standard concrete. A private source from the Philippines, where that was rife – allowed Harris Homes to cut its building costs by 15%, doubling of the norm for the industry profit. Applying all his native cunning, Charlie disguised the defective nature of the materials to escape the attention of those whose job it was to carry out, and be satisfied with building regulations. Only David Reeder, the company's in house surveyor, was alert enough to betray his suspicions by asking Charlie a few uncomfortable and unanswered questions. After which Charlie sacked him for 'gross misconduct' after setting him up on a fabricated allegation of misappropriation of building materials. A devastated David, unemployed in a recession with little chance of re-employment, thrown on the scrapheap – minus his £70,000 annual salary which he needed to keep his wife, mortgage and two children.

Reeder was found floating in the Thames near Maidenhead six weeks after being fired. When a plainly upset, 56-year-old secretary, Miss Warner, showed Charlie the report of the suicide in the *Daily Mail*, he shrugged his shoulders.

Charlie rarely travelled anywhere without his Aston Martin Vantage. His love of expensive cars had, however, been spoiled by a five year suspension of his driving licence after his conviction in 2017, for causing the death of a pedestrian by careless driving, an offence for which he got, thanks to the silky tongue of Robert Asquith QC, two years' imprisonment suspended for one year. So, he was able to observe the gates of Wormwood Scrubs from the street. All which meant a chauffeur. Ray Wallace was a godsend. Ex-soldier. Driver of jeeps in Afghanistan. Loyal as a German Shepherd to his police handler. Reliable as the minute hand of Big Ben. Discreet as a priest. The job offer was a mere formality. Married to a theatre nurse working for the local NHS hospital, Ray was the ideal man. No children, no baggage, on call for emergency needs.

'I'm a lucky bastard,' said Charlie to himself after Ray said he could start whenever Charlie liked. Like the following day.

'I've got a hospital appointment on Monday so I won't be around,' Ray said to Charlie, five months into the job, 'but my wife Debbie is off next week, so she can drive you if needed.'

Charlie accepted with some misgivings. He had an appointment with his bankers in the City in the morning. 'Tell her to be here at 8.30. Sharp. I hope she is able to bleeding drive.'

'No worries, guv. Before qualifying as a nurse Debs was on traffic in the police.'

Charlie's almost but not entirely imperceptible recoil, did not pass unnoticed by Ray. 'An ex-copper, eh. I hope you mind your bleeding p's and q's,' said Charlie to mask his mild discomfort.

Monday morning at 8.29, a knock on the door of the office of Charlie Harris. 'A Mrs. Wallace is here for you,' Miss Warner said. 'Says she's here to run you about while her husband Ray has an appointment elsewhere.'

As she came in Charlie was momentarily stuck to the carpet. Blonde, hazel eyed, the body of a 30-year-old Carla Bruni and with a

face to suggest that maybe Audrey Hepburn might have done with a bit
of plastic surgery to compete. A modest unblemished smile.

'Good morning, Mr. Harris. I'm Ray Wallace's wife and he's asked
me to stand in for him this morning.'

For a full ten seconds Charlie was speechless. His own wife was
a looker. But this was something else. A bit special. A bit classy. For
a few seconds the reasons for her being there at all escaped him. But
collecting himself he managed to reply, 'Let's go.'

Effortless handling of the Aston allowed Charlie to relax. Initiating
small talk which he had not indulged in since his marriage of 13 years.
What was her job like? Is the NHS really so inefficient? Why leave the
police force? To his surprise, and no little pleasure he saw she responded
by asking him about his business career, the length of his marriage,
and – maybe this was a give-away of sorts – his interests. On the drive
back to the office the conversation continued more freely, helped by
the success of Charlie's meeting which had resulted in an offer from
the bank of ten-year term £2 million overdraft at a fixed interest rate
of 0.82%.

'Thank you, Mrs. Wallace. It's been a pleasure.'

'The pleasure's been all mine. Mr. Harris. And call me Debbie.
You know where to get hold of me if I'm needed again, Mr. Harris. I'm
actually off duty in ten days' time for a couple of weeks.'

'Call me Charlie. All my friends do.

'There's a site which I'm thinking of bidding for in Harrogate,
Ray, and I need to test a sample of the earth before proceeding further.
All bids must be in by midday tomorrow, so you'll have to collect the
specimen direct from the seller's surveyor's premises and bring it back.
Take the Aston and I'll see you in the morning. 7 o'clock sharp.'

'OK boss. Let's have the address. Shouldn't take more than about
eight hours there and back I reckon.'

'Take it easy, Ray. Don't want any accidents.'

After summoning up the courage of a teenager about to go on

his first date, Charlie made the call. And with a feeble attempt at prevarication, Debbie needed little persuasion to meet Ray at a country inn 18 miles or so away from where she lived.

'An early lunch would be ideal for me,' said Charlie, 'as I have to be back in the office by 4.30 at the latest.'

'Suits me fine,' replied Debbie.

An Uber cab delivered Charlie at The Greedy Fox in the tiny Buckinghamshire village of Severalton, just as Debbie was getting out of her Ford Fiesta.

'Looks nice,' said Debbie as Charlie kissed her cheek.

'The sort of place for a dirty weekend. But don't you start getting any ideas mind,' she said with just a hint of ambivalence. She might have guessed that Charlie was beginning to entertain ideas of that.

The aphrodisiacal effect of Lobster Thermidor lubricated with a 1957 premier Cru Chablis proved overwhelming. The genesis of stolen hours of a secret liaison of sexual gratification grabbed at times when excuses for absence were sufficiently plausible to stop any suspicions of Miss Warner on the one hand and Ray on the other. Taxing on Charlie's powers of imagination as they were, he nevertheless managed to come up with something which justified an 'urgent secret meeting which nobody, not even Ray, could know about'. Co-incidentally at Debbie's off duty times.

'I can't imagine life without these special occasions,' said Ray post orgasmic bliss. 'Thank goodness my wife hasn't got a clue. One ounce of proof and half my fortune goes out the window. She's got a lot of qualities, but a readiness to forgive is not one of them.'

When Debbie failed to show on time for lunch arranged for 12.30 on Friday 25th May 2018, Ray having been dispatched to deliver certain documents to Charlie's lawyers, Charlie was not amused. Only two hours had been set aside for a very quick snack followed by a more than hurried session upstairs. After 20 minutes he started to worry. A further 15 minutes of waiting began to induce a sense of foreboding.

justified as it turned out, when Ray appeared. Who sat down. Who placed his hand firmly on Charlie's forearm as Charlie made to leave.

'A little talk, Mr. Harris. I'll have a large scotch if you don't mind.'

The conversation was effectively one way. The accusations from Ray. The acknowledgements from Charlie. The threats from Ray. The fear from Charlie.

'£100,000 in used fifties by Monday or Mrs. Harris gets a warning.'

Nothing could have scared Charlie more than the threat of disclosure to Charlie's wife. And Ray knew, as much as Charlie knew – and Charlie knew that Ray knew – that Mrs. Harris would have no compunction in taking Charlie to the cleaners.

The £100,000 turned out to be the first instalment. On reaching £600,000 over the following nine weeks, Ray became even greedier. 'A quarter of a million by next Thursday and no excuses.'

But excuse there was. 'Believe me Ray, I can't get my hands on it. Perhaps in a month's time or so.'

Further attempts at extortion were unsuccessful. This time an email. 'Mr. Harris. I am tired of waiting. It's either another 250 on top of the measly 600 or you will regret it. Perhaps we could have a little chat after work. Somewhere nice and private where your car isn't bugged or anything like that. How about "The Dog and Bone" pub near Isleworth. Say 7.30 this evening? You get a cab there. I'll drive the Aston on my own.'

Extraordinary though it sounds Ray had continued to carry out his chauffeuring duties as if nothing unusual were happening. All in the firm belief that Charlie would never dare do anything to compromise his marriage. Ray was the master. And Charlie knew it.

The following morning Ray had not arrived at work by 10 o'clock. Charlie asked Miss Warner to see if she could track him down. 'I'm sorry, Mr. Harris, but no sign of him. His mobile is switched off and there is no answer to his landline.'

'Keep trying, Miss Warner. It's not like Ray,' he said, with an air of unperturbability but nevertheless irritated to be without a chauffeur.

Despite all her efforts Miss Warner got nowhere. Ray had simply disappeared for the day. Or so it seemed. Not a sign. There was nothing else for it. Charlie rang Debbie's mobile. Answerphone. Every attempt at contact failed. The rest of the week passed with no progress in locating either Ray or Debbie.

At 10.15 on the following Monday morning Miss Warner knocked on Charlie's office door. 'A Detective Inspector Morrison to see you Mr. Harris.'

After the introductory pleasantries – possibly more aptly described as unpleasantries – DI Morrison came to the point. 'We've had a report from a Mrs. Deborah Wallace that her husband, Raymond Wallace, has disappeared. Not seen nor heard from him for five days. Can you tell me whether he has been at work during that period.'

Charlie explained that he too had not seen or heard from Ray.

'In which case, sir, I invite you to come to the station with me for further questioning. Meanwhile I am impounding your laptop and your mobile phone. And I need the keys of your Aston Martin as well as the clothes you were wearing when you and Ray Wallace were last in each other's company.'

'Yes,' said the Judge to the eminent QC appearing on behalf of the Crown. 'Be so good as to outline for the benefit of the jury the case for the prosecution.'

The case was R v Harris. The charge – murder. The accused – one Charles Harris. The alleged victim – one Raymond Wallace. As Robert Trowson explained to the jury: 'No body has ever been found. But the circumstantial evidence is not only powerful, but overwhelming. The defendant was being heavily blackmailed by Mr. Wallace. The defendant had, over a period of nine weeks withdrawn from his bank accounts £600,000, none of which he could account for. An email from Mr. Wallace recovered from the defendant's inbox not only strongly corroborates the relationship between the parties – that of blackmailer and blackmailee. But it implicitly threatens the accused with disclosure of what the Crown alleges had been his sexual relationship with the wife of Mr. Wallace. She will testify as to the occasions on which sexual intercourse took place between them. According to that email Mr. Wallace invited the defendant to meet at a specified venue to for, as he put it, "a little chat". An Uber driver has confirmed delivering the defendant there where he saw parked an Aston Martin saloon. Further evidence consists of bloodstains found on the front passenger seat of the defendant's Aston Martin. The blood matched that of Mr. Wallace. Mrs. Wallace will tell the Court that the defendant admitted to her that he was terrified of losing half of his wealth if his wife found out about the affair and commenced divorce proceedings. Mr. Wallace has not been seen or heard of since the alleged meeting with the defendant on that evening. A compelling case if ever there was one. The inference is irresistible. That the defendant, desperate to avoid being bled dry by Mr. Wallace, and equally desperate to avoid being found out by his wife, killed Mr. Wallace with an instrument which caused some blood to stain the front seat of the defendant's motor car. The learned Judge will tell you that it is not necessary to produce a corpse to establish guilt on a charge of murder.'

By a majority of 10-2 the jury convicted Charles Harris of the murder of Raymond Wallace, the Judge sentencing him to life imprisonment with a minimum of nine years – allowance being made for the degree of provocation in the form of probable blackmail.

As he was escorted from the dock to start his sentence, Charles Harris was heard to say that he had been set up. 'Just like Dave Reeder,' Mrs. Wallace was heard to mutter softly in the earshot of DI Morrison.

This time it was the turn of Mrs. Wallace to be confronted by DI Morrison, though under circumstances different from those in which she attested for the prosecution of Charles Harris. But not before he had ascertained her maiden name was Reeder, and that she had a brother David who had committed suicide after his sacking from Harris Homes. And not before a trace on her mobile phone established that she had been in communication with her husband after his 'disappearance'. And not before she had been put under surveillance and followed to a hotel in Carmarthenshire where she was seen to rendezvous with a man having a strong resemblance to a description of the victim provided by Miss Warner. But it was before a package containing £600,000 in used £50 notes had been retrieved by Deborah Wallace from the basement of her house and handed it to DI Morrison with a request that he give it to Mrs. Charles Harris.

The arrest and subsequent charging of both Raymond and Deborah Wallace was a formality. As was the release from jail of Charles Harris. But before he had served the first week of his sentence, the service of a divorce petition, as well as a broken jaw inflicted by a gang of prisoners to whom he refused finance for their illicit drug supply ring.

'On the sole charge of conspiracy to pervert the course of justice we, the jury, in the case of The Crown versus Wallace and Wallace, find that these defendants were more than justified in taking the action which they did. For Mrs. Wallace to have sacrificed her body and thus to lay the foundations for an elaborate plot to set up Mr. Harris as a prospective victim of wrongful conviction, was an act of nobility deserving of profound sympathy. All this to avenge the suicide of her brother which was caused by the merciless behaviour of Mr. Harris. Similar considerations apply to our opinion of Mr. Wallace who allowed his wife to prostitute her body in the cause of retribution, and who then feigned a killing. Those of us – the minority of two it must be said – who initially saw beyond the strict application of the letter of the law, understood what had motivated the behaviour of the defendants with increasing admiration as the evidence unfolded. The robust and enlightening discussions in the jury room gradually convinced the original ten in favour of conviction to change their minds, one by one. "How could we send heroes to jail while the villain goes free?", we asked ourselves. Our consciences are more than clear. We find both defendants not guilty. As the final jury member to change his mind was happy to admit: "It's a matter of justice".'

Never Say Never

'Have you seen this, Mr. Harrison? You won't like it, I guarantee,' Chloe Patterson said as he walked through the front door into his office reception on that May Monday morning at 8.25.

'Not now, Chloe. I'm late as it is. Due in front of his Lordship Mr. Justice Avery at the Old Bailey in 55 minutes on a bail application. It'll have to wait.'

'I think you'd better take a look, Mr. Harrison. Really, I do.'

It wasn't like Chloe to give up when she believed that it was in her boss's interests to persevere. As loyal secretary, receptionist and general factotum Chloe, 31, knew better than anybody else what he did – or didn't – need to know. This news she knew was a matter to engage his interest. At the foot of page 3 on the *Daily Mail.* 'Man arrested on suspicion of teenage rape and murder'. A headline which was nothing out of the ordinary. It was the identity of the man arrested which had caught her eye.

Marcus Illingworth, who ten days earlier had been acquitted of a particularly vicious killing and rape of a teenage girl on Clapham Common thanks to the smart advocacy of Anthony, whose cross examination of the chief prosecution police witness had exposed irremediable flaws in the interrogation of the accused. A victory for Anthony which had nevertheless left a bitter taste in his mouth which had not exactly been sweetened by his client's condescending protestations of innocence.

'Told you all along, guv, that I didn't do it. I'm thinking of suing for false arrest.'

143

'And I'm advising you to thank your lucky stars,' replied Anthony. 'Just keep your nose clean.'

Now it appeared that history had repeated itself. Anthony had been as certain as he could have been that his client had been guilty. This arrest more or less confirmed it. He felt sick to the stomach. But for his skill an innocent girl would quite possibly be alive instead of dead.

'My worst fears,' he said to Chloe. 'A more odious creature never walked this earth. I'm making this solemn vow to you now, Chloe. I will never again take on a murder case. I'm not going to be a hired gun for anybody. And I do not want to be responsible for a guilty person walking free.'

'Now, now, Mr. Harrison,' said Chloe, 'never say never. You never know.'

A disillusioned Anthony Harrison appeared before Mr. Justice Avery on that Monday morning to seek bail on behalf of client who had been remanded in custody by magistrates on the previous Friday on a charge of armed robbery.

'Bail is denied, I'm afraid, Mr. Harrison. The risks of witness intimidation are too high. Just a minute. What is all that commotion going on?' The Judge was being distracted by raised voices coming from Counsel's row.

The barrister instructed to act for the defendant in the next case had failed his Covid test at the doors of the Court. Prosecuting counsel was objecting to an adjournment which the Court clerk was seeking on behalf of the now unrepresented defendant.

'Easily solved,' said the Judge. 'Mr. Harrison. What are you doing today?'

'Oh, no,' said Anthony. 'You're not catching me out. Just because I happen to have a vacant diary…'

The Judge cut him short. 'May I remind you, Mr. Harrison, that the Lord Chief Justice has yet to make a final recommendation on the outcome of the disciplinary complaint lodged against you last month, and – if you weren't already aware – your behaviour is under surveillance.'

'But, my Lord, I made a vow not one hour ago that I would in future never act for any defendant on a murder charge, one reason being that I would not want to feel responsible for a repeat offence if I secured an acquittal.'

'Well,' said the Judge, 'you'll have no qualms in this case, because the defendant is charged with matricide.'

Twenty-four-year-old Percy Worthington seemed totally impenetrable. As if clothed in chain mail. He had no idea of conversation; for him dialogue consisted of one word answers and he never started any talk. It was not as if he was uncivil. Or rude. Or unpleasant. Or nasty. It was simply that he was a mere being. A human amoeba. Incapable of responding to a stimulus except to give the shortest answer.

When charged with the murder of his mother, 47-year-old Florence Worthington, his only reaction had been a shrug. The family had lived in a penthouse flat in Belgravia. The only child of a widowed mother whose late husband Dominic had been found dead in his office accompanied by an empty bottle of sleeping pills and a note which cryptically said that he had had enough. The coroner's verdict of suicide threw no light on why.

After a respectable period of three months' mourning, Florence had resumed her busy social life, with little compunction in attracting romantic interest. The dining tables of Sheekey and The Ivy saw more than one eager suitor on more than one day in the week. Any hint of lingering grief would have been hard to detect, such was Florence's gourmet gusto.

It was ironically in the kitchen of 17 Belgravia Court that Florence was to meet her fate. One clean stab wound with a kitchen knife though the heart. The police arrived at 8.45pm on the Saturday evening having been alerted by Florence's intended escort after he had been concerned at her no show at the Savoy Grill and no response to his mobile phone calls.

Percy Worthington had calmly answered the door, showed the police into the kitchen and surrendered without resistance. Since when he had refused to answer all questions put to him by police, lawyers, doctors, psychiatrists, prison staff and others interested in his welfare. He resolutely declined to assist in his defence, neither confirming, nor denying, participation in the stabbing, notwithstanding a clear set of fingerprints on the knife's handle as well as DNA evidence. Various duty lawyers had all suggested the possibility of a defence of insanity as the only hope of avoiding a conviction, but the received wisdom was that mere silence did not of itself necessarily imply lack of reason. Percy Worthington appeared to be wholly disinterested in his fate. In his all but inevitable conviction. In his life sentence of imprisonment with no parole for a long period of time.

And with no relatives and no friends, neither did anybody else. Except for one person who by chance happened to have been at the Old Bailey on that Monday morning. Anthony Harrison.

'I will require a good hour with my client, your Lordship,' said Anthony.

'Of course,' said the Judge, 'but from what I hear you will be fortunate if you find yourself inundated with instructions. The case is adjourned until midday. And good luck.'

By 11.30 the case was ready to be called. Anthony's attempts to obtain any meaningful instructions from his client proved abortive. Other than to confirm his name, Percy chose to ignore all Anthony's efforts to engage. It left Anthony utterly frustrated. This 24-year-old, unremarkable looking, polite young man of medium build, about to confront the most demanding ordeal of his life, behaving as if were about to spend the day on some kind of sightseeing trip with not a care in the world. Unwilling to undertake the slightest step to assist Anthony, immersed in his shell.

The jury was empanelled. The charge was read out. When asked whether he pleaded guilty or not guilty the defendant declined to speak.

'In which case,' said the Judge, 'I'll enter a plea of not guilty.'

Prosecuting counsel then introduced himself to the jury. Sir Terence Parkinson QC. And introduced Anthony as representing the accused. Then the police who attended the scene of the crime gave evidence. The arresting officer said what he found – the deceased, the knife in the heart, the defendant – calm as a cucumber who said nothing. Forensic evidence followed – the fingerprints and DNA. It was all very straightforward.

Anthony had nothing to cross examine on. The defendant remained passive.

Anthony rose. 'I call the defendant, Percy Worthington.'

Percy appeared confused. Non-plussed. He had not bargained on talking. As if in a trance he entered the witness box. The jury stirred. Their interest suddenly stimulated. Eyes fixed on Percy.

Anthony asked him his name but got no response. 'Are you Percy Worthington?' he asked.

'That's a leading question,' said Sir Terence.

'And that's a stupid comment,' said the Judge. 'Have some understanding if you would be good enough, Sir Terence.'

Anthony thanked the Judge. And then looked at Percy. 'I am your counsel,' he said. 'I am here to help you.' No reaction. 'I recognise that it is not an easy thing for you to admit that you need to be helped, but it is my job to do my best for you.' This time a tiny spark of recognition.

And then: 'Don't bother to waste your time.'

With anybody else a response of discouragement. With this defendant a chink of daylight. Anthony continued. 'Do you know where you are?' Percy nodded. 'Do you know why you are here?'

Another nod. 'Do you know why you killed your mother?'

Percy moved his lips.

But said nothing.

Anthony asked him again. Nothing doing.

'Forgive me, my Lord,' said Anthony as he walked from his position in counsel's row and up to the witness box.

'Really, my Lord,' protested Sir Terence.

'Sit down and shut up, Sir Terence,' interjected the Judge, 'or I will have you removed.'

By this time Anthony was next to Percy. He put a sympathetic arm round his shoulders. The jury were transfixed. 'Would you like to tell me about it?'

The pause – the silence – was excruciating. If a pin had dropped the sound would have been explosive. All eyes were on Percy Worthington.

'She told me that I had been a mistake. We were talking in the kitchen. A minor argument over the wine which I had bought and which she said was the wrong year. "A mistake. That's what you were. From conception. That was a mistake. From birth. Another mistake. When as a baby you kept me awake with your cries. Not suffocating you. That was a mistake. Not giving you up for adoption. That was a mistake. Saving you that day on the beach when a huge wave swept you away. That was an even worse mistake." She went on to tell me that my father, who I adored and who I thought adored me, secretly loathed me which was the true reason he committed suicide. Her voice was getting louder and louder.

'She continued to taunt me. I was a wimp. A weakling. With no mind of my own. I picked up the knife which was on the table. She dared me. "You're a waste of space. You haven't even got the guts".' Percy paused. 'I couldn't stop myself. Have you any idea? The utter feeling of rejection. She'd pushed me over the edge. My mother. Who I loved. Telling me all these hateful things. I lost all sense of reality. I lunged. The knife went through her heart. I'm so sorry.'

Percy's voice tailed off as he lowered his head. Anthony took a deep breath and looked towards the jury. At least five of them were dabbing their eyes. Anthony turned back to his client. 'Is there anything else you would like to say?' he asked.

'Yes, Mr. Harrison. There is. I would like to say thank you to you for giving me the courage to speak.'

'Are you unanimously agreed upon your verdict, members of the jury?' asked the Judge.

'We are, my Lord,' said the foreman.

'Tell us, Mr. Foreman. Guilty or Not Guilty?'

The foreman paused. An unintentional moment of high drama. He looked around at the other jury members as if for reassurance. 'Not Guilty, my Lord.'

'Mr. Harrison,' said the Judge, 'permit me to join with the defendant by extending my personal thanks to you.'

'I'll be perfectly honest with you, Chloe' said Anthony to his secretary on his return to the office, 'I still have a lump in my throat.'

'Just as well the Judge forced you into taking the case,' said Chloe. 'And that if there's a next time for a murder trial you won't reject it out of hand.'

'You're right – as always, Chloe. I'll remember your words. "Never say never".'

Timeo Danaos
(et dona ferentes)

*The line is from Virgil's Aeneid and means
'especially fear the Greeks bearing gifts'*

A blank is what you would draw if you tried to imagine a setting more quintessentially English than the clubhouse at Blenheim Park and its environs. Originally constructed in the mid-19th century to constitute the ornately Victorian designed 14-bedroom country pile of the Duke of Barkingside, it had latterly been acquired by a group of businessmen to make the clubhouse for those enjoying the 18-hole golf course which the Duke's heirs had built over a landscape of 250 acres.

'Parkland', is how such a course is described. The word itself, however, fails to do justice to the magnificence of the array of trees adorning the course. Oak, beech, elm, sycamore, maple. A visual cacophony which at the same time constituted obstacles to be surmounted – or avoided – on the journey from tee to green. The house itself had been converted in 1985 to accommodate everything a golf club needed – two generous, oak panelled bars a large dining room. Kitchen, card rooms, changing rooms, snooker table and administrative offices. The furniture Chesterfield. One could imagine it surviving in its present form for generations to come. An atmosphere of conservative gentility, geniality, civility, and respect for fellow members.

There was one problem, however. Blenheim Park Golf Club was running out of cash. If there was not an influx of 40 new members in the next year paying an additional £120,000, the club's money would run out in the following six months. Insolvency beckoned. Thus, behind the façade of solidity, lay a financial fragility of which those on the club's governing committee had recently become only too keenly aware. None more so than Jeremy Blakemore, the Chairman appointed the previous year for five years. The monthly figures showed a worrying forecast of declining membership and hence, income. It had become his paramount responsibility to try to steer the club through waters, choppy enough in the prevailing climate of economic austerity. What made it worse were the nakedly aggravating, aggressive efforts of the club's traditional local rival, Harvil Manor, to poach members. The Harvil promised new members discounted annual fees for three years. Blenheim's superior golf course afforded a major line of defence to Harvil's tactics, but it was by no means immune from the odd defection.

Jeremy Blakemore had been an investment banker until he retired two years earlier when he was 45. A fine golfer with a handicap of six. Married with three children – a teenage – wild child – daughter of 16 and twin boys of 11. A red Ferrari Dino parked in the space reserved for the Chairman in the club car park. Passionate about the interests of the golf club. Some said less so about the personal interests and welfare of its members. He was taciturn and arrogant. Cold of heart. And he had an almost desperate will to succeed to feed what was generally perceived to be an infinitely deep ego. His colleagues on the committee saw him as the ideal candidate to confront the impending storms. His reputation for turning the fortunes of sick companies with ice cool, objective, analytical, unsentimental logic, put them in total awe of his abilities.

'If anyone can rescue the club from disaster, it's Jeremy,' was the general opinion *nem con*. Hence any opposition to any proposition coming from Jeremy's lips would be unlikely to materialise – from the committee at any rate. It would be left to the smattering of members bold enough to question him, without fear of retaliation to try to dent his overbearing self-confidence. Notably, for example, Anthony Harrison who had been a member of the club for many years. He had seen Chairmen come and go. Some good. Others very good. Others not so good. Others not even as good as that. Time would tell into which category Jeremy Blakemore would fit.

'We'll call an EGM then,' said Jeremy to his seven committee colleagues. 'Something like this needs the approval of the whole club. It's beyond our powers to make a decision. Anybody disagree?'

Seven heads nodded obediently. The meeting had been called to consider a proposition. From Gardiners, a firm of solicitors based in Tower Hamlets, a registered letter came out of the blue. Gardiner stated that they were acting for a charitable institution – Golf 4 Kids – with substantial funds available to invest for the benefit of disadvantaged children. That its founding trustees had been advised that golf was an ideal activity for its beneficiaries.

Gardiners added, 'Young boys and girls, many suffering childhood domestic abuse, are perceived to be likely to benefit from the golf environment and all that it stands for: consideration for one's fellow players, sportsmanship, healthy exercise and character building. One of our client's trustees is familiar with your golf course and believes that with suitable investment it can be improved to a standard which will be the envy of the East Hertfordshire golfing community. We are accordingly instructed to say that in principle they are prepared to make available a grant of £2 million for the following purposes:

1. To build a three-hole junior academy course comprising two par threes and a short par four.

2. To install a new drainage system on holes 16 and 4 to alleviate the flooding which so frequently occurs on their fairways.

3. To replace every green with the most modern, state of the art, greens grasses and technology to be worthy of an English Augusta.

In return our clients would ask for a 20-year free corporate membership entitling, on any one weekday, a maximum of 20 persons of unblemished character employed by, or authorised by, the charity, as well as up to 20 juniors below the age of 13 to play on the junior academy course. The development's funds would be held in an escrow account in the joint names of ourselves and the club in readiness for expenditure where required. Please let us know whether this proposal is of interest to you. If it is not, then it is only fair to advise you that we are instructed that our clients will consider making a similar approach to Harvil Manor.'

The General Manager of the club was instructed to email to every member a copy of Gardiners' letter accompanied by a draft resolution that the Chairman be authorised to conclude such an agreement in line with those proposals as he may think fit. The date for the EGM – 26th May was 28 days after the notice. Meanwhile the committee instructed Jeremy to write to Gardiners to express interest in the proposals which, he would stress, would need membership approval. Thus, the scene was set.

'What do you reckon, Anthony?' asked Johnny Simons during a post-game discussion in the bar the following Saturday. 'I can't believe that charities have that sort of cash to chuck around.'

'Nor can I disagree with you,' said Anthony Harrison to his friend. 'In fact, there are a number of things that seem a bit fishy to me.'

'Like what?' asked Johnny.

'Like the involvement of Gardiners for a start. Not exactly a City Magic Circle firm. They're the "go to" people for the crooks of this world. Not your ordinary, everyday, shoplifter mind. More the heavy-duty mob. Drugs, racketeering, extortion. The odd murder or two. And lately gang warfare and knife crime. If I were Jeremy, I'd be asking a lot of questions about the provenance of the so-called charity cash.'

Johnny's face dropped. His misfortune was well known. A daughter. Serena. Beautiful and with the nature of a Florence Nightingale. Until ravaged by crack cocaine. Found in a gutter outside her home choking to death on her own vomit. Dead at 17. The supplier sent away for seven years. The prosecution tried to get him for manslaughter but had to be content with supply with intent. One of Gardiners' gang of clients enjoying life in Wormwood Scrubs.

The EGM was to prove loud. Strong views – for and against acceptance – being expressed passionately which might have been anticipated, given what was at stake. But all comparatively civilised until Anthony took the floor.

'If you don't mind, Mr. Chairman, perhaps I could have five minutes. I will try to be even handed. We are debating these proposals against a background of declining membership, aggressive competition, and failing finances. With the proposals in front of us – supported by you, Mr. Chairman – an objective observer might well argue that any person who rejects what is, on the face of it, an offer beyond generosity, must be out of his or her mind. At a stroke a solution to all the club's financial problems. Some cynics might even ask if it is too good to be true. The Greek scholars among us – mindful of the lessons of Timeo Danaos. But that aside, the benefits incalculable. Transformation from a rapidly deteriorating balance sheet to accounts brimming with financial health. A vastly improved golf course would be exactly what was required to attract those looking for the kind of golfing challenge needed to knock out competition from Harvil once and for all. And yet there is this lingering doubt in my mind. Unease perhaps is a better way to describe it. Let me start with Gardiners. I must be careful what I say, but the general character of their clientèle raised questions in my mind. I decided to do a little investigating. The firm acts for no other charitable institution. Golf 4 Kids was formed two weeks after the killing of Marty King, a notorious gangster from Manchester whose death left a huge vacuum in the Salford drugs distribution market. Further enquiries revealed that a week before the King killing, Ray Cansino, a convicted drug lord, was released after serving half of a 15-year sentence for drug trafficking. Who acted for him? Gardiners of course. It may, of course, be only a matter of surmise, but to me the whole thing is at least questionable, dodgy – and potentially dangerous.

There is a stash of cash to be concealed fast. I believe that we could risk being seduced into the trap of laundering money which could well represent the proceeds of drug crime. Members may wish to consider very carefully the moral aspects of being complicit in washing just about the filthiest, most morally reprehensible, lucre around – money received by the peddlers of misery and death – in order to enjoy a round of golf.'

'Why don't you get down from your fucking self-righteous, self-professed, high horse of moral superiority you stuck up prig? In a matter of ten seconds the illusion of civilised gentility shattered.'

A foul mouthed, but deeply felt, shout from the back of the room from Henry Porter who, in the past 24 years, had never been heard to utter anything more profane than 'dammit' after missing a 12-inch putt.

'What is wrong,' he continued, 'with taking advantage of what is on the face of it a perfectly sensible, commercial offer to invest money into this club through a firm of lawyers whose only offence is to act for clients according to the responsibilities which our legal system dictates? I for one can't see anything improper with the proposal. It's a win win situation all round.'

'Here here,' echoed round the room.

'It's time for the vote,' said Jeremy after the heat had abated and several other speakers had voiced their opinions. 'Would members please tick yes or no in the box provided on the ballot paper which you all have been given and hand it to the tellers who will collect and count.'

The tellers went to the next room to do the counting. The result expected to be a foregone conclusion if the mood music of the meeting was anything to go by. Twenty minutes later Michael Lamb, the committee member in charge of the count, appeared from the next door room and approached Jeremy.

'Are you absolutely positive?' Jeremy was heard to ask incredulously.

'Not a shadow of a doubt,' Michael replied. 'We've checked it four times.'

Jeremy called for silence. He stood. 'I have the result of the ballot,' he said. He paused. And looked around the room as if begging for some divine intervention. For the first time in anybody's memory Jeremy looked distinctly uncomfortable. The tension increased. 'I must tell everybody that there is no clear result. The votes cast are 133 in favour of the resolution to accept and 133 against. It's a tie. Under the constitution of the club the Chairman has only one vote – a casting one. That is, of course, now mine to exercise. I wonder whether, in the exceptional circumstances, you might all be good enough to allow me several minutes in which to make a duly calculated decision.'

The members approved.

When he resumed his seat, he cast his eye around the room and then looked towards those sitting in the front row. He met the eye of Johnny Simons. The bereaved father. His enduring plight ringing a strident, dissonant chord with Jeremy. Imagining, in one fleeting second – his own daughter ensnared in a drugs web such as had beguiled Serena Simons. Whose distorted features he could see being etched into the surface of every green financed with proceeds of crack cocaine. Johnny was fixing Jeremy with a stare which was heart-breaking, pleading and meaningful. It was a moment for Jeremy to come of age. His dilemma resolved. An almost imperceptible nod to Johnny.

'I cast my vote against the resolution,' he declared resolutely.

'In which case,' said Henry Porter, 'I, and others who think like me, will be off like a shot to Harvil.'

'That's up to you,' replied Jeremy. 'But in my opinion the association between the ostensible benefactor and Gardiners poses a risk which we will do well to avoid. Besides, we have an overriding moral question to consider as much as a commercial one. And the answers to each are not necessarily the opposite of one another.'

The financial year of Blenheim Park ended on 31st May. The same date as 57 of its members led by Henry Porter, left for Harvil Manor. Losing them meant the club had to get an emergency bank loan secured by a legal charge on its freehold property to ensure its liquidity. While Blenheim suffered Harvil flourished. Following Blenheim's rejection Gardiners had followed through with its approach to Harvil which was approved with little discussion – the Greeks being welcomed without any reservation.

The work started promptly on the Junior Academy and a comprehensive course improvement plan was adopted within days. Blenheim's loss was Harvil's gain. Even the loyalists in Blenheim's camp began to doubt the wisdom of the decision. Jeremy had called a committee meeting for 30th June to consider further the club's declining fortunes. He and his seven committee colleagues sat down at 6pm.

A knock on the door.

'I told you no interruptions,' shouted Jeremy.

To his irritation the door opened. In stepped two men in their early forties. Brandishing their IDs. Both Metropolitan Police Officers.

'I am Detective Chief Inspector James Richards and this is my assistant Detective Constable Simmons. We're investigating a serious case of money-laundering involving the disposal and washing of proceeds from various drug deals orchestrated by Raymond Cansino. In conjunction with his lawyers – a firm called Gardiners. The High Court has issued a freezing order on all monies belonging to, or owed to, Cansino, and we are here to check that this club has no interest in any such funds. Our inquiries show that at one point recently there was a prospect of your becoming involved in a Cansino sponsored operation and although we have intervened in the scheme involving Harvil Manor, we need your assurance that Blenheim Park is free of any such association.'

Jeremy's response was immediate. And to the point. He walked up to the Inspector. Took his head in both hands and kissed him firmly on both cheeks. Three times.

'I take that as a yes,' said the Inspector.

'What are we going to do with these?' asked Jeremy to his co-committee members as he brandished 57 re-joining applications – the regular July monthly committee meeting having taken on a remarkably optimistic tone. 'Every single one of the defectors wants to come back. And it's hardly surprising since Harvil's operations have been suspended. The club is under investigation for conspiracy to launder. It has been ordered to reimburse £250,000 of Gardiners' funds which it has already expended on ripping up some greens and a number of fairways. If we're not careful we'll be inundated with applications to join here from a load of their disaffected members. What was that Greek saying Anthony Harrison mentioned? – Timeo Danaos et dona ferentes – I fear the Greeks, especially when bearing gifts. It's Anthony we've got to thank for all this.'

'Don't underestimate yourself, Jeremy,' said Michael Lamb. 'Just ask yourself who it was that exercised his casting vote – and in which direction?'

Perfect Match

'Mr. Harrison,' said Judge Curtis Robertson, 'it is your misfortune to happen to be in my court this Monday morning when the defendant is unrepresented. He is here for one very good reason. He is charged with murder. He has indicated to the prosecuting authorities that he has no interest in enjoying – if that is the right word – legal representation since he has no interest in contesting the charge.

'As you well know, Mr. Harrison, the English legal system does not allow a person accused of the ultimate crime to submit to a trial of this gravity without, at least, the assistance of a solicitor, and preferably a barrister as well. It is therefore his good fortune – if not yours – that you, as well as being a solicitor/advocate and thus combining both specialities, are present at this time and uninstructed on any other immediate matter. This court therefore appoints you to represent the Reverend Jonathan Brinkley on the charge of the wilful murder of Peter Burnett.'

'But, your Honour, you need to know that I am booked for another case which is scheduled to start in four days' time.'

'Hard luck then,' replied the Judge with a sarcastic smile. 'Someone else will have to take it instead. Now I will allow you two days to take instructions. This case is therefore adjourned until Wednesday at 10am. Best of luck, Mr. Harrison. From what I understand you will need every ounce going.'

Anthony Harrison could not believe what had just happened. It had been pure chance that he had entered Court One at the Old Bailey on that March Monday morning in 2021, to retrieve a small file of papers which he had inadvertently left there on the previous Friday. And then to be hijacked to take on a case in which some nutty member of the clergy was intent in relinquishing any rights which the state afforded in these circumstances and as a result to lose out on a juicy case involving bribery, extortion and adultery, was any laughing matter. Now he had to persuade the Reverend to allow him to take on the case at all. And if he could get over that hurdle, to see whether there existed any possibility of persuading him to at least consider changing his intended plea of guilty. And to investigate whether there might be any grounds on which to put forward a credible defence.

Altogether daunting. Still, the life of an advocate is never straightforward. Were it otherwise what would be the point?

Consoled with a little bit of philosophy Anthony made his way to the cells of the Old Bailey for an in initial conference with his new client. But not before a half an hour meeting with the notoriously supercilious prosecuting counsel, Alistair Summers QC, who briefed Anthony on the essential facts of the case.

'Open and shut if ever there was one,' he told Anthony. 'When a deceased dies from a knife wound to the heart which is administered by the accused who not only admits to doing it but was the person who informed the police of the *actus reus*, and then seems almost happy to invite a charge of murder, the chances of getting him to plead not guilty, must be pretty close to zero. And even if the jury is asked to consider its verdict what is the likelihood of an acquittal, I ask you? You've got an unenviable, monumental task on your shoulders, old chap. From what I gather he's one of those obstinate types. Mind made up. And that's it. If you can pull this one off it will be a big feather in your cap, I can tell you. Damn waste of everybody's time if you ask me.'

'Great,' replied Anthony. 'I can't wait. I suppose one consolation is that it will all be over by Friday at the latest. And there is a more than faint possibility that I won't miss out on my next case. Meanwhile four days of unrewarding boredom and frustration.'

Anthony stood patiently outside the door of the consultation room in the Court basement awaiting the arrival of his new client. After ten minutes, under close prison officer handcuffed escort, the Reverend Jonathan Brinkley was unceremoniously dumped on a chair at the far end of the room and introduced – if that is not an exaggerated term – to Anthony.

'Your prisoner, Guv. Hope he's a bit more talkative to you than he is to me and my mates. I'll be outside the door if I'm needed.' The officer left the room, the door remaining ajar, although from the demeanour of the client, the risk of his perpetrating any physical harm on Anthony seemed unlikely.

'I sit here,' said Anthony. 'The rules. Prisoner at the end of the table furthest from the entrance to the room.' Jonathan nodded. Mouth securely closed. 'I was wondering if you are alright?' said Anthony trying to break the ice. 'I could not help noticing your slight limp. Nobody has roughed you up I hope, while you're locked up on remand in Belmarsh. A prison not noted for its serenity.'

'It's a trait I was born with. There's nothing wrong with me in the slightest. It's just the way I walk. That's all. So, you needn't worry about me. I'm getting what I deserve anyway.' And that was just about as far as Anthony got.

Every question about the events surrounding the killing was answered with a 'no comment'. Otherwise it was ignored. By way of confirmation of Anthony's prediction of frustration, Jonathan's stock response was a blanket clamping of his hands over his ears. Not a nod. Nor a shake of the head. A total distancing from reality.

After 30 minutes Anthony called the prison officer. 'I'm finished with this prisoner,' he said. An expression which intentionally, or otherwise, carried more than one meaning.

According to the written prosecution statements the basic facts of the case were these: According to his widow, at about midday on Saturday, 14th August 2020, the deceased had apparently visited the accused at the church manse where he lived. He had told his wife that there was a question which needed an urgent answer. 'Agitated' was the description she had applied to his state of mind. He had told her that he wouldn't be too long. He had given no clue as to what was troubling him.

At 1.17pm on the same day, the duty 999 operator received a hysterical call from a man who identified himself as the accused, to say that he had just stabbed a man in the kitchen of the manse and that the victim appeared to be dead.

At 1.29pm on the same day, an ambulance with two paramedics arrived, closely followed by a police vehicle and two uniformed police officers. The victim was pronounced dead at the scene. The accused's hands were covered in blood.

The assumed murder weapon a serrated eight-inch kitchen knife belonging to the accused, was similarly bloody. The accused was desperate to tell the police officers that he had 'done it'. That it was all his fault. And that he deserved God's punishment. When asked to explain his motive, he flatly declined to say. 'It's between me, the deceased and my maker,' was the only enigmatic response.

The forensic examination of the alleged murder weapon clearly showed the fingerprints of the accused on the handle. The additional presence of the fingerprints of the victim was assumed to have been caused by his partially successful attempts to get the knife from the grip of the accused during a fight which had broken out between the two of them.

The formidable scale of Anthony's task was clear. Enthusiastic, voluntary, freely offered under no pressure, the Reverend had confessed. It was corroborated by incontrovertible forensic evidence and constituted a mountain to climb even if he were to be able first, to persuade the judge to disallow the defendant's plea of not guilty, and thereafter to persuade a jury to entertain a reasonable doubt.

The current direction given by a judge to a jury is that 'they must be sure' of guilt. Could even Anthony Harrison beat that? 'Unpromising' was the way Anthony considered to describe his prospects of success. And not without good reason.

'I know this is very unconventional, Mrs. Burnett,' explained Anthony on the doorstep and through the letterbox of the Burnett home, 'but I wondered whether I might have a word with you. I am Anthony Harrison, the solicitor appointed by the Court to represent the Reverend Jonathan Brinkley, the person charged with your husband's murder. It's not of my choosing. I have no choice in the matter. I will entirely understand if you tell me to beat the hell out of here, but I am given to understand that you are the kind of open-minded person who wants to see justice done. I have all the ID that you might want to look at. Covid restrictions mean that we would have to meet outside.'

After what seemed like an eternity, for reasons which were not apparent, at least to Anthony, an apprehensive, nervous, Emily Burnett opened the front door.

'Let's have a good look at you,' she said.

They sat in the garden. The pre-spring sun had begun to seep through the earlier morning clouds. Anthony declined a cup of tea.

'What can I tell you?' she asked, 'beyond what I presume you already know. A good man struck down for no apparent reason. A fight, they said. But what on earth could have caused my poor Peter to get involved in violence? A more peaceful, sweet, loving, docile man you could never meet. Throughout our marriage people would comment that it was one made in heaven. "A perfect match" was the phrase so often used.'

Anthony was tempted to offer her a tissue with which to wipe away her tears, but Covid disallowed all that. He paused to allow her to collect herself. 'And you have no idea why he went to see the vicar in the first place?' he continued.

'None at all,' she replied. 'I've already told the police a thousand times that he just went off in very agitated state. Angry even. It was very uncharacteristic. All this is having such a terrible effect on us. That's to say me and Isabelle. There she is. Over there. Just coming on 11. She's still finding it very hard to cope, even though her father has been gone now for seven months.'

'So sad,' said Anthony to himself before taking his leave and thanking Emily for her time. 'Lovely girl you have there,' he said as he watched her daughter walking away towards the house. Her mother had not told her why Anthony was there.

Court Number One at the Old Bailey was as full as Covid restrictions permitted on that Wednesday. In addition to lawyers and court staff an array of accredited media reporters as well as many members of the public as eager to witness the sight of a murderer as to observe the administration of justice. Not, it had to be said, as many as one would expect to be the case in normal times, but nevertheless, considerably more than a sprinkling. All had undergone lateral flow tests at the entrance to the building as well as prearranged PCR tests the day before. All were presumed to have shown a negative result. Amongst them Emily Burnett and her daughter Isabelle who wanted to see her father's killer convicted and sentenced.

As soon as Anthony entered the courtroom Emily found herself having to explain her white lie about Anthony's visit to the house two days previously.

'How could you, mummy?' said Isabelle.

'To protect you, my darling,' said Emily.

Isabelle put her arm round her mother's shoulder. 'Sorry mummy.'

The defendant stood in the dock and confidently said 'guilty'.

'Yes, Mr. Summers,' said the Judge to prosecuting counsel. 'Are you ready to proceed?'

'I am your Honour.'

'And you. Mr. Harrison? Equally so I presume?'

'I am, your Honour,' replied Anthony in the tone of a top poker player whilst inwardly suppressing all his misgivings, as he had none of the ammunition which might be expected in the armoury of a well briefed defence advocate. 'But in order to allow me to make the best of my client's opportunities which, I might remind your Honour, you appointed me to exploit, I have two very unusual requests to make to the Court, neither of which I regret to tell you is supported by my learned friend, Mr. Summers, who regards the first of them as offensive to the principle that a plea entered cannot be changed and the second as an affront to convention and an insult to his standing in this case.'

The QC scowled.

'My client is proving less than co-operative with me. So much so that I have been unable to take one instruction of any profitable nature. He is being obsessively obstructive and refuses every offer of help which I have contrived to make. Since the alleged facts of the case are admitted in their entirety, I ask your permission to take my client through them as I see fit and to treat him as a hostile witness in a way which will allow me to ask leading questions and in effect conduct my own cross examination of him.' Anthony sat down.

Alistair Summers rose. 'An outrage, your Honour. It's nothing less than a preposterous attempt to manipulate the procedures which have dominated the regulation of crown court trials over centuries. The defendant has pleaded guilty. End of matter. On request number 2, may I remind your Honour that it is no part of a defence advocate's job to undermine that of prosecuting counsel. Both requests are each equally unusual and should be rejected.'

'May I perhaps remind you, Mr. Summers, that Mr. Harrison himself is highly unusual, but that is no reason to reject him. I am going to allow both of his requests. I record a plea of not guilty. And I invite Mr. Harrison to call his client as his first – and for all I know, his only – witness. Although I would add, Mr. Harrison, that you had better not be wasting the Court's time.'

When Anthony called the Reverend Jonathan Brinkley to take the stand, he did not have any more than three or four iotas of confidence in his ability to avoid a charge of time wasting. His knees quaking with anxiety he addressed his client in the witness box.

'This time, Reverend, I hope you will do me the honour of answering some simple questions. Just for the benefit of the jury, you understand. Nothing too intrusive, or too personal. The last thing anybody wants is to aggravate the ordeal which your presence here today must constitute.'

An initially tense, furrowed, Reverend Brinkley could be seen to unfurrow by the second.

After a series of simple, uncomplicated, uncontroversial questions to further put the defendant at his ease – his upbringing, relations with his parents, his education, his universal popularity – Anthony's phone buzzed. 'Sorry, your Honour,' he said whilst eyeing its message. 'I'll turn it off straight away.'

'I'm warning you, Mr. Harrison,' said the Judge. 'You know the rules. No mobiles. Next time and it will be confiscation. Is that clear?'

'Certainly, your Honour. I'm so sorry. Now Reverend,' he asked, adopting a subtly more positive, confident tone, 'I want to ask you if you could enlighten us as to the reasons why you chose, at the age of 32, to enter the clergy?'

Jonathan hesitated. Did he really want the world to know that he had been forsaken by the person whom he regarded as the love of his life for another.

'I would rather not say, if you don't mind,' he replied.

'Good,' thought Anthony. At least he is beginning to give a response to a challenging question, rather than say nothing at all.

'Very well then,' said Anthony. 'It's your privilege to maintain your silence. This time, however, I want you to think very carefully before answering my next question and then to give your answer in as honest and candid manner as your conscience dictates.' This caused a frisson of expectation amongst the public gallery as well as the press.

166

'Would you please let us all know whether the name "Isabelle" means anything to you?'

A question which produced an instantaneous, as opposed to a considered, reply, but was nothing less than electrifying.

'How do you know about Isabelle? Leave her out of it.'

'That's a yes, I must presume,' said Anthony. 'And what does the name Emily mean to you?'

'You tell me,' replied the witness, uncontrollably provoked by the question.

'It's your floor,' said Anthony. 'Just let it all out.'

The sight of a man about to unburden his soul was one which everybody in Court One would never forget. His account was to prove riveting. Whilst cooking his lunch on that August Saturday the previous year, he had been disturbed by a frantic knocking on the front door. On opening it he saw a man he did not recognise either as being a member of his flock or from elsewhere, except that it did seem to register as having perhaps belonged to a first time attender at his previous Sunday sermon.

'This person barged into the kitchen demanding if I ever knew one Emily Stonehouse, and that if I did to tell him the nature of our relationship. The mention of her name rang heavily on my heart. I had been deeply in love with her and had believed that she felt the same way about me. But one day – it was precisely one week after we had last made love – I received a message to say that she had fallen in love with somebody else who had simply swept her off her feet and that she had resolved never to see me again. I was heartbroken. I thought that I would never recover. My mental health suffered an almost total breakdown. But recover I did and discovered that my refuge lay in the church. Several months later I received another message from Emily to say that she and her new love were married, that she was expecting a child, and that I should never try to make contact with her in the future. I have continued to respect and honour her request. When I told the unwelcome visitor about my relationship with Emily he completely lost his cool. Told me that I must have been the father of their daughter, Isabelle, aged ten. That he suspected as much the previous Sunday when he noticed the similarity with which we both walked in the strange angle at which we project our right ankle to result in a slight limp. My protestations of regret and sorrow cut no ice. He simply went berserk saying that he would kill me. Shouting that I had ruined his life. The more I tried to reason and placate the more violent he became. He grabbed a knife from the kitchen table and lunged towards me. I just about managed to sidestep but we ended up in a clinch. He continued his crazy assault. The next thing I knew was that he was lying on the ground. Not breathing. That's when I called the emergency services.'

Jonathan had finished. Everybody had been held spellbound.

Anthony was the first to break the silence. 'Are you able to tell us why, ever since this awful event, you have continued to maintain your protestations of guilt to all concerned, including, in particular, this court?'

'It's very simple,' replied Jonathan. 'Emily. I did not want her to feel any responsibility for the actions of her husband who had plainly adored her and whose actions had been motivated by understandable uncontrollable jealousy. A devoted and faithful husband. A victim of deception throughout their marriage. How could she have been expected to live with the revelations? Better to allow her to believe that her husband was the innocent one. And how could I allow the daughter who I have never seen to find out that her father was not her biological father? My only regret is that I have allowed myself to lose my self-control and reveal the unpalatable truth.'

An overcome Emily shouted from the public gallery. Unable to maintain her silence. 'You have nothing to reproach yourself for, you stupid, wonderful man, You've been an absolute hero.'

'I take it you have nothing further to ask, Mr Harrison?' said the Judge.

Anthony himself overcome with emotion, could only shake his head. 'And you, Mr. Summers?' Close to choking prosecuting counsel could only do the same. 'And you, members of the jury? Do you need time to retire to consider your verdict?'

In unison they shook their heads, the foreman blurting out 'Not Guilty', before burying his head in a large tissue.

'You are free to go, Reverend,' said the Judge. 'But before this court adjourns perhaps, Mr. Harrison, you would be good enough to let us know what, seemingly, made you so certain that it was the victim, and not the defendant, who had been the initial aggressor.

'I will tell you Judge, since you ask. But I would rather that everybody in this courtroom agrees not to disclose what I am about to say before I say it. I entered with not a scintilla of evidence with which to establish my client's innocence.'

The Judge could hardly wait to make the necessary restraining announcement.

'It's like this,' said Anthony. 'I had noticed the defendant's peculiarity of gait when I first met him on Monday not 20 metres beneath this very spot. After I had plucked up the courage to visit the victim's widow later that day to fish for anything which might throw some light on what actually happened, inspiration arrived with the sight of Isabelle's gait. Its resemblance was striking. It could not be coincidence. It set my mind racing. Relying upon the goodwill of persons whose identity I will never reveal and who happen to owe me a favour or two, I managed to arrange a secret DNA test on Isabelle via the PCR swab taken as a precondition of her access to the public gallery.

'I also managed, through the same source, to gain access to a sample of my own client's DNA held on the police database. A likelihood of identical readings between persons unrelated through blood is one in one billion. The comparison between the samples taken of the accused and Isabelle showed identical readings There you have it, your Honour.'

'What do you mean, Mr. Harrison, there you have it? You have yet to explain how and when this information was disseminated to you at the same time as you were questioning your client?'

'Oh. Sorry your Honour. It was in that text message which you reproved me for getting when I was doing exactly that – examining my client. It gave me the confidence to follow through on my theory.'

'Yes, yes, yes,' said a progressively more impatient Judge. 'But what did the text message actually say?'

'It was from my secret friend. Only two words. And such beautiful words they were.' Anthony paused for dramatic effect which he simply could not resist. And then delivered them with all the power which they conveyed: 'Perfect match.'

CSRA

The thud was sickening. The scream shattering. Followed, as it inevitably was, by instantaneous death. Bang outside the front of Cansino's Club in the centre of town at 1am on that deserted early Monday morning. The last of the working girls would work no longer. A life cruelly stopped short by the reckless antics of the 25-year-old Audi R10 driver, Mark Cansino. He was pumped full of cocaine which he had enjoyed with at least three of the female staff. The owner's only son. The heir to the Cansino empire. Seventeen nightclubs in the major cities of England and Scotland. A – declared – annual turnover of £18 million. A son whose standards of behaviour, when put to the test, lacked the integrity even to stop; speeding away as he did, through a mixture of fear, panic, cowardice, and desire for self-preservation. He was sure there were no witnesses.

Except he was wrong.

Jean Bartlett, the firm's 33-year-old in-house accountant, had been furiously working late in her office on the top floor of the building, to put the finishing touches to draft accounts which would be the subject of HMRC scrutiny the following day, after a tip off from a Revenue insider that a tax raid was 'all systems go' for Monday morning.

Jean had barely emerged from the side entrance when she had the ill fortune to observe the event. The brand new white, Mark Cansino owned Audi screaming off. The fatally injured victim. Two police cars and an ambulance arriving within three minutes did not save the deceased. A distraught Jean Bartlett.

She was escorted to the local police station and given copious cups of tea which allowed her to regain control of herself and describe what she had seen. A sympathetic policewoman transcribing. The statement approved and signed. Still shaking from her ordeal, her mood was not exactly helped when, by an unfortunate coincidence of timing, she was confronted by her boss's son being walked in. She was frightened. What would happen to her two early teenage daughters? She was a single mother.

Summoned to Charlie Cansino's office four days later, she was confronted by two of the firm's big guns: Dawn Fraser – Head of Human Resources, and John Merriman, ex-senior partner of Merrimans, solicitors, retained as special counsel to dispense legal advice to witnesses whose memory might be vulnerable to manipulation. Barely a week would elapse without some or other crisis. Drugs raids. Licensing objections. Affray. Prostitution. Blackmail. It was not a do-good deeds club.

Jean was – initially at least – put at her ease by the lawyer. 'Nothing for you to worry about, my dear. Just a few minor matters which perhaps you could clear up for us. We do know that you have been having some problems with your eyesight lately. And we recognise that what you may have thought to have been Mark's car, could have been a different car. If you see what I mean.' A slight sinister edge of tone and a knowing look.

'My eyesight is fine, thank you very much,' Jean said at once.

'I thought that you might say that,' Dawn Fraser smiled. 'In which case we were wondering whether a tax-free bonus of £100,000 might persuade you rethink what you think you saw on the night in question.'

This time a long pause.

'I've done nothing – and nor will I be doing anything – to deserve such a bonus. Now if there's nothing else–'.

'I'm afraid that there is,' replied the HR head. 'Plans have been drawn up to move the firm's accounts hub to Edinburgh. Meaning that unless you are disposed to change your recollection of events or to reconsider the very generous award which we have in mind, your post in London will become redundant.'

The next time an out of work Jean saw either of them was when she looked up at the public gallery at the Old Bailey just before testifying for the prosecution at the trial of Mark Cansino for manslaughter. He was found guilty and the Judge sentenced him to a term of eight years in prison.

'Had I heard one word of contrition or remorse, I might have been persuaded to reduce the sentence by up to two years. But in the absence of any remorse I find myself unable to apply any such relief. Additionally, I must accord credit to the bravery of Jean Bartlett whose courageous testimony has helped to secure your conviction. I am satisfied that if she suffers any consequences as a result those responsible would be readily identifiable and punished accordingly.'

With those words ringing in his ears Mark Cansino was sent to the Category B prison HMP Wormwood Scrubs in West London to start a four-year all expenses paid holiday as a guest of Her Majesty. A physical and emotional disruption to a hitherto spoilt, selfish, self-centred, uncaring, inconsiderate, hedonistic, existence. Exposure to ruthless exploitation by his peers of any detected weakness or vulnerability, meant that any perceived notions of superiority on account of his wealth and lifestyle would be rapidly exploded. A fact of prisoner existence which Mark was slow to recognise. He would painfully discover that jail, like pandemic, is a great leveller. No respect was to be gained by boasts of unlimited women and recreational drugs. Survival depended on humility. A willingness to tolerate the antisocial behaviour of his cohabitants, unprotected by 'Daddy's' army of enforcers. Prison warps pride.

The only saving grace: the British sentencing rules conceded that one half of his sentence would not have to be served in jail. Instead, he would be released on licence with conditions imposed on his behaviour when at large as an incentive to avoid unacceptable conduct. Any infringement and he would be back behind bars.

It was a short – three-month – stay at the Scrubs. As a prisoner who had been unable to come to terms with the realities of equality, and who refused to repress his bragging tendencies, management saw him as vulnerable. Liable to physical assault from prisoners who would find his superior attitude objectionable. Proof followed when he was found one evening lying in a pool of blood in his cell with a broken nose. Fortunately for him he was seen as one whose risk of escape or breach of behavioural requirements was quickly downgraded to low, and thus seen as meeting the criteria for being placed in the more relaxed Category 'C' Establishment – this time HMP The Mount at Bovingdon, several miles north-west of London – to where he was transferred within days.

With a population of 1000 'clients', its accommodation was principally single cells. But nevertheless with a number of doubles. Most prisoners prefer to be alone. To enjoy their privacy. Mastery of their own abode. Often solitude – but not solitariness. Others want company. Often unhappy with their own. And it is those who, in theory, are selected for the double cell accommodation who are first subjected to what is called a Cell Sharing Risk Assessment – CSRA for short. A box ticking exercise to assess if one prisoner is safe to share a tiny cell with another. You don't put a convicted Muslim jihadi terrorist in a minute room with a rabbi who has defrauded his flock.

The prison officer hierarchy consists of various grades, the highest being Custodial Manager – CM for short. In charge of CSRAs and cell allocations at The Mount was CM Alex Langridge. He was 40 years old with 15 years' prison experience. And not cynical. He was one of the number of inspirational, dedicated officers preoccupied with rehabilitation and protecting those whom they are employed to protect. For him the box ticking was no mere sideshow. If he could, he would try to achieve a match which would get the best from both occupants. A challenge which he felt unable to resist, even though he knew he would be transgressing the limits in the case of Mark Cansino. Cansino's CV convinced him that the vacancy in the double cell occupied solely by Harry Parker following the departure of Harry's cellmate after he had finished his sentence was just about the only double space where Mark might respond to the challenge of company without provoking some kind of attack.

Unlike Mark, a single one-off offender, Harry was a career criminal. His metier was theft. Beginning at the age of 13 when he discovered the Artful Dodgery facility of clandestine supermarket sandwich removal but he was too brazen, so cheese and pickle robbery earned him a three-month spell in a young offender's institution. From supermarkets he graduated to climbing the drainpipes of affluent suburban houses. The Acacia Avenue theft led to his first substantial sentence – three and a half years. Once released he did not stop. It was the only lifestyle which he understood. Prolific reoffending led up to his current sentence of nine years as an accessory to armed robbery as the getaway driver in an Audi R10 from outside Barclays Bank in the City of London.

The product of a one-night stand between a teenage, on benefits mother, living in a two-bedroomed flat on a Harlesden Council Housing Estate, originally from Jamaica, and of a Nigerian father whose acquaintance he had never had the opportunity to enjoy, one could reasonably make the case for excusing the behaviour which his career would take.

CM Alex Langridge introduced the pair to each other on the Monday morning two weeks after Mark arrived at The Mount. The occasion would remain in Alex's memory forever. The expression of flabbergast on Mark's face did little to disguise the suspicion of negrophobia. Confirmed by his point-blank refusal to enter the cell.

'Don't worry, mate,' were Harry's first words, 'I won't eat you.'

'I never thought you would,' he replied with a glimmer of smile. 'But just so's you know. My dad always told me to never trust a black man. And ever since I was a child, I've been terrified of the lot of you.'

'This is your bed,' said Alex pointing to the small divan adjacent to the right-hand wall. 'Now I'll leave you two together. Be sure to look after him Harry.' Adding as an afterthought: 'If I had any genuine reason to believe that you harboured racist feelings there is no way that I would let you into this cell, let alone allow you to live in it.'

Fingers tightly crossed Alex left. At least he comforted himself in the knowledge that when it came to physical attributes, there could be only one winner. Harry sat on his bed. While Mark humped his bin liner containing his clothes and such possessions which prison rules allowed him to have in cell on to his and sat.

Conversation was stilted. Awkward. Each introducing himself to the other with the fewest words possible.

'Nice little box that,' were Mark's eventual ice-breaking words. 'You make it?'

'Sure did,' replied Harry. 'An obby of mine. Always been good wiv me ands. For making fings wiv as well as for nicking fings.'

Mark visibly relaxed. The time would shortly be bound to come, he supposed, when they would talk normally. Even discuss more personal things beyond the 'what were they doing time for?' Any family? Wife? Kids? Occupation? Interests? Meanwhile conversation centred on the jail itself, mostly prompted by Mark's questions. Who were the decent officers? Any decent food to order? How to get into the gym facilities? Any cushy jobs going? All questions willingly answered.

Harry added for good measure that they could share a newspaper every morning. An offer which Mark ignored. Maybe he hadn't heard. Instead, he switched the talk to his former lifestyle. How his father ran this huge club empire. Birds ten a penny. Cocaine no problem.

Harry could not contain his displeasure. 'I'm not fucking interested in your rich daddy. Or your fancy bleeding cars. Or your cheap women. Do you hear me?'

Mark was stunned into silence. 'Sorry,' he muttered sarcastically under his breath.

'You talk like that to some of the other boys in here, and you'll find yourself up in Healthcare before you bleeding well know what's – and who's – hit you,' was Harry's angry piece of advice. 'Now just shut the fuck up.' Followed by a distinct froideur between them. In fact, neither said a word to the other for a couple of hours. Mark sulked. Harry got on with a piece of carpentry. Then it was unlock for lunch – a cheese sandwich and a small packet of plain crisps.

'Do you fancy learning how to shape a nice little piece of wood?' Harry asked that evening after several hours of near silence.

Mark looked up. With a feigned reluctance he said, 'I don't mind.'

'Look here. I'll show you the basics.'

In truth Mark found it anything but basic, but he was prepared to persevere in the interests of collaboration if nothing else. His efforts were not a success. Lacking, as he did, any spatial or artistic skills.

Two days later Harry was reading the *Sun*. 'Want to have a look, Mark?' A shake of the head. Preferring to watch the television news. 'Do you fancy trying to learn how to read instead?' Harry asked.

'What do you mean?' Mark said tetchily.

'I think you know exactly what I mean,' Harry replied. 'Come here. Let's make a start with this headline.'

And thus was the genesis of the biggest challenge of Harry's life to date. How to teach a totally word blind individual to read. How to apply all his latent skills in unlocking the barrier to literacy which was lurking somewhere in the brain of his cellmate. How he would manage the challenge he had no idea. But for the first time since adulthood, he had the chance to do something rewarding. It would require patience. And application. And a visit to the prison library which had various basic reading manuals including, importantly, the Toe-By-Toe method of literacy tuition. An excited Harry booked a library visit for the following afternoon.

The process was, at best, frustrating, and more generally, soul destroying. Ten hours' slog failed to produce the recognition of even the simplest of two-letter words. On the point of giving up Harry finally lost his temper – hurling the *Sun* straight at Mark's face.

'At least you could make a pretence of trying, you lazy bastard,' he shouted.

Defending himself Mark caught the paper in his right hand, held it up to his face and shouted: 'The cat.'

'What are you talking about? What cat?' asked Harry.

'It says here something about a cat,' replied Mark.

'Show me,' said Harry. And dammit. There it was. At the foot of the right-hand column of the fourth page a small headline: 'LONG LOST CAT FOUND AFTER FIFTY DAYS'.

There was no holding back Mark's enthusiasm after that. It might be an exaggeration to suggest that he was close to acquiring the ability to embark on reading Shakespeare's sonnets, or Plato's *Republic*, but the ice had inexplicably been broken. A switch had been magically turned on. He was on the road. It would take perseverance. And some time. But there was to be no turning back. At that moment it would have been difficult to distinguish between the respective levels of satisfaction and joy experienced by each of Harry and Mark. For Mark it was nothing short of a miracle. Liberation from ignorance beckoned. To be followed in due time by liberation from jail. For Harry it was liberation of a different kind. From the blindness of self-interest. A recognition of self-worth. Could such a sense of impending self-fulfilment ever have been enjoyed so much by two such disparate human beings in detention. Dawn had broken. For each. Brothers in learning. The one through an exciting new window on the world. The other about himself.

They continued to cell share with no undue dissent or violent argument, other than when three solid hours of Bob Marley proved too much for Harry's capacity to tolerate. Mark's reading progress was spasmodic. But nevertheless tangible. A tiny light becoming ever more visible at the end of the tunnel. Harry's tuition invaluable. Neither doubted eventual fluency. And then, as if suddenly, there were two years left to run before Harry's release date. Meaning that he had become eligible for recategorisation of his status to the very low escape risk 'D', thus allowing him the potential to move to an open prison where restrictions on movement would be far more relaxed than those in a closed prison. Where prisoners can enjoy day release and local work in the nearest town. A taste of freedom denied to those in closed conditions. To be accorded Cat D status was, particularly for a longer-term prisoner, a prized ambition, and now Harry had reached the brink. With an exemplary prison record he was likely to be off at any time. And – not entirely unexpectedly – within a few days into the two-year period, a note through the cell door signed by the Governor, confirmed the change in Category. And a reminder that any transfer to a Cat D jail would depend on good behaviour in the meantime. In particular no nickings. No breach of prison rules.

For Mark it was bitter/sweet. Happy for his cell mate. But apprehensive about achieving total reading fluency by himself. But achieve he would. Of that he had no doubt. Or had he? Any failure would not, he convinced himself, be down to any lack of desire. But the confidence? Another question altogether.

'Heaven fucking knows how I'm going to manage without you Harry,' said Mark to his cellmate. 'I'm bleeding terrified if the truth were known.'

'You will mate,' replied Harry, none too convincingly. 'You will.'

'Off you go, Mr. Parker. It's time to get out of your cell and into your job in the library. You don't want to fuck up and be late on your last day here,' Prison Officer Jameson said.

'Why don't you fuck off and mind your own fucking business?' was Harry's intemperate reply.

'Get up and be on your way,' said the good-natured Mr. Jameson. 'I won't ask you again.'

Harry got up alright. But on his way, he looked the officer straight in the eye, raised his right arm, and told him 'to fuck off before I give you one'.

'You're nicked,' said the officer.

The subsequent prison adjudication found Harry guilty of deliberately refusing to comply with a lawful order as well as threatening an officer in the execution of his duty.

'Behaviour of the most unexpected and frankly uncharacteristic kind,' the Adjudicator, Governor Evans said. 'I can't imagine what possessed you to act in that way. You plainly could not have known that your Cat D status will now be automatically rescinded.'

'Are you completely mad, Harry?' asked Mark later that afternoon just as CM Langridge had escorted Harry back to his cell. 'Whatever possessed you?'

'Think about it, Mark. And then work it out. And if you can't you're a bigger prick than I took you for.'

The penny dropped 'You're a fucking, stupid, crazy, beautiful idiot,' was Mark's answer. An eavesdropping CM Alex Langridge was reminded of his CSRA almost two years earlier. Unable to resist an involuntary smirk. Even if Harry had taken matters a bit far.

No Holding Back

'Congratulations, Anthony. It's one that got away from us thanks to your uncompromising language which somehow or other had impressed the Bench. You did well, young fella. Too well if you ask me. My boss won't be very happy with me. We'd chalked this up as a stone cold certainty.'

The words spoken by Jeremy Carter, a senior prosecutor for the Crown Prosecution Service, to Anthony Harrison, who had a reputation for winning the unwinnable, defending the indefensible, and defeating the heavily odds on chances of a conviction in what any casual observer would regard as an open and shut case. A man whose professional progression was a testament to the powers of perseverance, having failed his solicitors' finals on no fewer than five occasions. No academic was Anthony. But compensation was bestowed from on high with the natural ability to read people as opposed to literature. An uncanny talent for anticipating the human response to a verbal stimulus allied with an intrepid capacity to attack. A fearless propensity to pursue and demolish any chink of weakness. More the confident, sometimes brash, aggressive United States trial lawyer than the British paragon of quiet reason. As well, it must be said, with the powers of imagination and stimulation.

A weaver of magic spells whereby his verbal dexterity could induce the belief in the possibility that black was white, and so sow the seeds of doubt necessary to achieve acquittal.

He was dealing with a case of alleged theft of a £75,000 necklace from Tiffany where, as a result of Anthony's skills the District Judge had been persuaded that it was a lapse of memory which had caused Pamela Romanewski to exit the shop wearing the article which the sales assistant had earlier put round her neck and while his attention had been subsequently distracted by her alleged accomplice.

'Thanks, Jeremy. Can't say I was overconfident, but that's the strange thing about this business. You can never be sure of the power of words and the capacity to induce a suspension of belief from whoever it may happen to be that has to deliver a verdict – be it a judge, a bench of beaks, or a jury. I must rush now, I'm afraid. I've got a potential "indecent exposure" client and his influential father, who's a major client of the firm and a bit of a pain in the arse if truth were known, to see at the office in 30 minutes. I daren't be late.'

Anthony left Court 1 of Westminster Magistrates Court where his client was waiting in the corridor.

'I told you I didn't do it,' she said to Anthony. 'Now do you believe me?'

Anthony gave her a wry smile. 'Let's just say that the Judge gave you the benefit of the doubt. And your seductive smile didn't exactly harm your chances. Now I need to go. And I don't want to see you again – at least under these circumstances.'

And with a quick peck on the cheek Anthony bade his client farewell and made off towards the street door. Before reaching which his path was blocked by a young, bleary red eyed man of about 19. Unable to hide his unconcealable terror. Shaking as if afflicted with influenza, voice about to crack into tears, he asked Anthony if he were Anthony Harrison.

'That's me,' said Anthony. 'I'm sorry, but I can't stop. Another time perhaps.'

'Two minutes, sir. I beg you. Please.'

It was an entreaty which Anthony felt unable to resist. He asked the young man what the trouble was.

'Thank you, thank you, thank you. I'll be as quick as I can. My name is Peter. Peter Graves. A second-year student at the College of Law. My father is a vicar living near Reading. I have a police record for possession of cocaine. Yesterday I was arrested and charged with having a quantity of the drug concealed behind the glove compartment of my car. It is a fit up. I know it looks bad, but I swear on my father's reputation that I am not guilty. But I reckon the police have planted the stuff to get back at my father who has been going on about their failure to tackle drug dealing in general, and cocaine dealing in particular. The case is on here this afternoon. I was stupid enough to believe that I could represent myself, but now reality has dawned and I am desperate for a good advocate to act for me. If I go down so does my future career. I was hoping – is there any chance that you might be free? I got your name off an ex-client of yours. Compared you to Leonardo da Vinci,' she said.

'I don't think he ever appeared in Court. I'm not only busy,' replied Anthony, 'but I would need time to prepare a defence, and time is a luxury that is not available I'm sorry to say.'

'The case is not due on until 2.45. That would give you two and three-quarter hours. I have all the papers here.'

'But I have an appointment with a client in just under half an hour. Sorry.'

Anthony made as to go. He reached the door. Out of what was probably something slightly greater than mere curiosity he turned round – to see a pathetic Peter Graves, who had silently followed him, on his knees in supplication. Hands out like a Neapolitan beggar. The eyes of a refugee child pleading for a morsel. It was too much.

'Let's go,' said Anthony. 'There's a consultation room round the corner which should be free at this time.'

At the same time as leading his newly acquired client along the corridor he texted his office to say that something had come up and that he would have to cancel his appointment until the following day. A text which drew a reply which, at best was hostile. 'This is your boss,

Mark. If you do not keep this afternoon's appointment I will fire you on the spot when you do eventually return. I will expect to see you within the next 20 minutes'. A simple 'Impossible – another case' was texted back. Followed by the switch off of Anthony's mobile. Followed by a short discussion about fees.

'Let me read the papers you've got here,' said Anthony. 'If it's a case that we should win you'll have me free of charge. If it's dodgy we'll have a discussion after the verdict.' There was little that could be said to be orthodox about Anthony Harrison.

'I'm beginning to like you already, Mr. Harrison,' said Peter.

'Everybody calls me Anthony, and you'll be no exception,' was the lawyer's reply. 'Now,' he said, entering the empty consultation room, 'let's get down to work.' But not before he put his mobile phone on charge. 'I suspect that you're going to be a busy boy this afternoon,' he said as he lovingly caressed his Iphone 6. Not the most sophisticated of androids but unfailingly reliable.

'Hm,' said Anthony after 30 minutes of evidence reading. 'I see what you're getting at. Not a shred of a suggestion that anybody saw you place the drugs in your car. Only that as a result of some anonymous tip-off, the police stopped your car, and while one of them took you aside for three minutes for routine questioning, the other took it upon himself to institute a search of the vehicle. And suddenly – hey ho – this time in your presence – he finds behind the glove compartment this packet of cocaine which you say the searcher must have planted. It's a story which is only too common I'm afraid. I need to make some calls so why don't you pop along for half an hour and I'll see you back here at two o'clock.'

'As you say, Anthony. You're the boss,' said Peter as he left.

Switching his mobile back on Anthony was met with the alerts which are such a feature of everyday life. He had missed six calls. All from Mark Heywood at the office. Plus three voicemail messages. 'Sod it,' Anthony said to himself. 'He can bloody well wait. I have more pressing things to do. Calls to make. Favours to call in.' And abandoning his misgivings as to whether he should have cancelled his meeting, he opened the contacts menu.

The case was opened by Jeremy Carter very confidently. 'Once you have heard the evidence, your Honour, you will entertain not an iota of doubt as to the guilt of the accused. "Red handed" is how we describe the manner in which defendants such as Mr. Graves, are caught.'

His opening address was followed by the evidence of PC Paul Streeter who explained how, following an anonymous tip off, they stopped the defendant's car and that following a search by his colleague, PC Colin Chambers, a package containing 20 grams of cocaine was found behind the glove compartment of the defendant's 12-year-old Vauxhall Corsa.

Anthony's cross examination was brief. He extracted the admission that Peter had not witnessed the initial searching being carried out by PC Chambers, and that when confronted by evidence of the find he disclaimed all knowledge of its presence.

'He expressed total amazement did he not?' said Anthony.

'If you say so,' replied PC Streeter.

PC Chambers then gave his evidence which matched that of his colleague.

Anthony rose. 'Your search behind the glove compartment caused a certain amount of damage to the back of it, did it not?"

'It did.'

'And that was a risk which you thought worth taking, was it not?'

'It was.'

'So, you must have been pretty confident about the reliability of the tip off, otherwise, you would be damaging the vehicle of an innocent motorist.'

'Correct.'

'There could of course be another explanation of your confidence

– the possibility that you fabricated the evidence and that you put the package where you purported to discover it while the accused was being questioned by PC Streeter.'

'That's a disgraceful insinuation.'

'Something that has never happened before I suppose.'

'Of course not.'

'Where is this leading Mr. Harrison?' said the Judge. 'You know that you cannot make unsubstantiated suggestions to a witness.'

'I do, your Honour.'

'This had better be good then,' said the Judge. 'Otherwise you'll be in a lot of hot water.'

'PC Chambers. Let me put it to you that you indulged in a bit of gardening after you stopped my client's car. Namely with a trowel to dig behind the glove compartment and a fork to plant the packages.'

'Rubbish,' said the witness. 'Absolute disgusting, defamatory nonsense. I have never heard anything like it in my whole career.'

'Really,' said Anthony. 'Does the name George Watson mean anything to you?'

It was as if a thunderbolt had struck. 'How do you know about that?' replied the witness. 'The investigation is strictly confidential.'

'You mean – to put it more accurately and precisely – a disciplinary hearing into your conduct following representations on behalf of the unfortunate Mr. Watson who was convicted on your subsequently to be discovered fabricated evidence of a find of cannabis in his glove compartment which led to the quashing of the jury's verdict and his acquittal on appeal.'

The witness stood in the witness box transfixed and open mouthed.

Jeremy Carter tried his best, submitting to the Judge that alleged conduct in another case had no bearing on the facts of this case. A submission which did not find favour with the Judge.

'How can I thank you enough?' said Peter to Anthony once he had been formally acquitted.

'Thank my contacts in the police force,' he replied. 'Now I'm off to face some music of my own.'

'Two nil to you,' said Jeremy. 'Well played.'

'You're fucking fired. I want you out of this office in 20 minutes. Thanks to you we've lost a major client. As you know only too well Trevor Perkins is a plumbing entrepreneur up there with the most enterprising of them. His Perkins Franchise is just about to take off nationally. The legal work which that would have generated for this firm would have produced projected annual legal fees of £2 million rising to £5 million after three years. For a firm of this size it's colossal. You're a selfish arrogant conceited show-off. Preferring, as I now know, to enjoy the plaudits of your admirers to the interest of the firm that feeds you. Now get out.'

And with that a deflated, self-questioning Anthony walked out of Mark's office.

'Maybe,' he said to himself, 'Mark is right. He certainly has a point. On the other hand, how could I have lived with myself if I had disregarded the plight of that wretched stranger.'

Anthony did not expect the phone call he got the next day.

'Mr. Harrison? My name is Jimmy Perkins. My dad is Trevor Perkins. We were due to meet last Tuesday afternoon but you put it off. My dad lost his cool. Pulled his business from the firm. Got me to instruct another one. But to be honest with you they're a load of bleeding rubbish. They tell me I've got no more than a five per cent chance of acquittal and that if I plead guilty my likely prison sentence will be reduced from six months to four. Big deal. Especially when the truth is I never did what I'm accused of, so why the fuck should I plead guilty. So, I'm ringing you, Mr. Harrison, to see if you'll let bygones be bygones and represent me. I know it's a big ask, but what do you say?'

It was a turn up for the book if ever there was one.

'Sorry,' said Anthony, but I'm unemployed and uninsured.'

'You won't be after my dad has spoken to your ex-boss,' said the young Jimmy Perkins.'

'Ten in the morning at the office OK with you?' said Anthony.

This time Westminster Magistrates Court was constituted by a bench of three: a District Judge as Chairman accompanied by two lay magistrates. One a 56-year-old man, retired religious instruction school teacher who was currently secretary of the Marylebone Temperance Society. The other a serving nun who had been given dispensation by an enlightened Mother Superior to join the magistracy 'in order to broaden your appreciation of the real world'. Hardly a favourable composition of the tribunal appointed to hear the case of R v Perkins.

After Jimmy had entered his formal plea of not guilty to the charge of indecent exposure to a group of schoolgirls, the prosecution conducted fortuitously, by Jeremy Carter got underway.

'If it please your worships, I appear for the prosecution in this case. Mr. Harrison appears for the defendant,' he began. And then proceeded to detail the allegations against Jimmy. 'That he was seen to be exposing and massaging his member by at least two girls aged 13 and 15 in the early evening of Tuesday, the 18th October, in the street, after having deliberately drawn their attention to his act by shouting out "ouch – what a relief – oops, sorry for the unintended pun," he said, followed by words to the effect "don't look". Words which the prosecution says were deliberately calculated to attract – rather than distract – their attention. To be fair to the defence, Mr. Harrison will submit that the accused's words must be construed at their face value. But do not be taken in by his silky arguments for which he is so celebrated – or should I say – notorious. You will hear the evidence for yourselves and draw your own conclusions.'

The first witness was called. Bridget Fairclough, 15 years old. A pupil at St. Anne's Convent in Marylebone High Street. Demurely dressed in the school's dark purple tunic. A young woman whose breasts were developing nicely. And as a convent girl that seemed a matter of shame rather than pride. Speaking in an unexpectedly confident tone she described the events of that evening. How at approximately 6.15pm she and six friends had come out from a local *Pizza Express* where they had guzzled a late afternoon giant Margherita before returning to the convent. It had just stopped raining. It was just getting dark. They had all just turned the corner into the next side street.

'And what happened next?' asked Jeremy.

'I heard this shout. Something like "Don't look. Look the other way." Naturally my first instinct was to do the exact opposite and try to see what was going on.'

'And what was going on?' asked Jeremy.

'The street was pretty deserted. I saw this young man – that's the one over there,' she said pointing at Jimmy, 'having what looked to me like a J Arthur.'

'A what?' interjected the nun.

'A J Arthur Rank. Wank,' said the witness. 'A Barclays is another way of putting it if you like.'

'A what?' said the nun in a display of innocent naivety.

There were, excuse the pun, titters in the Court. The Judge called for quiet. Jeremy became more embarrassed when the Judge asked him to invite the witness to elaborate. 'Is that really necessary?' asked Jeremy.

'It certainly is,' interjected Anthony. 'My client is entitled to know what is being alleged against him.'

'I agree,' said the teetotaller. 'I've never heard the expression before. I'm as perplexed as anyone.'

There then ensued a graphic description by the witness of her precise recollection of what Jimmy did. His trouser zip had been lowered, his penis taken out and held in Jimmy's right hand the fingers of which could be clearly seen to be manipulating. After less than ten seconds Jimmy had been heard to exclaim a huge sigh accompanied by the words 'what a relief'. Droplets could, she added, be seen to be leaking from 'his cock on to the ground'.

An involuntary peal of laughter drew a stern reproach from the Judge. 'We'll have no more of that.'

It was Anthony's turn to cross examine. 'You seem very well versed in the descriptive slang of masturbation.'

'You'd be surprised at what goes on behind the closed doors of a convent school,' she replied.

'As would we all, I suspect. Tell me, please. Did you complain to the accused?'

'No.'

'Why not?'

'Because what I had seen did not particularly worry me, to be honest. It was Jenny who took offence and insisted that we call the police.'

'It's correct to say that you did not observe any ejaculation. Merely – as you so graphically put it – a leaking from his cock. You confused his actions in shaking his penis with self pleasure, did you not?'

'I may have done.'

'It was your lurid imagination at work.'

'If you say so.'

'That's a yes, is it?'

No response.

'I'll repeat the assertion. It's a yes is it not?'

'Yes.'

'So, when Jimmy says that all he was doing was to have a pee–'

'Language, please, Mr. Harrison,' said the teetotaller.

'I repeat, a pee,' he said by way of implied rebuke to the magistrate, 'because he was absolutely bursting, you would not disagree that he could well be telling the truth.'

Once again there was no reply. This time Anthony simply sat down.

Jeremy called his next witness. Thirteen-year-old Jennifer Broadhurst. She too had been drawn to looking at what Jimmy had been doing by the language he had used – 'Don't look'. The mere sight of a male organ had been enough to shock her. The police had to be called.

Under a tactfully short cross examination, she agreed with Anthony that if Jimmy's account was true, he could not have had any intention to have caused alarm or distress to anyone who might happen to have seen his member – a critical element in the constitution of the offence.

'You accept, do you not, that Jimmy Perkins is here today because you and Bridget initially convinced yourselves that he was deliberately exposing himself in an act of self pleasure, when all he was doing was to relieve himself. And that if it had not been raining just beforehand he could have proved that the leakage was urine rather than a different liquid.'

A grudging nod from Jennifer and she was instructed by the Judge to leave the witness box.

Anthony stared meaningfully at Jeremy.

Jeremy returned the stare. Nodded. He knew when the game was up. Addressing the Bench, he explained that in view of the admissions extracted by his opponent, he was minded to withdraw the charge 'with the permission of the Bench'. A request which was quickly granted.

'That makes the score 3-0 to you then,' said Jeremy to Anthony. 'I suppose I have to congratulate you.'

'Not as vigorously as I do,' said Jimmy who had sidled up to them. 'You were fucking brilliant mate. Absolutely fucking brilliant.'

'Language, if you don't mind,' said Anthony. 'Not in front of a prosecutor. He'll have you for some kind of public order offence if you're not careful.'

Time to Retire?

Few trials in the criminal courts retain the public fascination in quite the same way as those alleging murder. Not where the evidence is all but conclusive to support a conviction based on the straightforward shootings, stabbings, the gangland pre-violent death tortures, the drownings and many others where the circumstances speak for themselves. Including cases where the accused's instructions to defence counsel constitute an almost crazy attempt to convince a jury to enter realms of fantasy. To suspend belief.

'I ask you to accept, members of the jury, that my client was suffering from a condition known as somnambulism – sleepwalking – when he opened the drawer, took out the gun, loaded the bullets and accidentally fired.'

Only a cock-eyed optimist might be willing to undertake that defence with any hope of success. Cases where there is a real, rather than speculative, possibility of doubt however fascinate, even obsess. Where the police have got the wrong person. Where the supporting evidence may be flawed. And where a fearless defender uses his forensic skills with all the bravery, and perhaps bravado, the situation demands. Where the exploits involving the unexpected magic of a 'Rumpole' to dazzle susceptible jurors.

The events leading to the arrest of George Maddox in the late evening of Wednesday 15th May 2019 on suspicion of the murder of Kate Lovatt, hit the residents of Amberley Crescent like a thunderbolt. The victim stabbed twice through the heart with a paper knife which made a good dagger. In the street. On the pavement. One hundred yards from where she lived with her husband James. A dazed George had been caught with the weapon in his right hand. Blood all over his hitherto white shirt. Cradling the deceased and weeping uncontrollably. Even as the police arrived, he was heard to be hysterically mumbling 'I'm so sorry. I love you. It's all my fault.'

A police search for witnesses only resulted in finding James Lovatt. Ostensibly heartbroken. He said his wife had stormed out of the house after an argument concerning her alleged extra-marital behaviour with more than one lover, the latest – George Maddox – with whom James had accused his wife of having committed unadulterated adultery. The two of them had reportedly been seen brazenly emerging from a local Travelodge at 4pm the previous day – when James had been at Lord's watching Middlesex play against Leicestershire.

His friend Charles Goodchild, himself no paragon of fidelity, was sure of what he had seen. Both arm in arm, laughing with carefree joy. 'Like a couple of teenagers out on their virginity losing first date' was his graphic description.

According to James, Kate had told him that he shouldn't be so judgemental. It wasn't her fault that he was impotent. 'I'm not the only victim of your erectile dysfunction,' she said. Marriage allows barbs. She was, she said, going out for some fresh air to get away for an hour or two and think about things. She wanted to be left alone. She had already told an inconsolable George she was seriously thinking of ending the relationship before it developed into something serious. She was at the same time angry – and contrite. But she said she still loved James and would tell George Maddox to his face, once and for all, that she wanted nothing more to do with him. Standing at the window James watched her leave.

After a minute or so he observed her being approached from behind by George. An argument ensued. He stabbed her twice in the chest. James rushed out, the mobile in his hand and talking urgently to 999. It was an emergency, he pleaded to the receptionist.

A packed Court 1 at the Old Bailey on Tuesday 10th December 2019 saw the opening of R v Maddox. The trial Judge Mr. Justice Redbridge was considered by practising criminal lawyers to be refreshingly enlightened. Especially when it came to granting exceptional latitude to the conduct of defence counsel to redress what he regarded as the imbalance of resources between the big battalioned prosecution and an often impoverished, legal aid funded defence.

The Crown retained Sir Andrew Forbes QC who had 31 years' experience of distinguished practice at the criminal bar. Formerly of an unparalleled reputation but widely considered to be past his best. His last – apparently open and shut – case involved his prosecution of a demonstrably aggressive pupil on a charge of raping a schoolmistress. He was acquitted. When the jury foreman announced the verdict, a disbelieving judge could hardly conceal his astonishment and contempt for the quality of prosecuting competence. Retirement beckoned.

By contrast George Maddox was represented by 25-year-old Joe Barnes, a solicitor who had – unusually at such a young age – acquired rights of audience to appear in a crown court. He had several high-profile victories under his belt – including the schoolmistress acquittal. He came into the courtroom on that Tuesday morning bearing an air of not so quiet confidence. Something was up his sleeve. His demeanour suggested a knockout. The battle lines were drawn. The young pretender versus the steady, but declining, old timer. The jury was sworn in, the charge read out to the accused. A plea of not guilty confidently spoken.

'Yes, Sir Andrew,' said the Judge, 'pray open your case.'

The dice are loaded in favour of the defence in one respect. An accused can speak openly and widely to his lawyer before the trial starts. Not that he may be told what, or what not, to say. Words cannot be put in his mouth – a rule not entirely strictly observed by some lawyers of dubious standing. But his lawyer may run through his evidence with him as a kind of rehearsal and explore, to clarify and explain certain weaker aspects of his testimony or of damaging evidence to be given for the Crown, to try to make sure that he is not caught by surprise by a deadly question in cross examination. A huge advantage. A prosecution witness has no such opportunity. Once his statement has been put in evidence, he may not discuss it with prosecuting counsel. He is left at the mercy of the defence cross examination with no rehearsal of the ordeal which he is likely to face.

'I'm sorry, Mr. Lovatt,' explained Sir Andrew to an agitated James before the trial began, 'but I am not allowed to discuss your evidence with you. All I can remind you is to tell the truth and do not be afraid to stand up for yourself. I cannot tell you how to react to questions which may be put to you. But I can anticipate the kind of defence strategy which might be adopted and prepare accordingly. It's a lonely existence giving evidence for the Crown I'm afraid.'

The prosecution evidence was powerful, even damning. Lovatt's DNA on the knife. The absence of any other DNA on either the knife or the victim or her clothing – save for that of her husband which was, according to Sir Andrew, easily explainable. The presence of the knife in the defendant's hand when caught. The words – spoken by the defendant to the policeman – which, the prosecution submitted, could only be construed as an admission of guilt – 'It's all my fault.' And vital the testimony of James Lovatt who witnessed the attack.

When advocates have nothing with which to discredit evidence given by a witness, they often try to discredit the witness him/herself rather than what they may have said. And so, hoping to persuade a jury to disbelieve, or at the very least doubt, anything that witness says.

As Joe rose to cross examine James Lovatt, he took out from his briefcase a thin file of papers. 'You will allow me to offer my sympathies on the tragic death of your wife,' was his opening. A classic gambit to elicit the sympathy of a jury. The witness nodded and uttered a thank you. 'I will not beat about the bush. In my hand is a transcript of your court martial which was held last year before you were dishonourably discharged from the Army for – and I will quote some of its findings – "deliberately and maliciously fabricating evidence of complicity in an act of violence against a superior officer by one Private Jones who was found to be wholly innocent". I take it that you do not dispute the transcript.'

James Lovatt looked stunned.

Sir Andrew jumped theatrically to his feet. 'My Lord. Where is the relevance of this piece of cross examination?'

The Judge was not having that. 'If, Sir Andrew, you are unable to discern the significance of asking the jury to disbelieve the word of an established and proven liar whose testimony is of a similar order to that which a court martial has found to be untrue – and deliberately so – then I am inclined to wonder whether or not you might wish to reconsider your objection – and perhaps – whether to consider your professional future.'

'Quite so, my Lord,' replied an apparently crestfallen, and humiliated, Sir Andrew.

'Pray continue, Mr. Barnes,' said the Judge.

'I am waiting for the defendant to answer the question,' said Joe.

'Correct,' said James, who realised the significance of the admission.

'In which case you will doubtless agree with me that there must be a doubt about the reliability of your testimony.' And before James could answer Joe sat down. The prosecution case left in tatters.

Joe saw no need to call George into the witness box. In summing up the Judge reminded the jury members of the glaring significance of the demolition of the character of the principal prosecution witness on whose evidence the prosecution relied and of the corresponding importance to the defence which had adopted the challenge to James' veracity. He told them in no uncertain terms 'that they must be sure' – the hallowed words – of guilt before they could convict. Each, the Judge proceeded to stress and 'to put it another way', had placed its eggs in the basket of Mr. Lovatt's testimony. The prosecution relied on its truth. The defence relied on its unreliability. 'It is not,' the Judge reminded the jury, 'for the defendant to establish his innocence, and his absence from the witness box is not to be held against him.'

A nod of approval from James was observed by the jury. Indeed, many of them appeared to nod in sympathy.

After two hours the jury returned. Joe tried to look solemn but inwardly congratulated himself on the forthcoming inevitable verdict.

'Are you all agreed upon your verdict?' the Court clerk asked the jury foreman.

James Lovatt who spoke, 'Excuse me, your Lordship, but may I say something?'

The Judge peered over his spectacles. 'You had your opportunity in the witness box. Do you know anything about this Sir Andrew?'

'The answer is that he doesn't, your Lordship, because he told me that I wasn't allowed to speak to him about my evidence. But he also told me that I was to tell the truth. Well, my Lord, there is more to tell and I've got Sir Andrew to thank for having given me the confidence to speak.'

'Really, my Lord,' Joe said, 'this is highly unusual.'

'So is the bravery with which the witness has addressed me,' replied the Judge. 'I will allow him to re-enter the witness box.'

As James did. 'My Lord, I wonder if you would be good enough to read this email which I have from the Court of Appeal?

James handed his mobile to the Court Clerk who in turn handed it to the Judge. Who read, and then reread what was on the screen, just to be sure that he wasn't about to err.

'Mr. Barnes,' said the Judge to Joe, 'I have just read the transcript of the recent, almost hot off the press, decision of the Court of Appeal in the case of this witness's appeal against the findings of his court martial. In short it asserts: "That the evidence given against Major Lovatt – as he then was – was completely false. A farrago of malicious, fabricated, lies. Major Lovatt has been the victim of a gross conspiracy and miscarriage of justice. His conviction is quashed and his discharge from the Army is revoked. His character is stainless."'

'I will need to reappraise my client's defence, if it pleases your Lordship,' said Joe to the Judge who replied that it would please him greatly.

At the Judge's invitation to speak Sir Andrew said that he had nothing to say. The jury was directed to put its findings into abeyance pending further developments. Which were not long in appearing. A plea of guilty, followed by a contrite, humble plea in mitigation in which Joe humiliatingly said how much he regretted the attack on James' character.

'We all live and learn,' replied the Judge, who told Joe that his verbal assault on James would have no influence on the sentence which he would impose. After due deliberation, he handed the mandatory life sentence with a minimum tariff – time to be served in prison – of 13 years. 'I'll see you and Mr. Barnes in my chambers, Sir Andrew,' said the Judge after the defendant had been led down to the cells below the Court.

'Do come in both of you,' said the Judge. 'There is a small matter which is troubling me, Sir Andrew. Perhaps you can help. I noticed that the email from the Court of Appeal was dated yesterday's date. Not only that. That while it was addressed to Major James Lovatt, it was cc'd to one Sir Andrew Forbes, QC.'

'True, your Lordship,' said Sir Andrew. 'As I recognised from before the beginning of this trial, the kind of tactics employed by Mr. Barnes would be those which he would, likely, and in the event did, adopt. But I seem to recall that Mr. Barnes was not slow to end his cross examination of my client after disclosing his conviction and dishonourable discharge. I did not see fit, or indeed able, given that I cannot give evidence – nor can I lead my witness to give evidence – to intervene further at the time, especially after the dressing down which you gave me. But I was confident that the witness would speak up. And expose, for what it was, the dangerous strategy deployed by a desperate defence lawyer whose arsenal was empty. I like to think to myself – strictly to myself you understand – that my silence played a part in leading Mr. Barnes into a corner of his own making.'

The Judge adjusted his spectacles. 'Maybe you're not quite ready to retire, Sir Andrew. I suspect that the Bar would be the poorer without you. What do you reckon, Mr. Barnes?'

Cupid

There really was little to compare. An Old Bailey attempted murder trial involving a meek and mild husband, a vicious tongued, domineering wife, and a judge who was irritable, and impatient with counsel and witnesses. He was tolerated only because of his peerless knowledge of the law. There had never been any appeal – let alone a successful one – from any verdict in a trial. Thirty-two years of stainless record. Could even Lord Denning claim that?

The case of R v Donoghue had all the trappings. The frisson of anticipation of the human drama about to unfold. When solicitor/advocate Anthony Harrison sat down in a row reserved for members of the legal profession not actually retained in the case, little did he know what lay ahead. It was his first time at a court since the suspension of his practising certificate 18 months earlier for 'Improper conduct'.

The Judge had reported him for 'behaving unnecessarily – to the point of unprofessionally – aggressively towards a witness' – a woman who complained of rape. The Judge saw her as the victim of an excruciatingly hostile piece of cross examination by Anthony representing the accused. The fact that the jury had acquitted was, according to the Judge – as well as the Solicitors Regulation Authority – neither here nor there. Professional standards had been breached. Never mind that the complainant was shown up to be a complete liar whose false evidence was calculated to stick her – as she had been compelled to admit – consensual sexual partner inside for seven years. Standards were standards.

So, it was thus a chastened Anthony Harrison who was present, on his first day of restoration to advocacy. He wanted to refamilarise himself with the unique Court atmosphere, and felt unable to suppress a wry smile when the Judge took the throne in Court 1. As the court listing had shown – Judge Hubert Donaldson. Anthony's executioner.

In the dock, stationed between two prison officers, was the accused. Lionel Donoghue. Donoghue was 41 years old. Charged with attempting to murder his wife, Clare Donoghue, at 2.30 on the afternoon of Sunday, 5th May earlier that year, with an aluminium rolling pin. The Crown alleged that he deliberately hit her with the pastry making implement over the back of her head three times in an attempt to kill her. The defendant ignored the advice of his solicitor and pleaded not guilty, thereby forfeiting the opportunity to enjoy a credit of up to one third off any sentence the judge imposed.

Barely had prosecuting counsel, Sir Geoffrey Harding QC, finished introducing the professional *dramatis personae* to the judge and jury, when defence counsel, Percy Silver, slumped forward for no ostensible reason. Paramedics arrived and treated Percy who was mercifully conscious, but plainly disabled. When Percy was taken to hospital, the defendant was not represented – his solicitor not having advocacy rights. The Court usher asked if there were any other barristers in court or available in the building.

The Judge told Sir Geoffrey that he had no alternative but to adjourn the trial until such time as fresh legal representation could be arranged.

Eighteen months out of court had not made Anthony shy. He rose to his feet. 'With your indulgence, your honour, I am ready, if the accused and his solicitor are agreeable, to undertake this defendant's representation.'

'Who are you?' scowled the Judge.

'If I may speak, your Honour, he has rights of advocacy,' said

Lionel Donoghue's solicitor who had had previous constructive dealings with Anthony and positively jumped at the possibility. After a huddled consultation with the Judge, Anthony was formally appointed.

The case was adjourned for one hour so Anthony could be fully briefed.

'It's not long enough, Judge,' said Anthony.

'Having read the papers, I consider this to be an almost open and shut case,' replied the Judge. 'An hour will allow you more than sufficient time to prepare. All back in court at 11 o'clock. And I hope I don't have to remind you, Mr. Harrison, to address me with the due respect to be accorded by an advocate to the Bench. If I say an hour is sufficient, it is not for you to question it.'

Anthony Harrison had been warned to be on his best behaviour.

An hour later Sir Geoffrey outlined the so-called facts of the case. 'It is of course for the prosecution to prove to your complete satisfaction that this defendant tried to kill his unfortunate wife, but you may well feel, once you have heard about the defendant's commendably frank admissions, that any doubts which you might have harboured will have been mere figments of your imagination, and that Lionel Donoghue's guilt is beyond any doubt. His Honour Judge Donaldson, will direct you on the law – the burden of proof and all that technical stuff. But you, members of the jury, are the judges of fact. The purveyors of common sense. You will ask yourselves one simple question. If you clobber somebody with a rolling pin, would you not expect the victim to be at risk of death? The Crown submits there can be only one rational answer. Leading to an inescapable *cul de sac* of guilt. I will now call my first witness.'

The 999 controller played a recording of Lionel Donoghue's frantic telephone message: 'I need an ambulance and the police. It looks as if I may have killed my wife who appears not to be breathing, but I thought I could detect a faint pulse. For heaven's sake come quickly.' Thus was established the identity of the perpetrator and his desire to call for urgent medical attention. Anthony would not be slow to emphasise the latter.

The first policeman to arrive at the scene told the Court. 'Mr. Donoghue was hysterical when we arrived. Was pleading with the paramedics to save his wife. Was more than frank in admitting that he had struck her three times in rapid succession with the rolling pin which had been lying on the draining board in the kitchen where the assault took place.'

The next witness was a scientific officer – Julian Sands – who gave his opinion on the degree of force used in the attack. 'Considerable,' he said. 'You can infer it from the indentations in the rear of the skull.'

When Anthony rose to cross-examine he was not in stiletto mood. 'Forgive me,' he politely asked, 'but as a forensic scientist for whom the importance of precision is critical, could you please tell the jury where they will find a linguistic definition of the expression "considerable force"?'

The witness stared blankly. 'Anyone knows what I mean,' he stated contemptuously.

'Then explain it,' said Anthony, 'for the benefit of those of us who don't fully understand.'

'It's obvious,' came the reply.

'I agree,' said the Judge. 'Most of us are capable of understanding what "considerable" means in this context. Now please either change your line of questioning or sit down.'

'I'm afraid that my client would not forgive me if I were to exercise either of your two kind options, your Honour. So let me be clear, Mr. Sands. There is no legal definition of considerable force, is there?'

'Put it that way I suppose you're right,' Sands answered.

'And in any event the force – however considerable – did not kill, did it?'

'Put it that way, I suppose you're right,' was the response.

'Put it any way you like,' said Anthony. 'The answer is still the same. Mrs. Donoghue is alive and healthy. With an indentation free skull. I have now finished with this witness Your Lordship.'

At least three members of the jury were seen to smirk while two tittered discreetly. Julian Sands left the witness box, a deflated figure.

The Court clock showed five minutes to one. 'Time to adjourn for lunch,' announced his Honour. 'We will resume proceedings at ten minutes past two. Meanwhile, members of the jury, I remind you not to discuss the case outside the jury room.'

When the Judge had left Anthony walked over to his client. 'Don't get your hopes up too much,' he told him. 'We still have a monumental hill to climb.'

The testimony of Clare Donoghue was always going to be the central plank of the prosecution case. Her written statement was clear, concise, and damning. During a particularly incendiary argument Lionel had walked calmly to the draining board, picked up the rolling pin, and struck her three times – as far as she could remember – around the head, causing her to collapse and lose consciousness.

The next thing she could remember was waking up in hospital with a headache from hell for which powerful analgesics were prescribed. She offered no explanation for the assault. She spoke clearly, unemotionally, and without rancour.

Anthony rose to his feet.

'Your Honour,' he said. 'I have an unusual request to make. For reasons which I hope will become clear in due course I would like to defer my cross examination of this witness until my client has testified.'

'And why should I defer to this highly irregular procedure, Mr. Harrison? Give me one good reason.'

'The interests of truth and justice, your Honour. Matters to which – if I may say so – the conduct of every trial should pay the highest regard.'

'Any objection. Sir Geoffrey?' asked the Judge morosely.

Counsel shook his head.

'Very well then, Mrs. Donoghue. You are released from the witness box for now, but be prepared to be recalled to allow Mr. Harrison to ask you some questions.'

And with that Clare Donoghue walked into the well of the Court where she took a seat to await the evidence of her husband.

'My name is Lionel Donoghue. I currently reside on remand at HM Prison Brixton and formerly lived with my wife at 17 Northcote Crescent, Ealing, the house we bought together when we got married eight years ago.' He went on to say that he was a physiotherapist employed by an NHS clinic. That his other interests included lay preaching.

'Is it right to say, Mr. Donoghue, that your wife did not approve either of your job or your interest in the Church?' asked Anthony.

'I'm sorry to say that you are entirely correct.'

'Do you have any idea why this should be the case?'

'I have my theories about it.'

'Would you please explain them to the Court.'

'Mr. Harrison,' the Judge said. 'Where on earth are you going on this? Are we to have a long psychological exposition on the state of the victim's well-being – or ill-being – when it is your client – the perpetrator – who is on trial here?'

'Against the backdrop of the requirement for a fair trial, the short answer is "yes" your Honour.'

The Judge rolled his eyes to the ceiling. Thought about it. And thought better of it. 'Proceed, Mr. Donoghue. We are all ears I'm sure.'

'I'll be as brief as I can,' continued Lionel. 'I first met my wife to be at St. Luke's Church in Pinner where I went as a lay observer at a funeral service held for her late father. A solicitor as it so happened. Pretty successful in the City. Clare doted on him. He had died in tragic circumstances when his car rolled over after hitting a bollard at high speed. That was bad enough. But he was not the only fatality. With him in the front passenger seat had been what had euphemistically been described as a lady of ill repute. It turned out she was a high-class call girl with whom Clare's father had been having a long – term relationship.'

He continued. 'Clare's mother had rheumatoid arthritis and with no siblings, Clare had been left to cope alone. Devastated barely begins to describe her state of mind. It was a long period of grieving during which I tried my best to comfort and console. We grew close. I suppose I was a kind of replacement father figure in a way. But the platonic nature of our relationship was torpedoed when one evening after we had eaten out. She invited me into her house. The pent-up passion simply exploded.

'Two months later we got married. Her mother, being too disabled to manage herself on her own, was mercifully found a beautiful care home where she is looked after to this day. To begin with things were quite wonderful and not only the sex. It was if we had been made for each other. She would provide a warmth and an understanding of my desire to help my patients as well as humanity at large. I would provide the solidity with which to buttress her insecurities, following the revelation of her father's relationship with the call girl. She wanted me home by 6pm every working day. She forbade me from attending church services on a Sunday or from undertaking any lay preaching.

'Then, but without actually saying so, she would imply that because my profession required physical contact with flesh, I must be tempted to have affairs. Nothing could be further from the truth; its effect was to first dampen, and then virtually eliminate, my libido. I began to realise that she drew some kind of perverse comfort in the exercise of control. I guessed that if her hero father could be unfaithful, she thought I was. Try as I did, I could not convince her that I was faithful. That I was not her father. But all to no avail.

'Then she began to develop violent tendencies. Called me useless because my cooking skills did not distinguish between the techniques to cook an omelette and scrambled eggs. I could sense my own sanity was being compromised. And to come to that fateful Sunday afternoon.

I had sneaked out earlier to see our local vicar for advice as to how to handle Clare's paranoia, and returned home to face a barrage of questioning about where I had been that morning.

'It was when she called me a pathetic piece of impotent uselessness that I picked up the rolling pin in a split second of anger.

'"Go on" – she screamed. "Hit me. Show a bit of manhood." She was hysterical. That was when I called her bluff and delivered the three blows. As soon as I had done so I came to my senses, phoned 999 and called for the emergency services.'

'Two questions, Mr. Donoghue,' said Anthony. 'The first is this. Did you, on that Sunday afternoon, attempt to kill your wife?'

'No – I did not. It was a stupid reaction to her goading which simply went too far.'

'The second question is this. Given the mental torment which you suffered at your wife's hands, did you not ever contemplate seeking a divorce, and if not, why not.'

'The answers to each of those are very simple. To question one, it is "no". And to question two it consists of four words "Because I love her". And I always will, no matter what. She needs me too much.'

Even His Honour, Judge Donaldson was moved to ask Lionel whether he would like a glass of water. The whole Court, lawyers and the public, sat motionless. Stunned by the sheer helplessness of this well-meaning, decent, man ready to tolerate his wife's hostile behaviour in recognition of her needs.

Sir Geoffrey tried his best stab at cross examination, but his tame efforts to suggest that anyone wielding a rolling pin must have been aware of the risk of killing were brushed aside.

'I recognise that now,' said Lionel, 'but at the time I was simply responding to Clare's cajolery.'

Wisely counsel refrained from pursuing the point.

'May I now ask Clare Donoghue to return to the witness box?' said Anthony.

Looking round he watched her shakily get up from where she had been sitting, handkerchief dabbing her eyes. After being reminded by the Judge that she was still under oath, and swallowing a huge gulp of water, she waited for Anthony's questioning.

'Is there anything which you would like to say, Mrs. Donoghue, in response to your husband's testimony?' he asked. 'Is there, for instance, anything which he alleged with which you disagree?'

'No, Mr. Harrison. I can't disagree with anything he said. It's all true. There is nothing further for me to add. Except to say one thing. To thank you, Mr. Harrison, for giving my darling Lionel the opportunity to express his true feelings for me. You are truly the Cupid of the legal profession. And long may you continue to be.'

It was no real surprise when the jury acquitted after a short retirement to consider its verdict. To the sound of rapturous applause from all those present.

'Thank you, members, of the jury,' said the Judge. 'A verdict with which I wholeheartedly agree. Thank you also, Sir Geoffrey, for the sympathetic approach taken by the prosecution during this – how can I best put it – unusual trial. And thank you, especially, Mr. Harrison, for your insight and understanding. Truly remarkable is what I say. Truly remarkable. Cupid, eh? You don't hear a description like that very often. Cupid. Cupid. That's a good one.'

What Would I Have Done?

The morning of Monday 1st July 2021. For Margot Preston it was the first occasion on which she had not felt suffocating panic since the sudden, premature death of her husband Paul two years earlier when he was only 28. The sudden end of a blissful marriage which had produced Jake. The apple of their collective eyes. Who, at the tender age of five, saw the paroxysms of anaphylactic shock suffered by his otherwise healthy father.

Margot's frantic efforts at reviving her husband before the arrival of the emergency services failed.

The postmortem demonstrated that an unidentifiable, unspecified, allergy was the only possible cause, unspecific as it was.

It was an unusually relaxed, contented, Margot Preston who, that July Monday morning, was gently chiding her son to finish his cornflakes to be ready to leave for school. She hardly noticed what sounded like a minor commotion at the junction of her cul de sac at the roundabout on the main road 50 metres from her house. She was more concerned at Jake's delay in bringing his satchel into the hall from the study where the desktop computer lived.

'Come along now, Jake. We don't want to be late.'

With no sign of a response Margot angrily entered the study. To be confronted with a wheezing, breathless Jake. Gasping for air. She remembered just that when her Paul had been the victim. With memories flooding back she dialled 999 for an ambulance and rapidly described her son's symptoms.

'It sounds like anaphylactic shock to me,' said the 999 operator, 'but there's a massive traffic jam at your roundabout which is causing a huge delay in ambulance availability. Your best bet is to drive your son directly to the Royal Berkshire Hospital. The road is clear on your side and with any luck you should be there within five minutes. Time is absolutely critical. Give me your name. Although it is not strictly my job, I will telephone the hospital to make sure that somebody is waiting outside the A&E department for you. Good luck.'

Margot gave her name, gathered her distressed son into her arms and, not without difficulty, managed to lay him across the back seat of her car. Then, double locking the front door in double quick time, she got into the driver's seat of her Audi A4, started the engine and turned left out of her drive towards the roundabout.

Where she was confronted by 35 self-styled demonstrators bearing white flags emblazoned by large red capital letters CCCCA – each capital letter respectively underlined with the lower case 'campaign for' 'climate' 'change' 'catastrophe' 'awareness'. Worse a middle aged, hippy like throwback from Woodstock, stood bolt upright in the middle of the road where it joined the roundabout, threatening to block her exit from the cul de sac. To block traffic totally one of the group lay on the ground across the exit, hands superglued to the roadway. No way through.

Desperate, Margot lowered her window and pleaded with the hippy to apply a fast acting dissolvent to the superglued member of the group to allow to her get out to the main road. He refused. When she tried to explain the urgency of the life and death threat to her son's very existence, she got a scornful comparison with the life and death threatening consequences of her fossil fuel burning car engine. It was a jibe too far. She had no time for academic discussion. One foot hard down on the accelerator and she was away down the road towards the hospital. A dead ex-demonstrator's hands stayed on the road, his torso, head, arms and legs, a bloody agglomeration of flesh, muscle, brain and bone.

The outstretched arms of a three-man medical team at the hospital's A&E entrance quickly identified Margot while administering jabs of adrenaline to the gasping Jake fighting for life. The reaction was pure magic. Within a matter of seconds, he started to breathe normally again.

'You have a very lucky son,' said the lead doctor. 'Sixty more seconds and his chances of survival would have been approaching zero.' Words which were closely followed by the sound of screeching tyres of a blue lighted police vehicle.

'You need to accompany us to the station,' said a serious looking uniformed police sergeant to Margot. 'I suspect you know the reason why.'

The public gallery of Court 1 at the Old Bailey was full on the morning of Monday, 29th September 2021. Spectators, several wearing CCCCA tee-shirts, keen to attend the trial of Margot Preston charged with the wilful, premeditated, murder of Rodney Wilson by deliberately driving over his prostrate body when he had no means to escape.

Margot pleaded not guilty. The prosecution then offered a lesser charge of manslaughter, which Sir Richard Blount QC, for the Crown, had put to Anthony Harrison, solicitor advocate for the accused. The offer was contemptuously rejected. The defence being one of justifiable homicide. A plea which, in turn, was equally contemptuously rejected by Sir Richard as being flawed as a matter of law and untenable as a matter of fact.

'Such a defence can only succeed, according to the authorities, where the perpetrator kills to prevent the victim from, at its lowest, causing serious harm to that perpetrator, or another, in circumstances in which the act of killing is a proportionate response. And since there was no threat of harm issued by the victim that defence must fail in this case, my dear boy,' lectured Sir Richard.

'We shall see,' said Anthony.

If Margot had been looking for a sympathetic judge, she was

unlucky. She had drawn the shortest straw in the judicial pack. His Lordship Sir Jeremiah Blackstone enjoyed a reputation for academic distinction. Any litigant in a civil suit, or defendant in a criminal case, would be assured that any issue which demanded the application of logic and of sound reasoning would enjoy an impeccable response. But the Judge had very little emotional awareness. An appeal to the heart would be destined to fail. A waste of time. Even – some would say – counterproductive. When addressing his Lordship on matters of sensibility words needed to be chosen with more than a modicum of tact. It might be not so much as what one might say as what one should not say. Anthony was only too well aware of the pitfalls ahead.

Unlike some of what would follow, the case opened with the standard formalities. The jury of seven men and five women was empanelled. The Court clerk read out the charge. Margot pleaded 'Not Guilty' firmly. Sir Richard started with his opening address to the jury, told them who he was and what he was doing there, and gave the equivalent information regarding Anthony Harrison.

Sir Richard then proceeded to recite the agreed facts of the case, emphasising the brutality of the killing. He went on to give a short, agreed discourse on the law of public protest and demonstration, not forgetting to inform the jury that a recent decision of the Supreme Court affirmed the legitimacy of the right of expression and assembly as per Articles 10 and 11 of the European Convention on Human Rights in pursuit of the demonstrator's beliefs provided actual violence or destruction was avoided. Disrupting people's lives was not in any way illegal.

Sir Richard then called his first witness, the middle-aged hippy, who testified as to his conversation with Margot and what happened next – in particular how she ran over the victim. With nothing to dispute, Anthony chose not to cross examine. No point in trying to disguise what had clearly happened.

The next witness was the arresting police officer who, under cross examination, readily agreed Margot had unhesitatingly explained that she had had no choice but to run over the victim to give her son a chance of survival. Further gruesome evidence relating to the corpse was given by the prosecution pathologist. And thus the case for the Crown was vividly demonstrated to the jury.

It was now the turn of the defence. Anthony Harrison called Margot to give her side of the story which she managed to give in a controlled, but at the same time, moving manner. Describing the moment when she decided to drive over the prone protester, she explained that while she would feel remorse for the rest of her life, she felt that she had no alternative but to act as she did. The Judge peered at the jury in mock disbelief.

The evidence thus concluded, Sir Richard, in his closing speech to the jury argued that according to the law, they had no choice but to find Margot guilty. His task was a good deal easier than that confronting Anthony. Nods of varying intensity seemed to follow almost every submission of Sir Richard. Those of Anthony, whose principal argument was that a mother has free rein to save a potentially dying son, consistently drew disapproving headshakes from most of the jury as well as from His Lordship.

'I am confident that you will do the right thing and acquit my client,' were Anthony's final words of urging to a progressively sceptical group of 12 deciders.

After deliberations lasting 16 hours, over three days, the jury returned to their box at 4pm. Eleven heads clearly bowed. As if in shame. That did not offer any encouragement to Anthony or his client to expect an acquittal. After telling the Judge they were finally agreed upon their verdict – drawing an indiscreet 'I can't believe what took you so long in this open and shut case', the foreman, himself a retired solicitor, asked the Judge whether, before confirming the verdict, he might give a rather fuller explanation of the reasons which lay behind it 'given the implications of the case and its impact on the accused and co-assemblers of the deceased, and any other protesters who may be of like mind as the victim'.

The horrified Judge hyperventilated at this impertinent request, divorced as it was from established orthodoxy, but allowed himself a quiet smile. 'Why not? It should be entertaining if nothing else. Is that alright with you two advocates?'

Sir Richard was unhesitatingly in favour. 'My Lord. It can't do any harm, especially since the verdict is now decided.'

'And you, Mr. Harrison, what do you have to say?'

'It's uniquely irregular, your Lordship, and I am frankly surprised, if not appalled, that you are in favour of the proposition, although given the undertones of your various expressions during this case, I daresay your confidence in a conviction is so strong that this gross deviation from procedure does not concern you.'

Anthony immediately regretted his outburst, especially when he glanced at the jury who were, for the most part, gazing fixedly at the floor, and in one case, was almost on the point of tears.

'It's like this, my Lord,' the foreman said, 'members of our jury consist of a wide range of citizens. If I say it myself all, bar one, have degrees and qualifications of some kind or another which make us ideal constituents of a jury panel. Me – a solicitor, albeit retired. A vicar. A university lecturer in moral philosophy. A poker player with a mathematics degree. A dental surgeon. An optician. Three highly successful entrepreneurs. An ex-soldier turned pacifist. A climate scientist. And – the odd one out – a domestic cleaner. We started our discussions with a more or less collectively expressed opinion of obvious guilt. Without any legal grounds to justify the defendant's behaviour. Following the words used in your summing up. We then adjourned until day two when your direction was questioned by an opinion given by one of us that the victim had brought his death upon his own head by supergluing himself to the highway. Our philosopher then reminded us that an invitation by a person to commit a criminal act against him herself, does not justify the commission of that act. *A fortiori* – to use a Latin tag with which you might be familiar – and if you are not it means "even more so" – it could not be said in this case that the deceased made any such invitation when all he was doing was acting perfectly lawfully. So, any argument that the defendant could be excused on the grounds that it was the victim's own fault, went out of the window.

'Then the vicar supported the commonly held leaning towards conviction. That killing was the most extreme of sins incurring God's disapproval, and what had happened came nowhere close to justifying a wanton act of murder. The poker player initially took a different view. If the victim was prepared to dice with death and call the bluff of any motorist ready to ride over him, let him take the consequences. The student from a university environment where the opportunities for protest should be actively encouraged, and not discouraged by allowing the public to take the law into their own hands, said killing a protester otherwise than where his life was being threatened by the victim was not justified. Most of us in the jury room nodded in agreement. There were, however, some who were not so sure. Not, of course, the pacifist, whose military experiences in Iraq been so traumatic as to turn him from a professional killer into an evangelist for peace.

'But the dentist began to harbour serious doubts. "This woman was not a killer in the criminal sense of the term," he said. "Nor does she have to be to be guilty of this innocent man's murder," replied the philosopher. "I suppose so," said the dentist.

'That was it for the first day, my Lord,' the foreman said. 'Further voting was deferred to the following day when I called a preliminary vote first thing – before any discussion. We were eight in favour of conviction. The other four wanted more discussion on the moral arguments. And whether there was any possibility that sympathy for the defendant's predicament could be reconciled with the strict rules to satisfy the requirements for legal justification. A task which proved to be beyond the capacity of any member. At 5pm yesterday we took another vote. This time 11 were for a conviction. Only one seemed unsure. We decided to postpone proceedings until this morning. The ninth hour of deliberations.

'The first thing which I did when proceedings resumed this morning was to ask everybody who had voted for conviction whether they were still of the same opinion. All nodded their assent. I then asked the dissenter to say if there had been any change of mind. The answer was no. Pressure was then exerted to persuade her to accord with the expressed vote. I can't recall how many speakers stressed that we had no choice but to bring in a verdict of guilty in accordance with our oath. And then – at last – we arrived at our unanimous verdict. But before I announce it, I wonder if you would be so indulgent as to allow the dissenter to explain her position?'

'Very well,' said the Judge, 'but now we are almost there can she please not take up too much time. I want to get sentencing over and done with today.'

'My name is Sarah,' said the jury member. 'This is what I decided to say to my co-jury members. My parents were both of the Windrush generation. Regular churchgoers who instilled in me from the earliest age the principles of rectitude and honesty. "Follow your conscience" they would say to me. "You will know in your heart whether or not your behaviour gains God's approval". All my life I have followed this advice. It is the same advice which I have given to my own five children, and the advice which I hope that they will pass on to their children. I am a domestic cleaner. I do not have any of your abilities. Your brains. Your powers of reason. Your capacity to take risks and make – and I suppose lose – money. But I hope that I do know right from wrong. I am not obsessed with so called legal principles. I am concerned with justice. So, as a mother of five adorable children, I ask myself the simple question. In the circumstances in which Margot Preston found herself that morning what would I have done? I had said my piece your Lordship, did my best to articulate my argument. I was exhausted to be honest. Relieved to have got my sentiments out of my system. I now ask our foreman to deliver the jury's verdict.'

'My Lord,' continued the foreman, 'the simple, straightforward, morally inspired question posed by Sarah constituted the essence of the case. It was a moment of revelation for the most sceptical among us. There was only one verdict to be reached.'

'And that is?' asked the Judge.

'Not guilty my Lord.'

The Judge inhaled deeply and audibly. Then exhaled as though indulging in some kind of yoga exercise. 'And that is the verdict of you all?' he asked. An unnecessary question since it was plain how happy every juror was with the decision.

'Most certainly, my Lord. One hundred percent unanimous.'

'A verdict with which I wholeheartedly agree,' said the Judge. 'Although I must admit that it took a remarkable woman to make me see sense. As it clearly did with the other eleven of you. A woman whom it has been our privilege to encounter. It's been some time since I had such a good taste in my mouth.'

The Statement

It was half past one on the morning of 15th June 1970 that my flatmate Teddy gave me the phone. 'It's for you, Hark (as I was known to my close friends), someone called Lesley says she needs to speak to you.'

The only Lesley that I knew was an ex-receptionist who had worked for my small law firm where I had practised in partnership with my brother since qualifying as a solicitor in 1963. She was 25, of immaculate appearance and speech, born in India of British parents who had enjoyed the kind of cocktail party life colonial wallahs did. Tiffin was served by deferential servants every day. Lesley drank too much but that did not interfere with her efficiency. On the contrary she was a credit to the practice of which she was the shop window. When clients arrived, they would be greeted with a welcoming smile. Her wedding to Joe, a client of the firm, in March 1968, was the last occasion on which I had seen her, having given up work to assist him in his business.

With no little trepidation I took the phone. 'Is that you, Lesley?' I rather stupidly asked given I recognized the voice. 'Has something happened?' a question the answer to which was most definitely yes.

'It's Joe. I've just shot him. The police are here and they want to speak to you.'

'Here' was a basement flat in Regency Terrace on the Brighton seafront where Lesley had been living with Joe and their one-year-old daughter.

When I talked to Detective Chief Inspector Crawford, I learned that Joe had been admitted to Brighton General Hospital with shotgun wounds to his liver and was undergoing emergency surgery. The DCI promised to call me if there were any further developments. Meanwhile she was to be taken to Brighton police station to be held on suspicion of causing grievous bodily harm.

'Whatever you do,' I said to Lesley on being put back to her, 'don't say anything to the police at this stage.' The standard legal advice given in those days.

At 6 o'clock the same morning I was woken by a call from the DCI with the news that Joe had died on the operating table. He suggested that I get down to the police station as soon as I could. He promised not to question Lesley before my arrival.

My experience of the Criminal Law was, to say the least, limited to cases of a minor nature. Only half a dozen cases tried before a jury had passed through my hands. I was somewhat wet behind the ears. Some would say green and thus irresponsible in acting at all. But this was no ordinary case. I knew the couple. I knew that Lesley trusted me implicitly, and besides I had a kind of inner confidence in my ability to handle the challenges posed by the events. The law is not so abstruse and complex as a non-lawyer might imagine. Much of it is hard common sense.

On arrival at the police station, I was greeted by DCI Crawford who kindly told me that Lesley had informally, and not even under caution, told them everything that had happened the previous evening and that they were considering what, if any, charges to bring. I expressed my displeasure at the breach of what I regarded as binding police promise to desist from questioning – to be told that Lesley wanted to explain what had happened. Being at a time before the introduction of PACE – Police and Criminal Evidence Act 1984 – a major piece of legislation introduced to combat widespread police corruption generally and the practice of 'verbaling' whereby evidence of what an arrested person was alleged to have said was, often as a matter of routine, fabricated, I had been particularly concerned to ensure that Lesley's right of silence would be respected.

'Take me to see her,' I demanded.

This was Lesley's account. Just before midnight Joe had returned home after a bout of drinking, which he often and often ended in domestic violence perpetrated not only on Lesley but on their daughter, Beatrice, as well.

Beatrice had been asleep in her bedroom and Joe had wanted to wake her to wish her goodnight. Lesley had resisted his demands. He began to be aggressive as he approached her. Believing that he would assault her and Beatrice Lesley picked up his shotgun to frighten him and it had gone off by accident just as he was nearly on top of her. She rang the police and ambulance service straight away. It sounded pretty plausible to me. And given that she had already effectively spilt every bean in the tin, I gambled that it would be in Lesley's best interests to make a full and frank written admission as to the events in the hope that the police would be persuaded to treat the death as an accident.

So, with all the expertise which I could muster, I resolved to describe with a passion, the violence and threats suffered by Lesley at the hands of Joe during the marriage, as well as the traumatic events leading to the shooting, all in an effort to gain the sympathy of the police – and at least suggest, if not establish, her innocence. I would stress her profoundly inconsolable devastation and deep remorse in killing of her husband and father of Beatrice.

Thus, I embarked upon discharging the responsibility of drafting a six-page statement which Lesley approved and signed. Within five minutes of presenting it to DCI Crawford she was charged with murder! My reckless, naïve and irresponsible gamble had backfired in such spectacular fashion that she might, if not should, have terminated my retainer there and then. But with the obstinacy of a disenchanted mule, Lesley retained not only my services but also an unshakeable, touching faith in my persuasive powers to pull it off where it really mattered. Whatever powers I might have possessed did not however stretch to an ability to convince her to change her mind.

Legal Aid was granted and the wonderful Lewis Hawser QC plus the eminent junior barrister Greville Janner – later QC – were instructed. Bail was out of the question and my conferences with Lesley took place in Holloway jail with its austere, depressing surroundings being unconducive to optimism.

The prosecution evidence was damning. Ballistics tests showed that the gun had been fired from a range of approximately eight yards thus contradicting Lesley's account of how close she was when she 'accidentally' fired. The evidence from a gun expert which described the gun's firing mechanism all but ruled out an accidental shot. To cap it, a statement from a reliable third party that Joe had always kept the shotgun loaded at home, did nothing to help any suggestion that Lesley may have believed that the barrel was empty. The omens were far from good. On the other hand, Lesley protested her innocence. The trial was set to take place at Lewes Assizes on 9th January 1971 by which time she had made no final decision on whether or not to plead guilty to the charge.

Counsel was reluctant to advise one way or the other and Lesley was in partial denial of the evidence, so convinced had she become of her innocence.

The morning of the trial date is one which has been uniquely etched in my memory. The local press front page headlines screamed the biggest murder trial in the area of all time. The press box, as well as the public gallery in the Victorian court, was filled to capacity There was an air of anticipation. Nothing had attracted so much interest in years. The public wanted justice for the wicked killing of a devoted father. With leading counsel assisted by his junior we all met in a conference room beneath the Court. After a good deal of discussion, but no decision, Counsel suggested that if the prosecution could be persuaded to reduce the charge to manslaughter to which Lesley would agree to plead guilty, he might be able to persuade the Judge to impose a suspended sentence. With Lesley's reluctant agreement he went into action.

Prosecuting Counsel was the equally eminent, future Attorney General Michael Havers QC, a decent man who agreed to reduce the charge conditionally on a plea of guilty. The Judge was less accommodating. Not only was he unsympathetic to the Crown reducing the charge – he appeared to be satisfied as to Lesley's guilt as charged – but he would give no assurance on the length of sentence which he might impose let alone whether or not it would be immediate or suspended, if the Crown did, in fact, accept a guilty plea to the reduced charge.

The audience in the Court was becoming increasingly restless and agitated. It was now 10.30 and they had been patiently in their seats for an hour. What was going on? Counsel returned to the conference room with the partially good and partially bad news. A decision had to be made. Lesley was dithering. Counsel told her that she would have to make up her mind and was ready to give his advice.

'I don't want your advice,' she said somewhat ungraciously, 'I want to speak to Anthony alone.'

Slinking out, tails between their legs, they left me to her. 'It's the moment of truth, Lesley. No more prevarication.'

'What shall I do?' she asked. 'Please tell me.'

She was desperate and I had the awful burden of responsibility in effectively deciding her fate. In a gentle but firm tone I warned her that the evidence against her, while not completely overwhelming or conclusive, was strong enough to throw considerable doubt on her version of events, that Michael Havers enjoyed the reputation as one of the country's most ruthless cross examiners, and that she would more likely than not crack under severe questioning. The risks of being found guilty of murder were sufficiently high as to persuade me to say that she should risk an immediate but less severe term of imprisonment on a plea of guilty to manslaughter and rely on the advocacy of her Counsel to persuade the Judge to suspend any sentence.

'OK,' she said with no hesitation, 'let's do it. Guilty to manslaughter and hope for the best.'

And so it happened that the charge was amended. I took my place in the row behind counsel. In a mood of foreboding, I felt a tap on my shoulder. It was Michael Havers.

'Are you the poor sod who drafted the statement of the accused which immediately preceded the bringing of the proceedings?' I nodded. I felt ashamed. 'Well, I have a lot of sympathy for your client and I will read her statement as part of the evidence which I must present to the Court in as sympathetic manner as I can.'

And did he just. Summoning all the eloquence and passion at his command his impressive address had a remarkable impact on not only the public but also on the hard-bitten press corps whose sympathies were plain to see. More important I could swear that I saw the Judge surreptitiously wipe away some moisture under the eye. One could easily have been forgiven for believing that Havers had confused his role as prosecutor with that as counsel for the defence. But he was mindful of a prosecutor's duty to present all the facts to the Court and not just those which may favour the prosecution case.

'I need not call upon you, Mr. Hawser,' said the Judge.

On his direction the jury returned an immediate verdict of manslaughter.

'Will the defendant please rise.' Lesley stood. 'Lesley Collins. You have been convicted on your own admission of one of the most serious crimes in English criminal jurisprudence, that of the killing of an innocent man, your husband and the father of your young daughter. The law demands that I impose such sentence as reflects the gravity of the offence. I therefore sentence you to a term of imprisonment of 12 years.'

The Court remained deathly silent and Lesley visibly swayed.

'However,' he continued, 'I have been moved not only by the remorse which you so sincerely expressed in the powerful statement which you gave to the police and which has been so fairly read to the Court by Mr. Havers but also, by the continual suffering which the deceased perpetrated on you throughout your relatively short marriage. I am therefore permitted to take the exceptional course of suspending your sentence for three years which I so do. This means that provided you do not commit any serious offence within that period the sentence will lapse three years from today's date. You are now free to go.'

Cheers erupted in the Court.

Outside the Court Lesley met with me and her two counsels. In a reversal of the ungracious way she had earlier dismissed them she said: 'Gentlemen. I cannot thank you enough for what you have done for me and I will remember it forever'

'Don't thank us,' came the reply, 'it's Anthony who you should be thanking.'

I was left with a lump in my throat. And then the enormity of it hit me. The statement. The gamble which ultimately paid off. But suppose fortune had not delivered the wonderfully considerate and percipient Michael Havers.

Suppose the Judge had not responded with such leniency and understanding. It was too much. I could contain myself no longer and burst into tears.

'It's your turn now, Lesley, to tell me what to do, making such a fool of myself.'

'Well, I know what I'm going to do. Off to the nearest pub. Fancy joining me?'

An invitation which I was hardly likely to refuse, even at 11 o'clock in the morning.